Kate Cann

Leader
OF THE PACK

SCHOLASTIC

First published in the UK in 2008 by Scholastic Children's Books
An imprint of Scholastic Ltd
Euston House, 24 Eversholt Street,
London, NW1 1DB, UK
Registered office: Westfield Road, Southam, Warwickshire, CV47 0RA
Scholastic and associated logos are trademarks and or registered
trademarks of Scholastic Inc.

10 digit ISBN 0 439 96870 4

A CIP catalogue record for this book is available from the
British Library.

Printed and bound in Great Britain by
CPI Bookmarque, Croydon, Surrey

Papers used by Scholastic Children's Books are made from wood
grown in sustainable forests

3 5 7 9 10 8 6 4

www.scholastic.co.uk/zone

This book is fiction.
It is dedicated to David Box, whose influence over his
London Scottish squad was entirely positive. It is
also dedicated to the boys themselves.
What a team!

Chapter 1

Angry.

Young.

White.

Male.

These were the four pillars Jack Slade's mind rested on. Right now they were how he defined himself, how he tasted his life.

Angry: all the time. Not just because his life felt small and mean and stupid but because of the screwed-up way things were run, the way people were, the way everything was.

Young: seventeen.

White: English white. Not racist, he reckoned, just sick of the way white boys seemed to be bottom of the pile nowadays, at school, in the media, everywhere.

And male – yes, very male. Very focused on being a man. In a world that didn't seem to want men any more, not the way it used to do.

Jack Slade slouched his way to the back of the bus, and sat

there, glowering at the people sitting in front of him. It was a Tuesday night in early September and he was on his way to the first rugby training session of the season. He didn't know why he was bothering. His team was shite. Last season had been shite. Sure, training kept you fit, but what was the point when it never led to winning any matches?

Life, thought Jack, is about winning. Too many people are content to be losers. Not him though. Definitely not him.

The bus trundled round the roundabout halfway to the rugby club, and he felt this sudden urge to get off, go back home. The thought of the forced enthusiasm of scraggy old Len as he gave his stupid start-of-a-new-season speech and then tried to put them through their training paces filled him with disgust.

But Jack was the captain. If he didn't turn up, it would be a serious betrayal, like saying the team was finished. And he wasn't ready to do that, not yet.

The bus slammed to a stop, the doors cracked open, and a couple of girls about his age minced on. "Slags," he muttered under his breath. They made their way to the seat opposite him, eyeing him up as they approached.

Jack was used to female admiration. He had strong, clear looks; deep black-brown eyes. He was tall and broad-shouldered and because he trained and worked out with weights at the school gym, he was muscular and fit. It was his confidence that was most appealing, though. The way he moved, the way he "fitted his skin".

The girls stared at him and he stared back, insulting, appraising. One was quite pretty, but they both had slaggy dyed hair and short skirts and tight tops and they were like a symbol of everything that was shoddy and trashy about everything today, and he hated them.

Sometimes he felt like he hated all women.

Jack had had quite a few drunken one-nighters, but he hadn't got a good track record with girlfriends. There'd been Sally, a first-love thing, who'd got hysterical when he'd dumped her and kept coming round to his house and making scenes in school, and then a couple of hopeless cases who lasted about a fortnight each, and then Amy.

Five days ago, Amy had dumped him.

The bus careened round a tight corner and the girls watched Jack as he sat there with grief and rage in his heart, thinking about Amy. He'd met her outside a pub on a hot night on the second of August and it had been like something exploding. She was a year older than him, at college in the next town. She'd been all over him, telling him how gorgeous he was, and they'd made it together that night and seen each other every day after that and he'd felt like he was being pulled out of his old self like a rope out of a bag, uncoiling, unwinding, and then. . .

And then at the start of the new term, she'd gone on about how far apart they lived and told him she had to concentrate on getting good grades so she could get into the university she wanted. And dumped him.

Jack Slade glared over at the two slaggy girls. They were pushed up close together, chatting and squealing, opening their mouths a lot. He knew they seriously fancied him, the way the pretty one was stretching out her legs sidesaddle on the seat, the way they kept nodding their heads about and flicking their eyes at him to make sure he was watching.

The bus lurched to a halt at his stop and Jack stood up and swaggered down to the door, sure the girls' eyes were on him every inch of the way. *Out of your league, darlings!* he sneered, silently, and jumped off.

It took ten minutes to get from the bus stop to the Westgate Rugby Football Club, where the youth training sessions were held. Jack could feel his legs dragging as he got nearer, feel this shuffling sense of shame to be turning up again one year on. We're not a real team, he thought, bitterly. We're *nothing*. And right now he needed something. Something to get rid of all the anger he felt. Sometimes he felt scared by the way he felt, so scared he couldn't even look at it straight.

He checked his watch, saw he was late, and jogged the last stretch round the side of the clubhouse. A glance at the lads grouped under the goalposts told him there'd been several drop-outs – unless anyone was going to turn up even later than him – and no new members. Thirteen lads, that was all. Two short of a full team.

Jack hiked his mouth up from its grim downturn, and nodded at them. Jamie, the joker in the pack, grinned at him; a couple shouted hi; most looked as fed-up and defeated as he felt.

"Glad you decided to join us, Captain my Captain!" Len called out, looking up from his clipboard and beaming. He always called Jack *Captain my Captain*. It was supposed to be from some old poem, and it pissed Jack off.

Len was looking pretty damn happy considering he

hadn't even got a team this year. Like a scraggy cat that had just slurped a huge carton of cream.

"OK, lads," he burbled, rubbing his hands together, "welcome, everyone, to the start of a new season. And you're not the babies any more, are you? You're the Under 17s! I can see we've got a few drop-outs – well, that doesn't worry me. Because it's going to be different this year. Oh yes. By the end of this season, we'll have players lining up to join us. Trust me."

Jack rolled his eyes at Jamie. More of the same old delusional crap supposed to rev them up for the weeks ahead.

Len brought his hands together with a resounding crack. "Right, lads! We'll get on with the training soon, but before you get your boots on I want you to come with me into the clubhouse. I want to *introduce* you." Then he beamed mysteriously and set off across the field at a creaking jog, sure his rag-bag team would follow.

"He's finally lost it," announced Jamie.

"What's it about?" demanded Jack. "He say anything before I got here?"

"No," said Jamie. "But he's pretty pleased about something. Maybe they finally got us team shirts."

"Well that'll really sort us out, won't it," snapped Jack scathingly.

"Thought you might not be coming, mate. When you was late."

"You saying I'm a quitter? You saying I'd let my team down?"

"What team? Thirteen players."

The boys stomped gloomily across the turf. "I'm gonna give it a few weeks, see how it goes," muttered Jack. "If it's rubbish, I'll pack it in before Christmas."

"Me too. Get in another team, a better team."

"Or give up rugby altogether."

"Blimey," said Jamie, "you're seriously pissed off, aren't you, mate? This mean the rumours are true?"

"What rumours?"

"About you and Amy—"

"Fuck off."

"So they're true then," gloated Jamie.

"*Fuck off.*"

"All right, all right. Don't get so narky. Jesus. At least you had it over the summer. Me – nothing. Well – one boozed-up tart who was so drunk she passed out before I—"

"Shut up, mate."

"What?"

"*Shut up.*"

Jamie shut up, and the thirteen boys continued to meander across the pitch. A large black crow alighted ominously on the goal-post cross bar and cawed down at them.

Chapter 2

"Come on in, lads, come on in," beamed Len, as the team butted through the clubhouse swing doors and clattered into the outer room. "Take a seat." He waved hospitably at the battered benches ranged along the wall.

Jamie nudged Jack. On a table in the centre of the room was a large cardboard box, open at the top, with some dark-blue cloth showing. "Right about the shirts, see?" he muttered. As they collapsed down on to a bench, Jack nudged him back and motioned towards the serving-hatch on the far side of the room. Leaning through it was a man they'd never seen before. He was in his mid-twenties, with dark brown hair cropped tight to his skull, and a scar that jumped from his cheek on to his neck. He was sizing the boys up, Jack thought, like a farmer at a cattle fair. No — like a wolf on a rock over a field of sheep.

Who the hell was he?

"All right, lads," began Len, "this won't take long. I know you're desperate to get out on the field and start getting into shape again after all that lazing around over the summer!"

Some of the boys groaned at this, some laughed. The face of the man looking through the hatch didn't change.

"Now – I know last year was tough. We never seemed to get off the ground, did we? A lot of you got disillusioned. But like I said – this year's going to be different. Oh yes. For a start, the Club has finally recognized the Under 17s need support, and they've dipped their hands into their pockets. First of all—" Len poked a bony hand into the cardboard box, came out triumphantly with a blue shirt. "Yes, we've got 'em at last. Team shirts." An obliging but half-hearted cheer went up from the benches. "You'll have these on your backs the first fixture we play. But more importantly than shirts – the Club's forking out for some extra coaching. Someone who's going to give me a bit of time off, I hope. Lads – I'd like you to meet Alan Box."

And he gestured grandly at the serving hatch. The crop-haired man leaned forward and for a surreal moment Jack thought he was going to spring right through the hatch. But he disappeared, and walked into the room seconds later. He was average height, lean, broad-shouldered, powerful looking. "Hi," he said, unsmiling, "pleased to be here."

"Alan's ex-army," gushed Len, "he played rugby in the army, flanker, and he's *good*. He's hoping to make a new career for himself as a sports teacher, and while he's training, he'll be practising on you boys, right? Boxy! Anything you want to say to the lads?"

There was a pause. "I don't think so," said Boxy. "Let's get out and get down to it."

An hour and a half later, Jack thought he was going to die.

8

He'd been sick twice, his legs were shaking and his lungs felt like they'd been scoured out with acid.

But part of him felt fantastic. Part of him felt cured, whole, *real.*

Beside him on the changing-room bench, Jamie was whimpering as he pulled his boots off. "Never again," he groaned. "*Never fucking again.*"

Jack ignored Jamie. He was too full of what had happened on the field. Boxy had made them run. Fast. Then he'd made them run with each other on their backs. He'd made them do press-ups. He'd brought out the tackle bags and if he was holding one you felt like the bag was boshing you, not the other way round. He'd laughed when one after another, they'd puked on the side of the field, and said his aim for the first session of the season was to make everyone throw up at least once.

Beside Jack on the bench, Jamie tried to stand up, then sank down again. "I'm gonna *die,*" he croaked. "I can't walk."

Halfway through the session, Big Mac had howled "*Fuck* this" and walked away, wiping vomit from his mouth. "Quitting are you?" Boxy had asked. Or rather – he'd stated it, like a fact you couldn't argue with. Then he'd turned back to the other boys, as though Big Mac had never existed.

"I'm gonna phone my mum," wailed Jamie. "Get a lift."

At the end, Boxy hadn't congratulated them on all their hard slog; he hadn't really said anything. But he'd pointed at a big black crow devouring a pile of puke, and laughed, and they'd just about joined in. Then he'd looked at them as though they were his team and said, "Saturday, eleven o'clock, boys. We got a lot of work to do."

"My back's killing me. Why'd it have to me who carried Big Mac? *Jesus,* I'm so knackered I. . ."

"*Jamie, for Christ's sake stop whingeing!*" Jack erupted. "You're like some bloody little gnat, buzzing away . . . listen – we gotta get Big Mac back."

"*What. . .?!*"

"He's a good prop. We need him. And Iz. I'm gonna see him, talk him into coming back."

"Have you gone *mad*, mate?"

"And then we need one more. Another flanker." He turned to Jamie, and his whole face was alight. "Then we got a *team*," he said.

Chapter 3

That same evening, Gem Hanrahan, seventeen, long glossy conker-brown hair, sexily-athletic, stretched out a slim bare foot and jabbed it several times into the back of the boy hunched at the computer. "Are you listening to anything I'm saying, Christian you wanker?"

"Yes. Stop it. Stop poking me."

"That's my foot. You can't poke with your foot."

"Yeah you can."

"What have I just been saying then?"

"That you fancy Jack Slade. Which is an idea so repulsive and revolting I'm going to ignore it, OK?"

"Oh, sod off. Why is it revolting?"

"Gemma – he's a *jock*. He plays *rugby*."

"You said you had good discussions with him. In the politics class."

"I said he was a right-wing bastard. Who unfortunately can string a few words together in a way that occasionally convinces other people he might have a point."

"That's cos he's got *charisma*," said Gem lecherously. "He's got this kind of *power*. He's got. . ."

"Muscles."

"Self-certainty."

"*What?*"

"Oh, you know. He knows what he's about. He's not a waster, not a follower. I need that kind of guy, Christian. To match me."

"*To match you?*"

She foot-jabbed his back again, hard. "I've got self-certainty too. Hadn't you noticed?"

"You've got a big gob if that's what you mean. *God*, Gemma, you disappoint me! Fancy fancying Jack Slade! You and half the aspiring sluts in year nine and ten. I thought you had more originality."

"Look, it's not about his looks and stuff. . ."

"Sure it's not."

"Well, it's not only about his looks. Something's just . . . *got* me about him!" She broke off. She wondered if she could be bothered to explain to Christian that after years of Jack blurring into a mass of sweaty, sporty boys at school she'd seen him one evening last term, training on his own on the field, and he'd looked over at her, and . . . somehow that was that. Somehow he'd seared himself all perfect into her brain and she'd felt she had to have him or burn up.

She couldn't be bothered to explain. Christian wouldn't understand.

"I heard he was seeing someone over the summer," she breathed, "and they broke up."

"Yeah, I heard that too. So *what*? It makes me sick, the way Jack's treated like some kind of *important person* . . . no one gossips about me that way."

"*Yes they do!* Is he gay? Is he straight? Is he bi?"

Christian smirked. "Wonderful! People ask you, do they?"

"All the time. And I tell them something different every time."

"Fab."

"Last time I told them you were into sheep."

"*Fab*. Next time, make it necrophilia."

"What's necrophilia?"

"Dead people."

"*God* Chris you're disgusting! And we're getting away from the point. Jack Slade's on the rebound—"

"And you're moving in before some other warped female gets there."

"If you help me, yes. You *know* him!"

"No I don't."

"You *do*! You grew up with him – you used to play rugby with him!"

Christian shuddered violently and theatrically. "*Must* you remind me of one of the most hideous times of my *life*?"

"Oh come on, Chris, your dad's forgiven you. . ."

"He may have done, but I haven't forgiven him! I shall need *years* of therapy."

"It's OK, baby – we'll get you through this!" mocked Gem, and she plonked her hands down on his shoulders and started massaging his neck.

Chris's dad was seriously into rugby; he helped run training sessions at Westgate Rugby Football Club, and still ran out occasionally for the Veterans. He'd taken Chris along to mini rugby at the tender age of seven, where he'd played alongside Jack. Jack had excelled; Chris had thrown tantrums and refused to go back.

"Jack used to bully me, Gemmy," wailed Christian, swooning backwards into the steady rhythm of her working thumbs. "How can you want to go out with someone who used to bully me?"

"No, he didn't – not really. That's just what you do in rugby. Anyway – what about that junior school play you told me about, when he was the Roaring Monster and you were the Busy Bee? You bullied him then."

"No I didn't – I *patronized* him. Cos he couldn't act. But he's so thick he didn't get what I was saying, so that doesn't count."

"Look, Chris—"

"*God*, I was a good Busy Bee. I brought it to a whole new level. It was the start of my shining acting career."

"*Chris* – this is gonna happen. All I want you to do is kind of . . . *speak* to Jack when I'm with you or something. It's so obvious if I just stroll over to him on my own. Yeah? Yeah, Chris?"

On the computer screen, a little red dragon leapt into view in a puff of green smoke and a digital voice said, "Hail Master Monster Prick! Your servant is back!"

"Oh – my – *God*," sneered Gem, stopping the massage dead.

"Gemma," gurgled Christian, "meet my familiar. Draggy."

"Where did it *come* from?"

"I was just offered it one day. You know – on screen.

It keeps trying to get me to sign up to anti-virus programs and stuff. I can make it say anything I want. Want to see?"

"No."

"It does philosophy. Song lyrics. Anything you type in. Plus it swears brilliantly."

"You're so sad, Christian."

"It's *company* for me. When one of my oldest and dearest friends neglects me because she's got a sick obsession for some meathead. . ."

"Oh shut up. Look – will you set this up or not?"

"Not."

"Why not? Oh God – I get it. You want him for yourself, don't you."

"Darling, I have better taste than that. Anyway – I'm not gay."

"Not this week, maybe."

Gem bent down and pressed her cheek against Christian's and for one brief moment his mouth yearned towards hers. "You wanna decide who you are, OK?" she murmured. "Gay or straight. And then act that way, and stop confusing people."

"I like confusing people!"

"Yeah, well, it gives me a headache. Look – tell me you'll set it up with Jack or I'll stab you."

"Bitch."

"With these scissors."

"Bitch."

"Tell me!"

"OK, OK. I'll do it."

"When?"

"Lunch time sometime. You hang with me – and I'll go up and speak to him. Or something. Now go away and stop torturing me."

Gem smacked a loud kiss on the top of Christian's head, then strode out of his room, all ease and energy and certainty, all the things Christian felt he lacked, all the things he hungered after. He turned back to his computer screen, where the little gambolling dragon was snorting out sprays of bright sparks. "Maybe Gem's right," he thought. "Maybe I should decide who I am." Edgily, he flicked off the machine and stood up. "Bully or victim. Masochist or sadist. Gay or straight." He paced his room, paced back again to the foot of his bed. "But on the other hand, why should I? Why can't I be all of it, take my pick, dip in and out of everything?" Then he let himself arc forward and fall face down on the duvet.

"That's why I like acting," he reflected. "Masks. Dressing up." And his mind trailed off into the folds of a silk gown, brushing against his skin. . .

Chapter 4

Jack was woken as usual on Wednesday morning by his mum standing at the foot of the stairs screeching, *"It's seven-thirty!"* He opened his eyes and let his brain shift into focus. And realized the weight wasn't there. The heavy dead weight like a concrete coffin lid on him every morning since Amy had dumped him – it wasn't there. He pushed back the duvet and sat up. His body felt like it had been trampled on, all the muscles in his body wrenched out of place. His legs ached as he swung them out of bed, his back stiffened as he stood up.

He felt wonderful.

He limped into the shower, let the hot stream pummel and soothe his body. Then he dried, dressed, and hobbled downstairs to the kitchen. "Hey, Ma," he said, "how are you?"

His mum jumped up from emptying the dishwasher and squawked, "How *am* I?"

"Yeah. I'm asking after your welfare, Mother. You OK?"

"I'm fine, Jack. *Fine.* Except I'm late of course – as *usual—*"

"I'll do that."

"What?"

"I'll finish unstacking. You get off."

Jack's mum stared at him. He grinned back, then opened the fridge, pulled out a pint of milk, flipped the top off and started drinking.

Jack's mum had learnt by hard experience not to comment on his moods. "Thanks, love," she said, faintly.

"I'm gonna get breakfast at school," he said. "I want something cooked."

Silently, Jack's mum opened her purse, took out three pound coins, and laid them on the counter.

"Thanks, Ma," said Jack, and turned to the dishwasher.

"Thanks, love," she said again, then she gathered up her bag and car keys and Jack's two little sisters and their bags and they all bundled out of the front door.

By eight-fifteen, Jack was marching through the school gates. Since term started just over a week ago he'd walked through raging and unseeing, not wanting anyone in his line of vision. But today he walked through looking. And noticed a group of kids from the year below him, all bunched up together chatting. Their heads turned towards him, mouths working, eyes slithering over him.

"You talkin' about me?" he yelled, heading towards them.

Almost involuntarily, the group tightened, shifted back. "No," said one of the taller boys sullenly. "What the fuck we want to talk about you for?"

"Good. Glad you're not. Cos that would mean you're

sad pathetic little bastards without any life of your own, wouldn't it?" Then he grinned at them cheerfully and continued on his way to the canteen.

Jack was sure of finding Big Mac there – he could be relied on to turn up for the subsidized breakfasts of bacon rolls and weak tea. Jack spotted him at the front of the queue, pushed past half a dozen Year Nines too intimidated to protest, and clapped him hard on the back.

"*Greeeugh*," responded Big Mac, mouth already stuffed full of breakfast.

"Fucking pig," Jack greeted him. "*Two* bacon butties?"

"Three. I'm eating this one before I get to the till." They both laughed, and Big Mac went on, "I need the sustenance, mate. Threw up so hard last night last Sunday's roast came up too. Did you stay to the end?"

"Yeah," said Jack, "I did." He smiled winningly at the woman behind the counter, who slipped an extra bit of bacon into a roll and handed it across to him. "I'm not a quitter like you, you fat git."

"Maybe not but you're obviously mad, mate. *Clinical*. Who else left?"

"No one."

"You're *joking*."

"Nope. We all stuck it out."

"Ah, you were just too scared to leave. Scared of that nutter who turned up to train us."

"We weren't *scared*."

"Who the hell was he, anyway? Some throw-out from the SAS? He was *barking*."

"Yeah, well. Listen, I know it was too much, it made us

all puke. But we felt *great* at the end. We were . . . we were all talking about it." Jack hoped that Mac, who could be clued in sometimes, wouldn't spot the colossal fib. "It was like – going through a pain barrier. Up to the next level. Len never knew how to train us, not like that."

"*Len?*" scoffed Mac, as the two of them handed over their money and headed for an empty table. "He couldn't train a pack of arthritic monkeys."

"Exactly. *Exactly*, Mac. We never had a chance when he was in charge! And this Boxy bloke – I reckon he knows something about rugby. I reckon he could be the missing link."

"The *whaaa*?" demanded Mac, chomping.

"The link between what we are – and what we *should* be," said Jack. "The thing that's been missing ever since we started out as a team. What we *need* – to go from being good basic material – to a team that can beat anyone we come up against."

"Yeah?"

"Yeah. Kick 'em right around the fucking paddock."

There was a silence, while Big Mac chewed and considered this. Jack, encouraged, plunged on. "Remember how shit it was, last season? When teams that looked like a posse of pussies ran *rings* round us?" Mac nodded bitterly. "Thing is, we weren't even *functioning*. The potential we've got – we hardly *scraped* at it. And from what Boxy was saying, we got real potential. If we work, we can go the distance. The whole distance."

Jack stopped, took a long swig of tea. All this stuff he was coming out with – he didn't know where it was coming from. Boxy had said nothing like it – he'd hardly said a word.

But something inside Jack had leapt into life after the training session, and it had felt brilliant, it had felt like a *cure*, and it was that talking now.

He leant across the Formica table and urged, "Give it another go, Mac. Come along on Saturday. Yeah?" Mac swallowed doubtfully. "We've got some good people in that team, and you're one of them. We've just never had a *chance*. Remember the game against Trojans? They had all these fancy tricks and manoeuvres, and they skipped away with it. Remember their prop? You *dominated* him. But he kept sticking it to you, taking the piss, jeering at you when they'd won. Wouldn't you like to put that right?"

Big Mac's face had darkened with the sour memory. "I'd like to walk his face into the ground," he growled.

"Well you'll be able to. *Trust* me. I've got a real hunch about Boxy. He can make us into a team. And we need you as prop, Mac – we need you. You're the business." Jack felt so fervent he felt like he was going to reach across the table, grab Big Mac's arm, *make* him agree to come back.

"I dunno," grumbled Mac. "I felt fucking awful after that session."

"It'll be better on Saturday. You'll be more used to it. Come on Mac – what you gonna do if you give up rugby? Squash? *Lacrosse?* Come on – it's your game. You give up – you'll be a fat waste of space come Christmas."

"Fucking hell, Jack! All *right*."

"*Yeah?*"

"Yeah. I'll be there, Saturday. I'll give it one more go. If that Boxy bloke's as good as you say he is. . ."

"He is. We can win this season."

"OK. Well I'm up for that, mate. I'm up for some serious revenge."

He grinned at Jack, who grinned back, swallowed the last of his tea, and stood up, saying, "See you Saturday, Mac. Don't let me down."

Jack walked away, convinced that Big Mac was convinced. And the thing about Big Mac was, once you'd got him fired up and on your side, he'd stay there. Hopefully even after he'd found out that Jack had been spinning him porkies about what the rest of the team felt and about what Boxy had said and – well, come to think about it, about everything.

He wasn't lying about the future though. It was going to come true. Jack knew that deep in himself. In his bones.

Chapter 5

"The thing that gets me," grumbled Christian, as he and Gemma toured the schoolyard arm in arm Wednesday lunch time looking for Jack Slade, "is that this is just another one of your horrible *projects*. Like when you started guitar lessons. Like when you decided that skinny cow Sara needed *saving* from herself. Like when you took up *kick-boxing*."

Gemma bridled. "And your point is—?"

"Those projects lasted on average five weeks each."

"That is bollocks, Chris."

"Well, near about. And you're submitting me to probable humiliation—"

"*What?*"

"When Jack at the very least *snubs* me or possibly physically abuses me – just for a five-week project."

"It could be a longer project. I could marry him and have his babies."

"Oh, *please.*"

"*Lots* of babies."

"I've only just *eaten!*"

"Anyway – why should he snub you or abuse you?"

"He hates me. He always has done. He hates anyone who does drama. He says we're a load of queens and calls us the Brady Bunch."

Gemma snorted with laughter. "That's quite good."

"Oh *thanks*. Thanks a *lot*."

"No, but I mean – you did all get a bit over the top doing that play last term, didn't you. Group hugging and all that 'darling you were fabulous!' stuff."

"We did not *group hug*. Anyway, I bet Jack *team hugs*."

"I bet he *doesn't*. He's far too macho."

"He does the macho equivalent, then. Come on, when he scores a goal he at least grunts in a sort of ... *celebratory fashion*."

"Bet he doesn't. He *expects* to be brilliant, so there's nothing to celebrate, it's just par for the course. Situation normal. And it's not a *goal* in rugby, it's a try."

"Just testing. And you've *failed*. Gem – I really am going to throw up. You've been learning about rugby, haven't you?"

"A bit."

"To impress him."

"To *understand* him. *Ssssss!*" Gemma suddenly stiffened and sank her nails into Christian's arm; he shrieked softly. "There!" she hissed. "Over *there!* Heading this way and he's on his own!" She snatched her arm out of Chris's. "Go on. Go and ask him about a politics essay. Tell him you wanna start playing rugby again. Whatever. *Go.*"

Christian rolled his eyes and veered towards Jack, arm outstretched in greeting.

Gem hung back, fiddling in the bag that hung over her

shoulder to give her an excuse not to join them just yet. She was feeling weirdly terrified.

Gem knew all about lust; she knew it was a complex process. She wasn't, for a start, sure of what Jack's voice sounded like. She'd only ever heard him shouting, and you couldn't tell from that. She knew that if she talked to him and he had a silly voice, or said stupid things, the lust would dwindle away.

And that would be sad, because this was fantastic major lust she was feeling. It was brilliant to feel.

Gem had an impressive track record with boys. She was good at running to ground the objects of her lust, getting them besotted with her too. They'd have a few glorious obsessional dates and lots of soppy phone calls and then – well, Gem got bored, and finished it.

She'd slept with two of them. Various people had told her this would make her feel more involved, more committed; almost certainly make the relationship last a lot longer. It hadn't, though. Part of her felt let down by this. Part of her wondered whether the lust was all in her mind, a projection she did because she was so desperate to fall "big time, all time" for someone, and have it last for a couple of months at least.

Well, now it was Jack's turn. She finished the mime of fumbling in her bag, mimed looking around to see where Christian had gone, and then strolled over towards him and Jack, miming mild annoyance. Christian turned towards her. "Hey, Gem," he said. "You know Jack, don't you?"

"I wouldn't say I *know* him," she said coolly, while her blood drummed.

"Everyone knows Jack, Gem. Captain of the team."

"Which team?" she said.

"Rugby, of course!" Christian cried, camply. He tended to camp it up when he was nervous. "Look at his thighs!"

"I can't see his thighs. They're covered up."

Jack laughed. He knew who Gem was all right. Everyone knew Gem. She was one of the class-acts of the school, but she was in with Holly and her bunch of über-bitches, so you didn't bother to think about her.

Although, staring at her now, he had to admit he liked her looks close up. And right now he was finding her snottiness quite sexy. He grinned all challenging and cocky and said, "Want me to take my trousers off?"

Gem didn't titter or giggle, just looked straight back, and said, "Go on then."

And then they both laughed, and kept on looking at each other.

Oh, *God*, groaned Christian, silently. *Here we go.* "*So*," he said, to fill in the unbearably vibrating silence, "*Jack.* Haven't seen you around for a while."

"I was in Politics. Monday."

"Right. So you were."

Gem, cringing, asked, "Is your team good?"

"The school team?" said Jack. "It's crap."

"So are you in another team?"

"Yeah. Westgate Under 17s. That's crap too. But it might. . ."

"Might what?"

"I dunno. We got a new trainer. It might improve."

The pause following this was too long for anyone to fill.

Jack shrugged, said, "Better go," and then he and Gem looked at each other again, then the three turned as one and wandered off.

As soon as they were out of sight round a corner, Gem gripped the top of Christian's arm like a vice. "I owe you one," she gasped. "Oh, *God*, I owe you one!"

"*Bloody* hell, woman, you're cutting off the blood supply to my head!"

"Sorry. Oh *God* though. *God*."

"So I take it you thought that dull little interchange was a success?"

"Oh, fuck off, Chris. Why d'you have to talk like an eighteenth-century vicar? *Yes* it was a success. *Yes* he's gorgeous. His voice is gorgeous too. Like the rest of him. Close up he's. . ."

"Gemma – I warn you. I shall *so puke*. Still, I s'pose it went OK. I s'pose the fact that he stood there and talked absolute bollocks with you must mean something else was going on—"

Gem yanked at Christian's arm. "*You mean you think he fancies me?*"

"Possibly."

"You could find out, Chris. You could ask him."

"No way. Our friendship doesn't go that deep. Look – I've given you your intro – what more d'you want?"

"Nothing," said Gemma, all conciliatory. "Look – I'm gonna try and book the darkroom some time this week. D'you wanna come along?"

Chris shrugged, enjoying the rare experience of Gem creeping up to him. Photography was one of the things that had cemented their friendship. It was how they'd met, back in year eight, at the school photography club, and now, as a huge concession from the school, they were both doing photography A level.

"Go on, Chris," she urged. "You got anything to develop?"

"A few bits."

"Yeah? What?"

"Some really cool fungus."

"Yuch!"

"It was just growing on this tree – it looked like a beautiful carving. Well – an evil carving. Well – beautiful and evil."

"Sounds scrummy. I'll put your name down next to mine."

The school siren screeched out, marking the start of the afternoon session and the end of their conversation. Gemma craned forward, and smacked a kiss on Christian's chin. Then they went their separate ways.

Jack, heading into school on the other side of the building, was mentally filing Gem away in his "Possibilities" folder. He had the strong feeling he'd been set up there, because Christian never came over to talk to him like that – their communication was generally just exchanging casual insults from a distance.

Being set up by Gem was quite a turn-on. So was she. He'd liked the look of her close up; he'd liked the energy off her even more.

Not that it was going to make him change his mind on

women, though. They were the enemy. You didn't let them in or they messed your head up.

And anyway, right now, he had other things to do.

Chapter 6

For the rest of that week, Jack worked hard. No MP unsure of his majority canvassed harder than Jack did. One by one, he collared all the Westgate Under 17s who went to his school, and talked to them. Jack Slade was one of the school stars, one of the key figures, and his team members were flattered to be collared in this way. With a heady cocktail of bullying, flannel and enthusiasm, he persuaded them all into turning up again for training on Saturday.

He kept Big Mac on the boil, too, and Big Mac, like a huge echo chamber, was good at reinforcing everything he said.

Jack's next major assault was planned for Friday night. Jamie and his two mates Iz and Dosh, the only members of the Westgate Under 17s who didn't go to Jack's school, lived on the far side of town. They were pretty inseparable as a trio and that might mean it would be harder to talk them round. Still, Jack meant to do it.

He knew where to track them down. Jamie's mum ran a thriving pub, The Crown, and she was generous about giving Jamie's mates the odd beer and letting them hang out in the big half-used cellar downstairs. Jack arrived there around eight-thirty to find Jamie, Iz and Dosh sprawled on a huge, stained sofa in front of an enormous telly, both items scruffy refugees from the pub lounge. "Oh, for fuck's sake," Dosh was squawking. "Slap 'er one. Go on mate. Stand up to her. You *pussy!*"

On the screen, a woman patronized a smirking, cringing man for not cleaning the toilet properly.

"Shove her head down the bog! Clean it with that!" yowled Iz.

"Fucking adverts. I hate 'em."

"Car adverts are OK."

"Except when they've got some *woman* cutting you up and acting all superior," chipped in Jack, as he walked into the cellar. Jamie, Iz and Dosh greeted him with minimal enthusiasm. Tuesday's punishment still stung, and because Jack was captain, they partly blamed him for it.

Jack slouched over and blocked their view of the TV screen. "The rest of the team are all up for training Saturday," he announced. "Big Mac, too. Just wanted to check you three were."

"No *way!*" jeered Dosh.

"You're having a laugh, mate," said Jamie. "Now *shift.*"

Jack turned to Iz. "Don't listen to these two mincers. You shoulda been there Tuesday. It was quality."

"*Bollocks* it was!" erupted Jamie. "Now *shift*, Jack, or I'll do you in!"

Jack grunted and moved away from the TV screen. Plan A – the fast one – hadn't worked. He'd have to make time for Plan B, that's all.

"Hey – that programme's on," said Dosh. "The Viking one."

"*History?*" snorted Jack, as he hip-barged a space for himself on the end of the sofa.

"Yeah, but it's good," said Iz, admiringly. "The Vikings – they were *animals*."

Further conversation was halted by a great explosion of metallic music from the TV. The screen filled with computer-enhanced images of slicing and slitting and slashing and the four watched, enthralled. Then, as the battle scenes gave way to an aerial view of Viking settlements, Jack waded in again. "You gotta give it one more go," he said. "On Saturday. Seriously, boys."

"No way," said Jamie. "I was crippled."

"But you're OK now aren't you?"

"Yeah, but—"

"Think how fit you're gonna get. Tonk as shit. Think of playing a real game."

"Think of chucking your guts up. Think of dying doing press-ups and that fuckhead not even noticing you were dead."

From the TV came the words, "Boys of fourteen years, thirteen even, were considered men, able to take on a man's role. A boy of strength and talent could rise swiftly up the male hierarchy." The four boys on the sofa stared sourly ahead as boy-warriors postured charismatically on the screen. Dosh flicked to a music channel; Jamie fetched four beers from a crate in the corner. "Don't your mum notice?" asked Jack. Jamie shrugged, decapped them on the side of the TV stand, and handed them out.

"I wish I'd lived then," Dosh groused. "In Viking times."

"No you don't," said Iz. "Even if you managed to survive a battle, if you'd got slashed on the leg or something, you'd get gangrene and die."

"Yeah, but supposing you didn't. Supposing you lasted. I mean – being alive, it meant something, then. You survived – you'd be special. A leader."

There was a pause, while the four boys swigged beer. "People our age – we had a lot more power back then," continued Dosh. "Not just Vikings – after that too. Like – supposing your family was starving. The *village* was starving. And you went out with your bow and arrow, and shot a fucking great deer. A stag. And carried it home. You'd get real respect then."

"How could you carry it home?" Jamie scoffed.

"OK, there were two of you. And you shot it together, and then tied its legs to a pole, and took one end each. . ."

"Its head'd be trailing on the ground."

"*What?*"

"Its antlers'd get all caught up in the bushes and stuff. . ."

Dosh raised himself a few inches off the sofa, then slammed down again, jabbing his elbow hard into Jamie's chest, who howled, then launched himself on Dosh. A brief furious punch-up followed, and over it, Jack shouted, "I know what you're saying. It's like, today – we live like little kids for years, till we're like – *twenty* or something."

"Longer, if you go to uni," put in Izzy, as Dosh and Jamie crashed off the sofa on to the floor and mutely called it quits. "My sister's still completely parental-dependent – and she's twenty-two."

"Yeah," panted Dosh. "We're no use – so we get no respect. Back in the day, when you brought back that deer . . . you got respect."

"You say that," said Jack, cunningly. "You go on about wanting to be like a Viking warrior and stuff. But the one chance you got to be like that, you run away from it. Just cos it's too hard. Too physical."

"Oh for fuck's sake, Jack – you on about rugby again?"

"Yeah, I am. Sport is one of the few places people like us can get respect."

Silence, apart from the slurping of beer. Then Iz said, "My uncle was on about that the other day. Sport is war, and stuff. How football hooligans ought to get put in the army."

"Boxy was in the army."

"Who?"

"The new trainer. The one that nearly killed us all."

Afterwards, Jack looked back on that evening, and wasn't sure how he'd done it. It was just a combination of chewing it all over and the right words dripping on the right places in their minds. That, and several more beers each. Anyway, around eleven o'clock Jack stood up to leave and Dosh and Jamie said again that they'd give training one more go. And then Iz said in that case he may as well check it out too.

As Jack left, he laughed. He felt a bit pissed and unsteady on his feet. "See you Saturday, boys," he slurred. Then he turned back. "Hey – where we gonna get another good flanker from?"

Chapter 7

Saturday, eleven a.m. sharp. The whole team was there, under the goalposts. Not only all the boys who'd been there on Tuesday but Iz too, and Leo Brown, who played flanker on the school team and had been press-ganged by Jack into repeating it for Westgate.

Jack felt full of prideful achievement as he waited. He watched Boxy striding towards them across the pitch, waiting to see his face light up, waiting to hear him say how great it was to see such a turnout. Such a *team*.

But Boxy hardly glanced at them. He just dumped his sports bag down, stripped his sweatshirt off and said, "OK, lads, let's get down to it. Warm up – two laps round the pitch."

Jack felt crushed as he jogged off. He'd wanted Boxy to acknowledge – even with just a *look* – that he knew all this was down to him, Jack. That he knew who'd put the work in on everyone. Christ, he thought to himself, why'd I bother?

He speeded up, moved out to the front of the runners. He suddenly felt angry at himself for being so bothered about *recognition*. I bothered for *me*, he told himself, then he speeded up more, like he was trying to outrun his disappointment.

This training session was even harder than Tuesday's. Lunges, sprints, push-ups, hitting the bosh-bags. Then on to team work: ball handling, playing skills. Boxy was strong on criticism, which he bellowed out like a drill sergeant, and short on praise. Big Mac threw up again; so did Iz and Karl and a couple of the others, but they kept going because it would have taken too much sheer courage to stop.

After seventy minutes, Boxy gave them a break. They lay wheezing and gasping on the ground and Boxy stood over them, looking down at them in silence. Then he said, "Boys – we got the making of a good team here."

The wheezing stopped; everyone gawped up at him. Iz rolled over and croaked to Jamie, "I thought he thought we were shit."

"You put the work in and you can be first-rate," Boxy went on. "You can meet any team and take 'em apart. But you gotta put the *work* in. *Major* work. First – fitness. Half of you haven't got any. You gotta sort that out, big time. At least twice a week – as well as training – you run, you sprint, you do step work. For your upper body, come to the gym here."

"We can't," piped up Jamie. "Not allowed. Too young."

"We'll see about that, won't we. If I'm there to supervise there's no reason you shouldn't."

Glances were exchanged. Jack and a couple of others had applied to use the gym last season and been turned down flat.

"You gotta be serious about your bodies, boys," went on Boxy. "Make physical fitness your number-one priority. Like the Spartans did."

"Who were the Spartans?" demanded Big Mac.

"Wanker!" scoffed Jamie. "They were those warriors, weren't they. Ancient Greece or something."

"Well, ancient Sparta, yeah," said Boxy.

"They were dead hard."

"They used to leave newborn male babies outside on the mountainside," said Boxy. "Overnight. Then find out if they were alive or dead in the morning."

"Blimey," said Dosh, "bit harsh, innit?"

"It was so the weaklings would die off."

"Yeah, well. We got incubators nowadays."

"You're missing the point, Dosh," put in Jack. "As usual. They *wanted* them to die off. They wanted to sort out the weak from the strong."

There was a pause, as they digested this.

"Any of you lot got put in an incubator when you were a baby?" Boxy demanded.

Jamie, who had been, suddenly felt there was no way he could admit to it.

"So," went on Boxy, "first, fitness, second – *skills*. Like I say, I see potential. A lot of the ball handling's shit but practice will sort that out. And trust me, we're gonna practise till you hate the sound of the word. But look, boys – it's gonna be worth it. I like the way you work together. I like the communication – I like the guts."

More glances exchanged – and grins too. Len never talked like this. Not all dramatic like this. Len was jolly and practical with a good larding of paternal encouragement. This was like a film or something.

Boxy picked up his sports bag. "OK, boys, let's call it quits for today. You did well and you're all beat. Now – next Saturday. I wanna see how you hold together under attack, pinpoint what you need to work on. Basically you can practise with each other all you like but there's no substitute for the real thing. So for Saturday, I'm gonna fix up a match."

Amazed muttering followed this announcement. "But," said Dosh, "Len used to make us train right up till November at *least* before we got a game. . ."

"Yeah?" said Boxy. "And did you win when you got one?"

Jack laughed. "Never."

"Point made, then. Keep doing the same things – get the same results."

"Who we playing?" demanded Will.

"Brayton Bridge, if I can sort it."

"Shit, they were up in the league last season, weren't they?"

"No point playing a team that's not going to give you proper outing, is there? One more thing. If we got a match Saturday, I want to do Tuesday as usual – and an extra session Friday night. *Don't* get your knickers in a twist," he went on, over the outraged outcry, "I only want you for an hour or so, early."

"Yeah, but there's a big party Friday!" squawked Karl. "This rich kid in the year above us – Lewis Banks – it's his *eighteenth* . . . his mum and dad, they've hired a proper club . . . he's a real geek, got no friends, so he's lettin' us lot in to make out he has—"

"*Look* – you can go to the party *after* training, OK? Just so long as you don't get too drunk and if you get laid you make her do all the work. Now boys – on your feet. Laps."

"I thought you said we was finished?" groaned Big Mac.

"We are. Laps is just cooling off. And that reminds me." He turned to look at Mac, who suddenly felt like a blowtorch was aimed at his face. "I'm glad you decided to come back today, Mac. But if you walk away from me again, that's it, OK? *You're* finished."

There was a silence. Then Mac grunted, "Yeah, OK."

As the team jogged wearily off, Boxy laid a hand on Jack's arm to stop him. "Hey," he said. "Captain."

Jack's gut burned with pleasure at the word.

"I know you must've done a lot of work this week," said Boxy, "to get this lot to show up. And it's gonna pay off. We're gonna be great."

Jack nodded, unsmiling. Boxy was looking at him like the two of them were in on something together, like he was talking about a lot, lot more than just a rugby team.

"Trust me," Boxy said, then he turned and walked away.

Jack started jogging after the others. He felt weird, excited. He felt like some kind of hurricane had sucked up all his anger and misery and now it was spewing it out into this *focus*, this channel outwards. He speeded up and caught the others up before they reached the end of the pitch.

Chapter 8

"Hi, Lewis," purred Gemma, manoeuvring her slim, stylish body into the empty canteen seat opposite Lewis Banks.

Lewis nearly choked on his chips. The only thing that Lewis could be said to have going for him was the fact that his folks were well off. This meant that he had good clothes that sat ill on his scrawny body and lots of spending money, which meant people would come out with him, and now – his big eighteenth birthday shindig. Not in some boring echoing church hall but in Cascades, a proper club with great music and – it was rumoured – *free drink*. Lewis had never felt so popular. And now *this*. . .

"Hi, Gemma," Lewis squeaked. "You're still coming, aren't you?"

"On Friday? Wouldn't miss it! I just wanted to check something out on your guest list. . ."

Lewis sighed. Quite a bit of this had been going on. Girls making out they liked him just to get some stud on the list, blokes coming on all matey just to get some girl included. . .

"I just *wondered*," breathed Gemma, leaning across the table a little, "whether you'd asked Karl and Mac and . . . you know . . . the rugby boys."

"Yeah, I did. They're all coming."

"Jack?" she asked, all offhand. "Jack Slade?"

"Yeah," sighed Lewis. "I think he's gonna come."

Before Gemma stood up she smiled straight at Lewis and put her lovely hand, still brown from the summer, briefly on his. Thirty seconds later he too stood up and swooned his way over to the canteen exit.

To be accosted by Jack Slade, who said, "All right, mate?" and dropped a heavy arm round his shoulders.

"Yeah, I'm great," Lewis peeped. "You?"

"I'm fine. Looking forward to your party."

"Really? Yeah . . . fantastic."

"I was just thinking – you asked Gemma? Gemma Hanrahan?"

"Um. . ."

"Oh, come on, Lewis. Don't tell me you left all the best-looking girls off your invite list."

"No," sighed Lewis. "I'm pretty sure she's coming."

The arm round Lewis's shoulders tightened till his bones grated. "Good stuff, mate. See you Friday."

And Jack Slade sauntered off.

Seven-thirty Friday night, at the Westgate Rugby Football Club. Training was finished; it'd been hard but skills rather than fitness-based, so it hadn't been too physically shattering. Boxy had been restrained in his comments; there was the general feeling he was waiting to see how they held up in the match on Saturday before he really started in on them.

He confirmed he'd set up a game with Brayton Bridge but he wouldn't discuss their form.

The thought of the match – and the feeling Boxy was calmly waiting to see whether they got slaughtered or not playing it – made the boys on edge, nervous, like before a battle. Which made them anxious to get to Lewis Banks's party and get a couple of drinks down.

The whole team – minus four lads who had other stuff on that night – showered and changed at the club, planning to go straight to Cascades. Jack had taken it on himself to invite Jamie, Iz and Dosh along, even though Lewis had never set eyes on them before.

"You sure we gonna get in?" asked Dosh, doing up the buttons on his jeans.

"Sure I'm sure," said Jack, breezily. "I'll tell that prat Lewis you're part of my team."

"Maybe they got bouncers."

"Then we'll *negotiate*," he scoffed, miming a hard-arm shunt to the face.

As the eleven boys headed out of the grounds, eager for a beer, Dosh said, "What you reckon this team's gonna be like on Saturday?"

"Dunno," said Jack. "Boxy just told me their front row was pretty strong."

"We'll get hammered," groaned Iz.

"Dunno," said Jack again. "Maybe not."

"He's dead serious, isn't he," grumbled Big Mac. "Wanting us there an hour before kick-off."

"We need to warm up properly," said Jack. "If we're gonna play good, we got to warm up."

"Can we shut up talking fucking rugby?" snorted Iz. "I wanna concentrate on getting pissed. And pulling something classy tonight, all right?"

Jack grinned, thinking of Gem. *Pulling*, that was it, that was the word. No more *involvement*.

They reached the bus stop and a bus heading into town drew up and they all piled on.

Eight o'clock Friday night. Gem was putting the finishing touches to her look. She'd decided to show her legs – a long stretch of them. Loads of people told her how great her legs were. Not only were they long, but what with her running and athletics, they were pretty toned and shapely. Gem reckoned Jack – as a sportsman – would seriously appreciate them.

She faced herself in the mirror. The top she'd put on was too low-cut and tarty with the short skirt. She'd go for a plainer top and lower sandals so she could move . . . yes, and just a few coppery-coloured bangles, and a ring, nothing else. Nothing over the top. Leave her long brown glossy hair loose and simple.

Her instinct told her Jack was the sort to like natural, understated looks in his women. And as that was what she intended to be, that's what she'd aim for.

Eight-fifteen. The eleven boys got off the bus and on a shared impulse went straight into a seedy-looking pub called The Anchor. They would have died before admitting to each other that they needed a beer or two to give them courage before arriving at Cascades, but that's what they all felt. Ever since they'd turned sixteen, well over a year ago now, they'd used Big Mac and then Jack to get the drinks in pubs – they'd never had any trouble. They downed the first pint almost in silence, then Jamie said, "Get some more jars in. We'll get knocked in the club – fiver a drink."

"Criminal," commented Iz, and Karl said, "I heard the drinks were free."

"*Yeah?*"

"Well – maybe. I'm sure Lewis said something about his old man putting a stack of dosh behind the bar. You know – five hundred quid or something."

"For *fuck's sake*, Karl," exploded Jamie, "why didn't you tell us that before?"

And as one, the eleven boys picked up their glasses, emptied them into their throats, and stood up. Big Mac burped loudly; Jack, chivvying them out, barked, "Move it! Let's get there before some other bastards drink all the fucking money!"

Eight-twenty-five. Gem's friend Holly had just been let into Gem's house by Gem's dad (who had tried not to stare at her large breasts in her tight coral-pink top) and now she was hobbling at high speed in killer shoes up the stairs to Gem's room. The girls had been friends since they were eight years old and it was really only their joint history and the fact that they lived three doors away from each other (handy for shared three a.m. taxis home or shared boring Sunday afternoons) that kept them friends now.

Holly was pretty much top bitch of the best-looking group of girls at the school. These were girls who – if not particularly naturally good-looking – worked hard at being gorgeous, with lots of time spent shopping and grooming and lots of attention paid to fashion and beauty magazines. They dressed to slay, even for school. They wouldn't date boys from the school, though, only older guys, preferably ones with cars. They acted gorgeous and desirable and created round themselves an aura of success that made them seem even more gorgeous and desirable.

Because of her friendship with Holly, Gem dipped in and out of this group. Holly felt she was generous towards Gem – tolerant towards her eccentricities. Like her friendship with that camp weirdo Christian for a start, and the way she sometimes *made her own clothes*, and carried a camera around with her, and refused to come out clubbing or pubbing very often with Holly and the girls. Holly would bitch mildly to the girls about all this and they'd tell her they didn't know why she bothered with Gem. At which she'd glow with loyalty. "I don't drop old mates," she'd tell them smugly. "I'm not like that."

Now she burst into Gemma's bedroom and squealed, "Haven't you got changed yet?"

"Oh, charming, Holl. I *am* changed."

"*God* – aren't you gonna dress up a bit more? It's at Cascades! It'll be really smart!"

"Are you saying I look crap?"

Holly, staring at Gem looking all fresh and healthy and beautiful, was beginning to feel overdressed, artificial even. Gem – who had a natural sense of style – often did this to her. "*No*, babe!" she cried. "Just – it's a party! Put some heels on at least."

"I can't *move* in heels."

"Yeah you can!"

"Not the way I want to."

The two girls stared at each other like a standoff across the bed. Gem could be quite scary and overpowering when she got like this. And Holly didn't want to get into an argument because they were running late and a fight might mess with her make-up. "Did you say your dad was gonna give us a lift?" she cooed, placating. "Only we should go."

"Yeah, he is," said Gem. "Let's go."

Five to nine. Gem's dad's car disgorged Gem and Holly on to the pavement just outside Cascades at the exact same moment that the eleven rugby boys came thronging round the corner. Holly sneered at them, then accentuated the sexy sway of her walk as she headed for the club door. Gem hung back, eyes seeking Jack's.

"Hi!" he croaked, flanked by all his mates.

"Hey!" she squeaked back.

And that was it. They couldn't even look at each other again. Two screwed-up magnets repelled by the sheer force of their mutual pull.

Separately, they shuffled up the stairs and into the club.

Ten o'clock. Lewis's eighteenth birthday party had been roaring for at least an hour. Karl had been right about the free drink. Everyone – getting through it as fast as they could while they weren't being charged for it – was either very well lathered or acting that way, so as not to stand out.

The weird thing about Lewis's party was that just about everyone from the sixth form was there. Normally, tribes kept to themselves and avoided other tribes. Kids wanted to be with kids who dressed, spoke, thought and acted in the same way as they did. But this was like some glitzy rehearsal for the end-of-school prom, with everyone all mixed up together.

The dominant tribes from both years had staked out various parts of the club. Jack and his sporty mates were all near the bar. Christian and the drama bunch were on the other side, lounging theatrically by some silver-edged mirrors and a huge potted yucca. The kids into music were grouped near the DJ, influencing his choice and loudly reacting to each new tune. Holly and her A-list girlfriends were on the move, touring, promenading, making sure they were seen.

Gem was with them, but her senses, every one of them, were trained on Jack.

Who was similarly focused on her. He thought she looked sensational, even better than she looked in school. He couldn't take his eyes off her legs, her hair, her body. . .

"Fuckin' hell," Dosh groaned at his side. "Fucking *look* at her."

"Who?" barked Jack, possessively.

"Jenny Baker. Christ, look at her tits. She don't have them in school. *Fucking* hell."

"She's a bitch, man."

"Yeah, but she's hot. And she's pissed. She looks like she'd be well up for it."

"Go and find out, mate."

"Which one you fancy?"

"All of them," lied Jack. "But they won't touch us. You know that."

"If they're pissed they might. Coming with me?"

"Yeah. In a minute."

But Jack wouldn't cross the great exposed stretch of floor to speak to Gem, not when she was in amongst those tarty harpies anyway, and Gem couldn't find the courage to walk over to the loud, all-male . . . *very* male . . . group of rugby boys.

"Oh, I'm fed up of this!" squawked Holly suddenly. "Just wandering about! Come on – let's dance!"

And the girls took the empty centre of the floor, and started to dance. It was something they often did, something they were well practised in. Because of the immense tightness of their clothes and the height of their heels, they could only do a kind of constrained, erotic writhing, but they flowed together, interacting and mirroring each other as they moved, and all of the eyes in the club were on them. It was like some strange act of self-worship.

Gemma hated the way they did this. She hated the ostentation; the way the whole point of it was not so much to have fun but to be watched. She thought they looked like a soft-core lipstick lesbian floorshow.

"C'mon, Gemmy!" squawked Holly, shimmying opposite her. Gem responded in as small a way as she could, just this side of not actually moving. It satisfied Holly, who quite liked a backdrop to her own lavish dancing. Gem told herself she'd give it a few cringe-inspiring minutes, then go and hide in the bog. And the route to the bog would take her past the rugby boys. . .

But the big beery group he was with – it was still an insurmountable barrier. Gem found herself scuttling by with downcast eyes, hoping Jack was at least looking at her. Inside the ladies', she applied more mascara and gave herself a pep talk. "Just go over there!" she nagged herself. "What's the worst that could happen?"

He could ignore me. He could do a massive put-down on me so that all his friends laughed.

Gem rammed her mascara wand back in her tiny bag. She knew she wasn't going to be brave enough to do anything. Then she walked back through the door, and straight into him.

Chapter 9

"Hey – sorry!" grunted Jack, as she rebounded back in the tiny vestibule that had both ladies' and gents' toilets leading off it.

"S'OK!" Gem gasped.

The split-second contact had been overwhelming for both of them. Each other's scent, touch, closeness. . . They stood back and tried and failed to meet each other's eyes.

"You finished?" demanded Jack, immediately mentally shoeing himself for how crass that sounded, especially as he knew she'd finished – he'd followed her in here.

Gem nodded, pulled open the main door and went through, holding it for him to follow. "Enjoying the party?" she asked, loud over the music.

"Not a lot," he shouted back. "Liked the free drink though."

"Oh – has it all gone?"

"Yup. They started charging half an hour ago."

"Shit – I only got two drinks!"

"Well I had one of yours then. Hey – I'll get you one."

"Thanks," Gem smiled. *It was starting!*

"What you having?"

"Vodka and lots of ice, and lime please."

She followed him to the bar, triumphant. After being that hungry for him, that focused on him all night – God, this was good. This was like tearing off and chewing and swallowing great hunks of meat when you were starving; it was fantastic.

But it was one thing to stand next to him and admire his strong brown arms on the marble of the bar and cast lecherous glances at his fantastic profile, and something else again to restart the conversation when he turned and handed her her drink.

He looked equally stumped.

"So what's wrong with it?" Gem demanded, taking a sip, adding, "Thanks. For this."

"Wrong with what?"

"The party. You said you weren't enjoying it."

"Oh, it's OK. Not really my thing, parties like this."

"Yeah? What kind you like?"

"Oh – you know. Saw you lot dancing."

"Yeah? You shoulda come and joined in."

"Not really my thing, dancing."

God but this is hard work, thought Gem. Conversations with Christian just . . . went. They swooped and soared and cartwheeled and caroused. But this . . . "heavy going" didn't come close to describing it, it was like wading through mud. *Cement*.

Maybe because with Christian the conversation was everything, whereas now . . . she wanted to touch Jack, show her interest in him, but her hands were frozen round her glass, her body was rigid, her face wouldn't flirt.

Jack felt the same way. He wanted to go into the routine he did with a girl he fancied, signalling with eyebrows and body and tone of voice that he was up for it, but he felt as inept as a twelve year old.

What was wrong with them? What was wrong with these normally confident kids that they couldn't communicate how much they liked each other?

"Sorry," Jack said, unexpectedly. "I'm knackered."

"Yeah?"

"Yeah. We had a training session early on. Got a big match tomorrow."

"Yeah? Who you playing?"

"Brayton Bridge. You heard of them?"

"No."

"Oh."

From the corner of her eye Gem saw the rugby boys surge towards them on their way to round up Jack, and in desperation she said, "I've always wanted to see a rugby game."

"Yeah?"

"Yeah. You know – find out what everyone goes on about."

"Well, come along. Twelve o'clock kick-off."

"Might do that. At the Westgate Grounds?"

"*Jack!*" Big Mac bulked up next to them, leering cnviously at Gem. "We're off. Gotta get our early night, haven't we? Anyway the price of beer here's a fucking *joke.*"

Jack cursed silently. He wanted to stay, but he wasn't at the stage with Gem where staying was an option. I mean, face it – she'd let him buy her a drink but her sort boasted about never paying for anything, didn't they, it needn't mean she liked him. And it was going really badly. He felt like a great block of wood. Supposing he stayed, and Gem cleared off five minutes later to rejoin her friends? He'd look like an idiot. "All right, hang on," he said – and then immediately regretted it, but it was too late.

Suddenly, the music stopped, and the club echoed with voices. Then the DJ called out, "Come on, we all know why we're here tonight. . ." and the tedious timeless tune of "Happy Birthday" jangled out.

"Oh, shit, look at the Brady Bunch," growled Big Mac. "I'm gonna have to go over there and sort 'em out. . ." On the far side of the club Christian was prancing around, conducting a semi-circle of his friends, who were all singing loudly. Lewis the birthday boy was standing nearby looking visibly moved.

"Jesus, come on," groused Jamie, "before I puke. . ."

"Yeah, come on if you're coming, mate," said Karl.

"See you," muttered Jack to Gemma.

"See you," she replied.

Chapter 10

"No way, no way, not now, not ever. . ."

"Chris, don't be a bastard."

"No, no, no, NO."

"Chris – please. Or I'll curse you. I'll make a wax model of you."

"No."

"I've got some of your hair. And nail clippings."

"No you haven't. Anyway I don't care. No torture you could inflict from the Black Arts could be worse than standing on a rugby touchline. I mean it, Gemma. *No way, no how, not now, not ever.*"

"All right, all right. No need to come on all *Cat in the Hat.*"

"How can you even *ask* it of me? It would be like returning to the scene of my earlier child abuse. No – it *would* be doing that!"

"I'll pay for your therapy—?"

"You could never afford the amount I'd need. And anyway – think what they'd do to me! A fully-paid-up member of the Brady Bunch, watching their game! They'd aim a *scrum* at me – I'd disappear beneath a *ruck* and never be seen again."

"Chris – I said all *right*! Forget it! I'll just have to make Holly come with me. But she'll be embarrassing."

"Well, there *is* an alternative. You *could* return to the land of sane people instead, and not go."

With dramatic emphasis, Gem stopped dead in her tracks, causing two girls behind her on the stairs to stumble and curse. Lewis's party was at an end, and the last of the guests were straggling tiredly and drunkenly down towards the exit. "I *have* to go!" squawked Gem, moving on again. "We were – I nearly pulled him, Chris! He bought me a drink! And then his stupid team turned up and . . . we were just outnumbered, it got awkward. I think he's shyer than he seems."

"*Shy?* Jack Slade *shy?* You've lost it, Gem. You need electric shock treatment on your fast-disappearing brain. Jack's about as *shy* as a charging rhinoceros."

"Oh sod off, Chris. Look – if I turn up to watch he'll know I'm interested, won't he. Then he'll have the confidence to make the next move. I never seem to bump into him at school, and anyway there's always too many people around to get anywhere. . ."

Christian grimaced with disgust. "God, Gem, you really are serious about this, aren't you?"

"Yes."

"I s'pose I thought – *hoped*, for your sake – that once you'd talked to him – seen his *criminal* lack of any kind of clothes sense—"

"Oh *piss* off—"

"—he dresses from *Just Sports*, Gem! His idea of a major label is the *Gap*!"

"I don't care."

"Well you should do! You've got such *style* – the way you put things together, the stuff you make up – no one's got a better feel for clothes than you have!"

"Apart from you, darling!"

"Well – true, apart from me. Together we've made you an icon, Gem. I mean it! People copy you! And now – you're planning to be seen in public with Mr One-Hundred-Per-Cent-Nylon-Sports-Top. . ."

"Chris – for Christ's sake. I've told you. I'm interested in what's *inside* his gear, not what it looks like."

"Oh, you depraved slut. You . . . *creature.*"

"Sorry, Chris," Gem gurgled. "I'm only being honest."

There was a huffy silence from Christian. They walked into the cool early-morning, early-autumn air, and she linked arms with him to walk along the street.

It often happened that they ended up going home together, after parties, concerts, whatever – even if they hadn't arrived together. They had some of their best, most honest, most open conversations then, after everything was over. Christian would go home with her and settle like a faithful dog on the floor of her bedroom on a pull-out bed and they'd talk more, right into the dawn. Gem's parents were quite happy with this arrangement because it meant Gem got seen safely home and anyway, they thought Christian was gay because he liked to join in their daughter's extravagant clothes-making sessions and he let her put nail varnish on him and even eye make-up sometimes.

"I suppose I should be glad it's all just *physical*," said Chris, finally. "I mean – if you really started to like him, like what he *was*. . ."

"No chance of that, babes. It's his chopper I'm after."

And they both hooted with laughter, and hurried on.

Gem knew how to handle Holly. She phoned her up the next morning, enquired after her hangover, then asked her to come to a rugby match with her at midday. Over Holly's squeals of derision, she told her that Karl (the best-looking of the team after Jack) really fancied her, then she promised to go shopping with her afterwards and treat her to a late lunch.

Within two minutes, Holly had agreed to come to the match. She loved it when boys fancied her, even if she didn't fancy them back – she bathed in their attention like scented oils. And she adored shopping and she couldn't resist a free lunch.

What she told Gem, of course, was that she'd do it for the sake of their friendship. "What are mates for, Gemmy, ay? Call for me, yeah?"

For his part, Jack hadn't given Gemma much of a second thought. He wasn't given to thinking about girls – not about plotting how to get off with them, anyway – it either happened or it didn't. The space Gem occupied inside him was like a sense of loss, a yearning, all messed up with what he felt about Amy dumping him, something he didn't really understand, not yet.

It didn't take up anything like the space that was focused on the match.

Chapter 11

Saturday morning, eleven forty-five a.m. The warm-up was over; Westgate were back in the changing room. First, Boxy gave out the brand-new dark-blue shirts like he was handing out breast-plates blessed by the king. Number one – Big Mac. Number two – Ben Worthing. Number three – Rory Knight. All the way up to number fifteen. The boys received them in solemn near-silence, stripped their training shirts off and put them on.

And now Boxy was talking to them. It was nothing like the cheery, encouraging pre-match chat that Len gave – running over techniques and reminding them about moves they'd practised and saying "do your best, lads".

This was life and death. This was a council of war.

Boxy stood, they sat. He didn't ask for their attention – he didn't need to. A tractor could've ploughed through the changing room and still all eyes would've stayed fixed to Boxy's dark, fervent face.

"I heard some of you earlier," he said, "talking like this match didn't really count. 'First one of the season, no real training, what can he expect', all that crap. Well, I'll tell you what I expect. I expect you to show me what you're made of. I expect you to show me the kind of team we can become."

He paused, scanned the faces in front of him, one by one, like he was rating them, assessing them. Jamie crossed his eyes in an effort not to glance away. Big Mac's fists were balling and unballing with tension.

"You're gonna make mistakes," Boxy went on. "I know it; you know it. Because we're not a team, not yet. But this is the *start*. This is the start of making us into a team. Now – you play it safe, you prat about, make a mess of things – that's the start you've made. That's the team you're gonna become. D'you want that?"

Jack shook his head; a few others copied. "*D'you want that?*" repeated Boxy, twice as loud, and Jack shouted back, "No!" and everyone copied him, shouting and head-shaking, Dosh wagging his head frantically because he was afraid he was going to start laughing if he didn't.

"You haven't got all the skills yet," Boxy growled. "No way. You haven't got the fitness. You're not together. You're a fraction of what you could be – what you *will* be. But right now – here on this field in five minutes' time – this is where you *start to work*. And I wanna see you make a good start, the best start. I wanna see you work with your heads and your hearts and your bodies. I wanna see you work for me, for each other, for your*self*. Cos everything else is gonna come from that. You gotta go out there and put your bodies on the line for what you're gonna become. OK?"

There was a silence. He scanned their faces again, and

they tried to meet his eyes unwavering. Then he barked, "Right. On your feet."

"Fuckin' *hell*," muttered Iz. Everyone got off the bench, some springing, some slow.

"Grab a shirt," said Boxy, and the boys formed a circle, slung their arms round each other's necks and backs, took hold of the brand-new, dark-blue shirts on each other's bodies. "You're a unit. You're a team. Look at each other. Who you gonna let down? Who you gonna give less than a hundred per cent to? This is it. This is the first match you're gonna play for me, there'll never be another first match. OK, lads. Make your choice. Make a start. *Make a start*. OK, Jack. Over to you." And he walked out of the changing room door.

Jack didn't know what to say. After everything they'd heard, there didn't seem to be much else to say. But he wanted to communicate the urgency he felt, the feeling that this could be the start of something big. "Let's go for it, boys," he croaked. "Let's show each other, fucking Brayton Bridge, *ourselves* – let's show who we are. Like he said – this is the start. *This is the start!*"

The circle broke apart, and Jack turned and ran, heart hammering, through the door and into daylight, his mates on his heels. He felt like a great roar should greet them, not just the patter of supportive parents clapping. As he led his team on to the pitch, he glanced over to the other training room door.

And there, jogging out slowly, meandering almost, were their green-striped-shirted opponents, Brayton Bridge. From the sheen of privilege and confidence on them he guessed they were mainly private-school boys, used to top-class trainers, used to winning.

Expecting to win this time.

His team milled round him. "Look at those bastards," he muttered. "Look at those smug, *cock-sure* bastards."

"Pretty sure they're gonna win, ain't they?" snarled Ben, the hooker.

"Let's take 'em apart!" growled Jack. "C'mon. Let's *do* it."

"Take 'em apart!" echoed Big Mac, scowling hideously.

"Go in hard from the whistle, like Boxy said and don't let up. C'mon. *C'mon!*"

The ref tossed the coin and blew up, and Iz booted the ball down the pitch. Jack was in a focused red haze as he thundered after it. He shouldered one green-shirt out of the way, dump-tackled the one with the ball. Then he was on it under a pile of players. He thrust it out of the ruck, saw Dosh sieze it, throw it wide. To Iz, who sidestepped his opposite number, and sprinted. Fast, faster, two greens on his heels, and—

Right over the line.

Chapter 12

Amid explosive triumphant cheering from Westgate, Jack raced up to Iz, whacked him on the back, gave way to Mac, who bear-hugged him, then he shouted, "OK, back, *back*! Keep focused, boys! They're not gonna let us get away with this!"

Brayton Bridge didn't know what had hit them. They were still half asleep; they expected this team to be, too. Their captain gathered them round, berated them in tones that said *no way* were they going down to a team of this standard.

Karl missed the conversion, so it was 5-0. Play restarted; five minutes later it was clear Brayton Bridge *had* woken up. Both sides battled on furiously. The ref had woken up too. He was a stickler for standards and fair play; he blew up for Big Mac having his hands in the ruck, awarded a penalty to the greens. Their leggy number 10 skilfully booted it over. Five-three.

And Boxy's roar from the touchline, "C'mon boys! You've made a great start! Now *take it back to 'em*!"

Jack took it back to them. He stepped up a gear; he tackled and battled, and the blues fought their way bit by bit up to the green line. Karl fumbled a catch but Iz saved it, spun it wide to Jamie. Who caught it, swerved back inside – and sprinted it over the line under two tackling greens.

The ref blew his whistle for a try. "Double movement!" erupted the green captain, shrill with indignation. "He put it down this side!"

"I didn't see that," said the ref, firmly.

"It was a *clear* double movement!"

"Don't argue, lad – I've made my decision!"

A couple of the Brayton Bridge parents were shouting out complaints in high-bred voices from the touchline, backing up their seething captain, who'd give away a penalty if he talked back any more.

"Keep your temper, pussy-boy," taunted Jack.

"*Fuck off!*" snapped the captain.

"*Ooops,*" said Mac, pressing up close to him. "Chucking your toys out the pram, ay?" Then he walked back, laughing – and roared in triumph as Karl booted the ball through the posts.

"Twelve-three!" Jack yelled. "*C'mon!*"

Things were really hotting up. The shouting from the touchline doubled in volume, green and blue parents moving apart now, antagonism towards each other growing with their involvement in the game. Brayton Bridge were rattled, playing their hearts out, desperate to get a try on the board before half-time.

Jack sensed rather than saw Boxy on the touchline, approving it all, urging them on.

And then, like a knife slash, the ball spun out sweet to the long-haired green centre, and Jamie missed the tackle, and the centre was clear and away, belting down the pitch towards the line, the blue fullback thundering to catch him, but sliding over the line on top of him, right under the posts.

The leggy number 10 converted the try with ease.

The greens roared their triumph; Jack's team was back to only two points ahead.

The whistle went for half-time.

"Jamie – it's past," Boxy hissed. The team was huddled round him as Karl handed out the water bottles on the side of the pitch. "You fucked up and they slipped one in. They got lucky. That's all it was. Up till then we dominated possession and we dominated territory."

"We was nine up!" groaned Iz.

"So we've lost a bit of ground. You gonna keep thinking – *if only, if only*? Roll over and get shafted if that's what you're thinking."

"It's past," urged Jack. His heart was hammering with the need to win, to *make the start* Boxy had gone on about. "We screwed up, but we're still ahead, and we can beat 'em!"

"What you gonna do now?" demanded Boxy.

"Come back twice as hard!" growled Big Mac.

"Come back, yeah. *Three* times as hard. They're pussy-boys. They can't take it in the ruck. I been watching them. You keep *taking* it to them and *taking* it to them – don't give an inch!" The whistle went. "Don't miss tackles," urged Boxy. "Don't let up!"

As Jack led his team back into the middle of the pitch his battle-narrowed eyes took in a couple of sexy female shapes on the touchline, one in a really stupid pair of high-heeled sandals. *Shit,* he thought. *Gem!* She *came!*

He was grinning as he turned to stare down the Brayton Bridge captain, whose face was all twisted up with the affront of being behind this undrilled team. The Brayton Bridge captain glared at him. *Don't get distracted by Gem, you prat!* Jack told himself, and glared back. Gem here, though! It added spice to the rage he felt inside. The whistle went and he threw himself into the fray like a madman.

Brayton Bridge, scalded and stirred by their half-time talk, came back at Westgate like tigers.

On the touchline, Gem was watching, open-mouthed. It was crazy, the way they were mashing and bashing into each other – insane! But somehow it was terrific, too. "*Oh – my – God!*" squealed Holly, as five bodies crashed to the ground a metre or so away from her. "They can't be *enjoying* this! Hey – which one is Karl anyway?" Gem couldn't find the breath to reply.

Ten minutes in, and a penalty was given to the greens, right on the edge of the pitch. "He'll never get it over," breathed Jack. "Not with that angle."

But the ball soared between the posts and the greens erupted in triumph. Now – at last – Brayton Bridge were one hard-fought point ahead.

Jack could feel his team sagging, sinking. "*C'mon!*" he roared, "take it back to them! *C'mon!*"

"OK, boys," yelled the Brayton Bridge captain, as they kicked off. "We've turned it around! Now let's get a decent score on the board!"

"Arrogant *fucking* bastard," seethed Jack – and hurled himself back at them. Infected by his heroism, his team went with him, and in a last, desperate, exhausted effort, they worked the ball up towards the green line. And then Big Mac, wrecked and gored in the ruck, somehow bulled the ball out, two greens hanging off him, and stumbled towards the line. . .

And touched it down.

Westgate and their supporters erupted with delight, the ref blew up for the try, Jack's team raced together, jumping on each other's backs, hugging. . . The Brayton Bridge captain, his face a pinched white mask of rage, started the march towards the posts for the conversion kick. Big Mac bounced at him, arms open like he was going to grab him and hug him. *"Turned it around have you, you wanker?"* he roared.

And the captain, snapping like a taut wire, threw a punch at Mac's face.

Within seconds, both teams were pitched into an all-out battle, fists flailing. The ref was dancing round them alternately blowing his whistle and screaming, *"Calm it! Calm it!"*

The Brayton Bridge trainer and several of the players' fathers belted on to the pitch. Boxy remained on the touchline. "Aren't you going to try and *stop* them?" shrieked Karl's mum. "Before someone gets *hurt?*"

Boxy smiled, shook his head. "They're big boys now," he said. "They wanna scrap, they can sort it out."

The fight was beginning to level off. Jack, having got in a few good smacks himself, was starting to steer Big Mac away, and two of the blue dads had their captain's arms pinioned. "Play is *abandoned!*" shrilled the ref. "I'm not continuing to referee this game! Game *abandoned!*"

Seething and swearing, the two teams started to separate, blues with blues, greens with greens. Gem's eyes were fixed on Jack. He had a cut above his left eyebrow, sealed up with congealing blood, and she felt like she wanted to clean it, kiss it. . . "*Wow!*" breathed Holly. "Does that sort of thing usually happen in rugby?"

"Shhhh," breathed Gem. She was waiting for Jack.

"OK lads!" shouted Boxy, moving fast on to the far side of the pitch, away from the greens. "This way – to me, here!"

Jack lurched around and as he turned, he waved in Gem's direction. She waved back but she wasn't sure he saw it because he was already staggering off after Boxy. The team grouped round their trainer, listening as he spoke to them. His fist was clenched and he was pounding the air for emphasis.

"Giving them a bollocking," said Holly, "I expect. For fighting."

The girls waited on. They watched Boxy finish speaking, then turn and lead his team into the changing room. Gem stared at the back of Jack's head, willing him to turn round.

But he didn't.

"Charming!" said Holly. "They might at least've said hello to us."

Gemma was silent.

Devastated.

"You gonna wait?" Holly went on. "I'm not bothered. Karl looked a bit of an idiot to me. You wanna wait?"

"No," said Gemma. "Let's go."

Chapter 13

The team had indeed expected a bollocking, like Holly said. Last season they'd got into a fight, not nearly such an all-out one as this one, and old Len had whinged on at them for ages afterwards, saying he was disappointed in them and it wasn't in the spirit of clean play and letting your temper get the better of you meant you lost focus and on and on and on, blah blah blah.

But all Boxy said was: "OK boys, so you had a ruckus. There'll be all sorts of talk going on right now, on the touchline, about how you've let yourselves down. Well, in my opinion, you haven't let yourself down – you've proved your mettle."

Through his exhaustion, Jack felt a stab of excitement. He shot a look at Big Mac, to see if Boxy's words had struck him in the same way. And Big Mac looked back at him, and grinned.

"You had to pitch in, didn't you?" Boxy went on. "You had to defend a teammate. Their captain had it coming. Mac goaded him and he couldn't take it. End of story. What's important to me is – you made a good start. A *great* start."

"We fucking *won*," said Iz.

"Yeah, you did," said Boxy. "Never mind that 'game abandoned' bollocks. You won the game, and you won the fight. You *won*." The exhausted boys huffed with pleasure, and he went on to talk about their game, where it was strong, where it was weak – what they were going to work on. He talked about how, in just a couple of months, they were going to be so strong and so good no other team could even put up a fight against them.

The boys were a solid, triumphant unit as they headed off towards the changing room. Jack was vibrating with it. It was only at the changing room door that he remembered Gemma, and he turned in time to see her walking away across the pitch with the other girl, the one in the stupid high heels.

When Gem was seven years old, she'd trapped her fingers really badly in a drawer she'd slammed. The pain was shocking, horrible, and it had grown, mushroomed until she'd wanted to be sick with it, with fear that it was going to keep on and on and on growing. So to control it she'd pretended it hadn't happened. She'd shut down on it, hard, shut the hurt out of her mind, and in the bath that night her mother had been horrified to see the red and purple weal across her fingers, upset that her daughter hadn't run to her for comfort.

Shutting down on pain was what Gemma was doing now.

She walked across the empty pitch beside Holly and she chatted to Holly about her part-time job in the bakery (and how the manager was mean to her because deep down she was jealous, well, she was bound to be, wasn't she, the dried-up old cow, no wonder her husband had walked out on her) and inside she clamped down on the fact that she'd laid herself open to Jack, she'd made all that effort to go along to watch the match, and he'd ignored her.

She clamped down on it so hard that it somehow ceased to exist.

Finished, she told herself. *Over.*

Chapter 14

Seven long weeks went by. The half-term holiday sped by. Halloween, crammed with plastic skulls and pumpkin heads, came and went; at night the sky was full of fireworks. The end of the endless autumn term was almost in sight.

Boxy had kept his pledge to the Westgate Under 17s. They trained hard every Tuesday night, and on Saturday morning there was nearly always a match; if there wasn't, there was extra training. Boxy also kept his promise to swing it for them to work out in the Club gym, even though they were, strictly speaking, underage.

The boys loved the way their hard training was paying off. They loved the way their muscles were building, their stamina was growing, their team skills were improving week on week. They'd played four more local matches and only lost one and immediately, Boxy had booked a rematch. "Next time," he said, "we're gonna paste 'em. Show 'em who rules." Impressed by Westgate's success, quite a few more lads turned up at the Club to join. It was Club practice to welcome anyone who came, but Boxy gave all the newcomers a trial and only took on the best seven. So now they were a real squad, and could cope with injury. Boxy was scrupulous about making sure all the players got a run out, unless it was a really hard match, and then only the top players got on the field.

There were mutterings from the older men in the Club, of course – the "alackadoos", as Boxy called them. They muttered about Boxy's arrogance, his extreme methods, about the way he was increasingly sidelining Len and taking the team over. But the boys didn't care about mutterings. They were a team, and they were on a roll, and Boxy had their absolute loyalty. They loved the aura of anarchy around him, the subversive way he looked at life. Like the evening they'd been poring over tabloid coverage of football rioting in Scotland, and Rory Knight was banging on about all the arrests and saying that rugby was a better game than football because its supporters weren't thugs, and Boxy, walking into the changing room, had said, "Those so-called riots – they weren't a problem. The police made it into a problem." They'd all looked at him, impressed, and he'd gone on, "Those shopfronts that got smashed, the street furniture that got trashed – it'd never've happened if the police had left well alone and not gone charging in."

"Oh yeah?" Rory had scoffed. "What about all the men that got beaten up?"

"They'd agreed to it. That battle – it was arranged. They were on the phone to each other for days before, fixing it up. It was *consensual*. Know what consensual means, Rory?"

"Yeah," said Rory, needled. "Both sides consent. Agree to it."

"Right. They weren't out to grab some innocent bystander and beat him to a pulp. Just each other. It's in our blood, see? Battle. War. Men *need* it. Our sort of men anyway. Have done since time began. What's the difference between arranging a street battle and arranging a rugby match?"

"You don't bring weapons to a rugby match," said Rory.

"We don't need weapons, we're hard enough without."

The boys grinned and Dosh said, "Rules?"

"You think they don't have rules? And yeah they get broken, but then so do ours, right? Truth is, there isn't all that much difference. Two gangs of men, arranging to fight. *Consensual*. That's the word, lads. If those guys want to fight, who's gonna tell them it's wrong? Why should we accept some nob at the top with muscles like a chicken telling us which way we gotta live our lives, arresting us when we step outta line?"

It was exhilarating. It was like you could break the rules and keep your honour – increase your honour. Honour was big for Jack, but he didn't talk about it, or about what was happening. Nor did any of the other boys, but Jack sensed they were feeling the same way he was. It was there like a pulse whenever they were together. It was as if they'd all begun to get a sense of what they were alive for, and it was enough just to live it. Every time they won a match, their pride increased, the pulse strengthened. At school, and among the people they knew, their status increased. They were talked about and pointed out and some girls started seeing it as a challenge to pull them, because they wanted a share of their success.

It was brilliant.

On the second Tuesday in November, Jack, Karl and Mac, the first to arrive in the changing room, were pulling on their training gear in a leisurely way when Dosh burst in yelling, "*Quick!* It's kicking off! Len and Boxy – in the clubroom!"

As one, the four boys surged out of the door and across the tarmac, then they ducked down in front of the clubroom windows and peered in. Boxy and Len were standing in the middle of the room, glaring at each other. Boxy had his arms folded over his chest; Len had his hands in his pockets but his back was rigid with tension.

"They're only *talking*," muttered Mac.

"Oh, what – you thought they'd be kicking the shit out of each other?" snapped Dosh.

"Shhhh!" hissed Jack. "Listen!"

"Look, Alan," Len was saying, far more loudly than he needed to with Boxy standing only a foot or two away from him, "you're taking this the wrong way. No one's criticizing what you've done. You've transformed a failing team into one with drive and a future, and we're all very pleased. It's just – well. Some of the parents are getting a bit nervous with the . . . with the *intensity* of it all."

"I'm not training the parents," retorted Boxy.

"No," agreed Len evenly, "but you're training their sons. And as I say, there's been comments about you working 'em too hard, running them into the ground. The mums are worried about the amount of injuries sustained during matches."

Boxy scoffed out a laugh, as though worrying about what the "mums" thought had to be a joke. "Well, that's rugby," he sneered. "It's a tough game."

"There's another concern. The general thought is your idea of the game sails a lot nearer to what most of us would call illegal, and Jack and the lads have taken that on. And it's . . . *well*, it's not acceptable."

"I see. So the winning is *acceptable*, but my methods aren't?"

The four boys crouching in front of the window exchanged glances, grinning.

"Alan, I'm asking you to meet me halfway here," said Len, sounding pained.

"I'm not a halfway type of bloke, Len."

"Look – OK, I'll say it. The last couple of times I've turned up to help train, I've felt in the way."

"In my book, there's only room for one trainer on the pitch."

"I see!" Len was outraged. "Message understood! So I get left to manage the fixtures and paperwork, do I?"

"You want to come back and train the boys, come back and train them. But I won't be there."

Len's face was pale with something approaching shock. He thought he'd just have to say a few words, and Boxy would wake up, as it were, and promise to mend his ways, but *this*. . .

Saying nothing, Len walked away, his mind a blank of not knowing what to think.

As soon as he'd gone, Boxy said, "OK, lads, you can stop creeping around like a load of spying schoolgirls, and get changed, and get on the pitch."

They converged on him as he left the clubroom. "Wow, man – you were *harsh*!" gloated Dosh.

"I just told him what was what."

"What you gonna do if he calls your bluff?" demanded Jack.

"What – turns up to training? I'd leave."

"Well, we'd leave with you!" grunted Mac. "We don't want that sad old git!"

Boxy, eyes straight ahead, smiled.

Chapter 15

At school, ever since the Brayton Bridge match, Gem had avoided Jack like a disease. It was easy to change her route to keep away from him, or be engrossed in talking to someone else when he walked by. She'd convinced Holly, all the other girls – and even, sometimes, herself – that there was nothing up with her, nothing at all. But she couldn't convince the ever-perceptive Christian. He niggled and probed and wheedled away at her until one day she exploded, "For *fuck's* sake Chris you bastard! OK! OK! *No* – I'm not happy. *No* – I'm not my 'old joyous self', as you call it. I still fancy Jack. I watched him the other day, on the sports field, and he looks better than ever. He's all pumped up and he was jumping about like he owned the pitch and. . ."

". . .some sickeningly depraved part of you finds that attractive."

"*Yes*. So now you know, can we drop the subject please?"

Christian leant back in his stainless-steel café chair and let the hurt and disappointment that Jack Slade was still an object of desire to his beloved Gem settle down inside him.

When it reached a manageable level he reached across the smeary tabletop and took hold of her hand. "Oh, Gemmy," he crooned. "Poor old Gemmy."

She snatched her hand away. "Shut up. Shut *up*! Don't *patronize* me, Chris! I know you hate him. You're *glad* he behaved like such an arsehole to me."

"Gemma, how can you say that? I'm not *glad*. I'm not glad at *all*. I hope his head explodes. When he's weight-lifting. I hope he overdoes it, and an excessive rush of blood to the cranium shatters his skull and—"

"*Chris* – I get your point."

"OK. But that's what I hope. I hope that for anyone who upsets you. Bastards."

Gem sniffed, then slid her hand back across the table to lie beside Chris's. "Sorry," she murmured. "For yelling at you. Why do I want that meathead when I've got friends like you, ay?"

"This is true."

"Sorry."

"S'OK. But God, Gem, it's time you talked about all this. It's time you let it out."

She smiled. "I thought I just had?"

"I mean let it out *sensibly*. Analytically. So you can begin to deal with it."

Gem groaned. "Here we go with the amateur therapy again."

"Hardly amateur. Mr Robins said my last piece of psychology coursework was the most *perceptive* he'd—"

"I'll *slap* you, Chris!"

"Promises. Sweetie – you need help. You've done the

emotional equivalent of putting a tiny sticking plaster on a great, pustulating, infected sore."

Gem grimaced. "Nice."

"You think if you just ignore it it'll go away. Well, it won't. You've got to bring it all out into the open, talk about it. . ."

"And then it'll go away, will it?"

"You'll be able to deal with it."

"What's to *deal* with? It's just – *there*. I really, really fancy him. I can't stop thinking about him. Even though he couldn't even be bothered to say hello to me when I turned up to watch him play."

"Oh, Gemmy – I know how *humiliating* that must've been—"

"*Fuck* humiliating! I don't care about humiliating! I care about the fact that he doesn't give the tiniest little *toss* about me! If I thought he did, I'd probably put myself right out to be humiliated again!"

There was a kind of shocked silence, broken only by Chris stirring his last dribble of coffee round and round in his mug with a plastic wand. Both of them realized they were on dangerous ground. They'd started using voices quite different to the teasing, mocking, affectionate voices they usually used with each other. Both of them wondered how much raw honesty their particular kind of friendship could stand.

"You don't mean that, darling," murmured Chris, at last. "You're just upset. You'll get over him. It'll fade."

Gem sighed. "I wish it would get on with it and fade, then. Sometimes I think I'm *obsessed*."

"Obsession can be cured."

"What – with electric shocks or something? Anyway, I don't know if I want to be cured. He's – he – oh *Christ*, Chris – I dunno."

"Want another coffee?" Chris asked.

She nodded and he trooped up to the counter and ordered two more large lattes. In his mind, he was formulating something to say to her, something that might comfort both of them. While the lattes were being prepared, he went to the gents', peed, washed his hands scrupulously, then studied himself for a few seconds in the black-edged mirror. Then he came back, collected the two tall latte mugs, and returned to Gem. She looked as though nothing about her, inside or out, had moved since he'd gone. "Thanks," she murmured, as he put the mug in front of her.

"Gemmy, I've been thinking," he said. "You're in the grip of this . . . primal urge."

She groaned. "Tell me about it."

"No, look, I don't just mean the urge to . . . do whatever disgusting thing you want to do with Jack Slade for its own sake. I mean – a procreative urge. The ancient urge to mate with the toughest and strongest in the pack. Natural selection. You know – Darwin. Like a doe wanting the stag with the biggest antlers, the stag who beats the crapola out of all the others, because then her young will be healthy, and safe."

Gem's eyes were glittering dangerously. "That's not how I see it, Chris."

"Hear me out. Some part of you – and I love you for

this, Gemmy, don't misunderstand me! – some part of you is seriously tapped into that old primal thing. You see a . . . a *specimen* like Jack Slade and you respond. Lots of girls respond. But yours is deeper, more gripping, because you're more full-on and you're more in touch with your primal side."

"Chris – what's your point?"

"My point – *also* due to Darwin – is that we've evolved. We're multi-faceted now, with lots and lots of different sides that evolved at different times. The old primal drives are still there, but nowadays we don't have to be ruled by them. We don't have to be ruled by what will keep our species going. You can say *no* to your primal side."

Gem's mouth twitched for a moment, then she burst out laughing. Chris sat back, mortally offended. "Sorry," she gurgled, "sorry. It was just the way you put it. Like – 'say *no* to underarm odour' or something. No . . . please . . . go on."

Christian shrugged and took a slow, meaningful sip of coffee. Then he said, "What I'm getting at, is if you *see* it as just that old urge, that old lust, you'll understand the mechanics of it, you'll be on the way to being free of it. For God's sake bring your *brain* into it, Gemma. You're too intelligent for someone like Jack Slade, and you know it."

This time Gemma took a slow sip. "Do I?" she said at last.

As for Jack Slade himself, he'd had very little time to brood about Gem although, somehow, she was always there with him. She occupied a space inside him like a mist, a wraith, curling round everything, but never seen properly and not really part of his world. Whenever he caught sight of her in school it delivered a blow to his groin that spread desire all through him, but he chose not to follow up on it. He'd never admit it to himself but he was alarmed by it, by its intensity. And of course the longer he left it, the more impossible it was to speak to her, to apologize for just letting her walk away across the rugby pitch after she'd made the effort to come and see him play. He avoided her like she was avoiding him.

Anyway, the new team was everything to him now; it was how he defined himself. It took up all his energy, all his focus, most of his free time. The boys were more than his mates, they were his brothers in arms. And every day, his belief in Boxy grew. Boxy would weave words into his team talks that sent Jack's head careening off into worlds that had just been fantasy before, worlds full of epic events, manned by heroes, worlds where he longed to live.

Jack felt a little uneasy about the total sidelining of Len, they all did, but they buried it under aggressive loyalty to Boxy. The Saturday after the showdown between Len and Boxy, the boys were stripping off triumphantly after yet another crunching Westgate win, with the noise level through the roof and Iz chanting, "*We're* the business! Westgate *business*!", when Jack chucked his boots down and announced, "Reckon there's more trouble brewing."

"Yeah?" demanded Mac. "What?"

"Len heard Box telling me to end their number ten's game."

"*Which* you did!"

"*Course* I did! I smashed the little fucker!'

"You hear what Len said?" demanded Jamie.

"Yep. *We all know tactical injuries go on but to actively encourage lads of seventeen to put the boot in is just not right, Alan.*"

A roar of jeering approval greeted Jack's imitation of Len's slightly querulous voice. "Reckon the alackadoos are getting their knickers in a right twist," gloated Iz. "You see the way they were all bunched up together at the end, talking to Len?"

"Didn't even clap us off properly!"

"*Bastards! Fuck* 'em!"

"They can't stand it that we're winning everything! They can't stand it that Boxy's a better trainer than they'll ever be!"

"Everyone's got it in for him," said Karl. "My dad was telling me how everyone's getting worried about him meeting up with us for a beer, after a match."

"Oh – *whaaat*?!" exploded Dosh. "What wrong with that?"

"Dad was going on about how there should be like a . . . *division,* between trainer and team."

"He's just fucking jealous we don't let him come!"

"He reckons a trainer shouldn't be too *involved.* Or there could be all kinds of problems."

"*What* sort of bloody problems? They reckon he's a paedophile?"

There was a huge roar of mocking laughter, and the subject was dropped.

*

Saturday night post-match celebrations were already a team institution. They generally went to The Fox, which was a seedy and depressing pub, empty even at weekends, so the landlord couldn't afford to be picky about the boys' ages or the fact that they made a huge amount of noise. Boxy always bought the first round of drinks and if you wanted to leave early, to go on to a party or out with other friends, you were jeered at and made to feel you were letting the team down. Increasingly, no one left early. Increasingly, various girls – girlfriends and friends of girlfriends – would turn up and join the boys, and other girls would wangle an invitation to come along (because it was understood you had to be invited) and get high on the energy the team put out. They were all referred to scathingly by Boxy as "the groupies" but the boys loved it, loved the attention. Even Big Mac finally lost his cherry when the sheer triumph of being in big part responsible for the win that day gave him the confidence to chat up a girl he'd hardly dared make eye contact with before.

As for Jack, he'd had three drunken one nighters, only one of them involving actual sex. All of them left him feeling a bit hollow, although he'd enjoyed the boasting and the joking with his mates afterwards. Then that night on the second Saturday in November, Jack got drunker than usual at the Fox celebrations. And something, he wasn't even sure what, made him remember Gem walking away across the field, and regret took hold of him like an iron fist, and he practically collapsed against the bar. "Fuck it," he muttered into his beer, "*fuck it.* Why didn't I look back earlier? Why the *fuck* didn't I catch her before she went?"

Jamie's arm came down heavily round his shoulders. "You all right, mate?"

"Yeah. Knackered. Pissed. I hate women. Why'd they always walk off too soon?"

"Dunno, but they do, don't they. Have another beer."

"Go on then."

"Forget women, mate," slurred Jamie. "The team. *We're* the thing."

"Yeah. *Yeah*. We're the thing."

Then three days later Jack ran smack into Gem as they were both heading into the school canteen.

Chapter 16

There was nowhere to go, no one to hide behind.

"Hi!" squeaked Gem, hating the way her voice sounded like a dying hamster.

"Herrgh," grunted Jack, eyes dilating in panic and excitement.

The air between them was humming with static. The silence screamed. *Sod this*, thought Gem, and turned to go, just as Jack, flogging his mind for something to say, came out desperately with, "Enjoy the game?"

"What game?" She sounded waspish, and she didn't care.

"You know – back at the start of the season . . . you came. . ."

"Oh yeah. God, that was months ago."

"You should come to another. We've upped our standard. You shoulda seen the game last week, against Millport. We *caned* 'em."

Gemma felt a spurt of pleasure at this sort-of invitation, and clamped down on it, hard. She couldn't meet Jack's eyes, so she stared down at the bag she was swinging in her hands and told herself, Chris is right. It's *hopeless*. He thinks I came to see the rugby. And out loud she said, "Good for you."

There was another pause, then Jack gruffed out, "I came to look for you, after. You'd gone."

"Er – yeah. Everyone left. I didn't fancy standing on the touchline like a solitary lemon."

"I waved—"

"Yeah, and then pissed straight off with the team."

"Well – Boxy called us to him."

"Fine," shrugged Gem.

Another static-filled silence, both on the edge of just hopelessly walking away from each other. Then Jack cranked out, "Sorry 'bout that, Gem."

"Look – I said – it's fine."

"You don't . . . *understand*. I couldn't come over to you." The words coiled out of him like a heavy chain. "I really couldn't. It'd be – it'd be as bad as running off the pitch in the middle of a game to talk you."

"Oh come on!" she snapped, and looked up at him at last. "How could it be?"

"Trust me." This time, Jack looked away. "The talk at the end – you gotta be there for it. It's vital."

"Fine. So why didn't you come over when the talk was over? Before you all went in the changing room? Would that've been *bad* as well?"

Too late, Gem realized she should be sounding cool, unconcerned, indifferent. Jack was scuffing at the floor with his trainer, like he really didn't want to answer. Then he muttered, "I got stick just for waving."

"Yeah?"

"Remember it ended in a fight?"

"Course I remember. You all went mental."

"Well, afterwards, Boxy was making these gags about how maybe if the captain hadn't had his girlfriend on the touchline he might've kept order on the pitch."

Gem flushed up rapturously at the word *girlfriend*, forgave herself for not sounding cool and indifferent. Then she said, "OK then. But after that – you just walked into the changing room."

Jack scuffed a bit more and muttered, "I forgot you were there."

Gem's rapture drained away. "Charming," she croaked.

"I was just – *look*. It wasn't personal. I'd've forgotten anyone, the state I was in. It was just so fucking amazing, I can't tell you. We'd won, we'd really stuck it to them and—"

"I thought the match was abandoned."

"It was. But we won all right. *And* we won the fight. And the talk Boxy gave – it was awesome. We thought he'd give us stick for fighting but he didn't. He said he was dead proud of us. That we got stuck in. His view of the game, it's – we're going places. We're one of the hardest teams in the area now."

There was a pause, and at last they both looked at each other. Gem wanted to push freeze frame to give her time to think, to work it all out. He'd *forgotten* about her. But he was also talking as if he was trying to make her understand – like it really mattered to him that she understood. She couldn't think straight. Standing this close to him made thinking impossible. "I know," she said at last, "I've been hearing about you."

"Yeah?" Jack said, grinning. "What?"

"Well – that. That you're a bunch of psychos on the pitch."

Jack laughed, and moved slightly closer to her. "We just wanna *win*," he said. The nearness of her was filling every part of him. He took in a deep breath and demanded, "Listen – d'you wanna come out with me?"

And Gem took in a deeper breath and gasped out, "OK. When?"

That evening, Jack headed over the bleak, wet sports pitch for Tuesday's training session, rerunning the way he'd finished his conversation with Gem. He'd tried to look normal and talk calmly about meeting outside the Odeon on Friday to see this new, highly-hyped film about Elizabethan sea battles while all the time he felt like throwing his head back and crowing like a cockerel. Which he recognized would almost certainly have put Gem off. He wondered if she'd felt anything like he did. If she'd managed to seem so steady and cool while underneath she was . . . *electrocuted*.

He fucking hoped so.

"Awright?" Jamie called out to him.

"Yeah," he said, dumping down his kit.

"So what's new? What you been doing?"

Jack grinned. The boys checked on each other constantly, policing new friends, new events, anything that might take them beyond the team. "Not a lot," he lied, adding, "you know Gemma Hanrahan?"

"Yeah?"

"I'm going out with her. Friday."

"Yeah? You took your time."

"What d'you mean?"

"She turned up at that first game, didn't she? Brayton Bridge? Why didn't you ask her then?"

"Couldn't be bothered," Jack sneered.

"Is that right. Well, you seem pretty chuffed about her. Been getting the balls up, ay? To ask her out?"

"*No.* I only now got round to it, OK?"

"Round to what?" demanded Boxy, who'd come up behind them.

"Jack's got a new girlfriend," gloated Jamie.

"She's not a girlfriend," snapped Jack. "I'm just going to the cinema with her."

"*Sweet,*" said Boxy. "So you're gonna hold hands in the back row, are you, Jack?"

"Make sure you buy her some popcorn, OK?" put in Iz, who'd joined them.

"Girls *love* popcorn," said Karl, and suddenly it seemed the whole team was round Jack, grinning and jeering, and Big Mac was idiotically chanting, "Gem-*ma*, Gem-*ma*."

Jack's response was to shoulder-barge Karl sideways and get a bit of a domino effect going through the boys. "Some of us need sex," he yowled. "Some of us can't live like fucking monks, can we?"

"No one's talking about entering monastic orders," said Boxy. "Seems to me there's quite a bit of business on offer after one of our sessions at The Fox."

"There is," affirmed Big Mac, nostalgically.

"I'm not into little dirtbags," scoffed Jack.

"Is that right?" demanded Boxy. "And why not, if you're just after getting laid?"

"You're not, though, are you, Jack?" asked Jamie slyly. "You want a *relationship*."

Jack resisted a strong impulse to smack his hand across Jamie's face, and said, "*No*, Jamie. *No*, I do not."

"You wanted one with *Amy*."

"Who's Amy?" demanded Boxy.

"She broke Jack's heart!" yelped Karl.

"When she dumped him!" crowed Cory.

Jack knuckled his fist into Cory's neck, then jumped on Jamie, who swung back at him. "Break it up, boys!" Boxy yelled. "Fighting over a *woman*?! That's a bloody disgrace. I'll tell you something about women. They make you weak, right? And we don't want weakness on the team. My view on girls is – you can do what you like as long as it doesn't interfere with your rugby." The boys laughed and cheered and Boxy added, "Now – can we stop the Agony Aunt column and *get some fucking work done*?!"

Chapter 17

"I am pleased," Christian said for the fourth time into the phone. "I *am* pleased for you, Gem, honest. If it's what you want."

"You know it is," she said. "God, I've gone on about it enough. Major lust, Chris. *Rrrrrowwwl.*"

"Oh, *God*, must you?"

"Yes."

"Fine. Well – enjoy yourself. Why you bothering to see a film with him first?"

"Don't be crass, Chris. It's courtship, isn't it. We're kind of circling round each other. . ."

". . .like a pair of scorpions on heat."

"*What?*"

"Scorpions do this huge ritual, this dance, to make it clear they want to mate – in case one of them gets the wrong idea and gets its sting out."

"Shut up, Chris."

"The more deadly the couple, the more elaborate the dance."

"I said shut up!"

"OK. Just don't let him change you, OK?"

"*Change* me? How's he gonna do that?"

"Oh – I dunno. If you get all smitten and in love and start *wearing your ha-air just for him. . .*"

"Chris – stop singing."

"The late, great Dusty Springfield. She was *fab*. All I'm saying is – just don't end up adoring him too much, OK?"

"I won't. He's just a phase, right?"

"A physical phase."

"Exactly."

"And you'll still love me best?"

"Course I'll love you best. You and I – we'll be *mad* about each other for *years* after I've forgotten all about Jack Slade. Hey – I want you to help me develop these photos I did last week."

"What of?"

"Seagulls. Screaming for food. My God they were *savage*. And they were all over the place, flying, but I think if we crop the frames properly I'll have some great stuff. . ."

"Sure, babes. Tell me when." Christian knew he was being thrown scraps here, scraps off her over-laden table like the pet dog he was, but there was no resentment in his voice.

"So don't be a shit," she said. "Wish me luck."

"Good luck, darling. Phone me when you get home Friday. I want all the details, OK? All of them."

And Gemma put the phone down and wondered if this thing they did – this making out they adored each other, making out like Chris was her Courtly Love Knight – had more power for him than it did for her.

But she didn't wonder about it for long. She was halfway through making some sharp adaptations to a skirt she'd bought cheap because the zip was broken, and she wanted to finish it for Friday night.

Friday, four-thirty. Gemma, glowing from her after-school session in the gym, hurried towards the sports hall exit.

"You sweaty thing!"

Gemma groaned silently as Mr Olsen, the new trainee teacher, beamingly blocked her path.

"I'm gonna shower at home!" she huffed. "I'm going out."

"Yeah? Hot date?" he leered. He had this cringe-making habit of flirting in a jolly way with the sixth-form girls. Someone, Gem thought, should explain to him that his attempt to be one of the lads was a profound failure.

"Very hot," she said, deadpan. "I gotta look spectacular."

Mr Olsen went very slightly pink. "Great, good, well – look. Gemma. Netball, Saturday. This flu that's going round – we're two players down. Couldn't you—"

"Mr Olsen, you know I don't play netball."

"Come on – you've got speed and you can pass a ball around—"

"I hate team sports. I'm not a team player."

"You're missing out, you know. The buzz when you win, the comradeship—"

"Hate it. Sorry. Now – I gotta go."

"Sure," he said grumpily. "Hot date."

*

Friday night. An hour before they were due to meet, Gem and Jack were both feeling more nervous than they thought was sane. Gem dealt with this by changing into three different tops, one after the other, and doing an intensive manicure. Jack dealt with it by masturbating in the shower. It calmed him down and he reckoned it was a good move in case things hotted up later – he didn't want to froth over too soon, did he?

He was hazy about where this might happen – maybe her place, if her parents were out – but he continued to tell himself that he was only after Gem for sex. And the reason he was after Gemma and not some little scrubber was scrubbers didn't turn him on the way Gemma did. But it was still just physical. None of that crap he'd started to feel with Amy. Like Boxy said, women made you weak. Women were the enemy.

They were both five minutes late, which meant they walked up to the doors of the Odeon together. They breezed through saying hello and getting the tickets (Jack paid and Gem gave him the exact money for hers and he didn't protest) and finding their way to their seats. They managed a bit of basic conversation as the adverts blared at them, then the film started and there was no need for any more talk.

Touching was out of the question. They had never touched each other before, not even, Gem reflected, accidentally. They hadn't kissed when they met, they hadn't held hands. Gem felt like there was a forcefield between them as they sat there, humming with energy, keeping them apart.

The film started. It was packed with violence, action and shouting but to Gem it was weak and pale compared to what was thudding inside her. Then, halfway through, Jack leaned in close and hissed, "D'you reckon this is shit?"

"Well—"

"Cos I do."

Gem huffed with laughter. She hated it but she'd thought – as he'd chosen it – that it would be Jack's kind of thing. "It's crap," she whispered back.

"Only there's this new bar opened – on the high street."

"Shhhh!" said the man in the seat behind Gem.

"You *shhhh*!" snarled Jack, twisting round. "It does two meals for the price of one," he went on, much louder, turning back to Gem, "if you get there before nine o'clock."

Embarrassed about the man, excited about what Jack had suggested, Gem scrambled to her feet. "Great – I'm starved," she whispered. "Let's go."

And outside, as though they were accomplices now, as though they'd formed a bond, he took hold of her hand all casual except it wasn't casual, of course, it was absolutely momentous for both of them. They walked along laughing about the film, feeling pretty superior because they'd made the decision to walk out instead of just sitting there putting up with it. "You know what?" Gem said. "That film really pissed me off. The way it focused on all the nasty bits, chopping off that guy's foot, and the cold and misery and the storm making them throw up. . ."

"Turned your stomach, did it?"

"Yeah. I nearly threw up, honestly. They were so

graphic about everything. Revelling in it. You know – this is life when it was cheap and brutal."

"And real," said Jack, fast.

"Why real? It's still as real now."

"Well it doesn't *feel* it, does it? Machines to do everything for you. Drugs to stop you feeling stuff."

"You're not saying you'd get rid of washing machines and aspirin."

"No. Just – OK, things can still go wrong, you can get mugged, or hit by a car – but mostly we're so cushioned, aren't we. *Protected* from everything."

There was a silence, then Gem said, "That's what got me about the film. Like we're leading such soft lives we gotta see something like that for a fix. Remind ourselves we're still alive. You know – made up of blood and bones."

Jack felt suddenly incredibly turned on. He clamped down on it, praying his hand wasn't going all sweaty in hers. "Right," he said, "a virtual reality fix," and they both laughed. He walked on, step in step with her, amazed. He couldn't remember ever being turned on by what a girl had *said* before. By one of her *thoughts*.

They reached the new bar; they could see from the outside that it was packed solid. "We're never gonna get a seat!" wailed Gem as they pushed the door open on to heat and noise.

"Yes we are," answered Jack, as he towed her through the crush of people. He glared around him; he had to sort this out, he'd look like a loser if he didn't. He collared a thin man who was carrying a couple of towers of glasses back to the bar and said, "We still in time to eat, mate?"

The thin man glanced across at a large, ruby-red clock on the wall, and said, "Yeah. Ten minutes, then the price goes up."

Jack turned to Gem. "C'mon, let's order."

"But there's nowhere to sit!"

"There will be." He elbowed a space for both of them near the bar, then picked up a menu from a nearby table. An ordinary-looking couple in their late twenties were sitting at it; they'd finished their meal and were drinking coffee. "May I?" he said loudly, too late, already reading the menu. They ignored him. Jack edged a little closer to them, then handed the menu to Gem and said, "Choose something, yeah?"

They decided on the Special Burgers; they ordered them, and beer, and waited. "Jack," hissed Gem, "stop crowding that table!"

"What?"

"You're practically sitting in their laps!"

"So?" Jack grinned, and moved in closer still. The woman he was just about on top of looked up and shrilled, "Excuse *me*!"

"Yes, move back a bit, mate," said her boyfriend.

"Sorry," said Jack, companionably. "There's just no room in here, is there."

"You could move back against the bar—"

"Yeah, but I don't wanna stop people reaching the bar, do I?"

The woman screwed up her paper napkin and chucked it peevishly on the table. "Oh, come on, Nev," she spat. "Let's just *go*."

"I haven't paid yet!" Nev grumbled.

"Well, pay at the bar." She stood up.

Jack thumped down into her empty seat while Nev was still pulling his jacket from the back of his chair. Gem waited until they'd gone, then slid into the other chair, saying, "God, Jack!"

"What?"

"D'you always act like this? Like – bullying people? That poor couple – and the man in the cinema?"

"The man in the cinema should have kept his nose out. And those two were finished, weren't they? Come on Gem – you gotta push, haven't you? Survival of the fittest."

She laughed. She wasn't sure if she was appalled or impressed by Jack's behaviour – maybe a bit of both. Jack, laughing back at her, thought: This is the business. Seats sorted, beer in front of us, food ordered, all down to me. . . I bet she's impressed. God, she's gorgeous.

"D'you mean that," she asked, putting her beer down on the table between them, "d'you really believe in survival of the fittest?"

"Yeah," he said. "I do. We're going down the pan in England, aren't we. Cos we let the weak survive."

"*What!?*"

"Doling out money to wasters and letting 'em breed."

"*Jesus.* Chris told me you could double for Hitler."

"Chris? Oh, your faggot friend."

"He's not a faggot. He's great. And I want to know if you really mean that shit you came out with just then."

They faced each other, eyes lit up with pleasure at the fight. Gem knew she should be turned off by what he was saying, but only a part of her was. Another part scanned his face and felt hornier by the minute.

"OK, I was harsh," said Jack, "but I do reckon we support no-hopers too much. Everyone's a bloody victim nowadays, aren't they. And the government keeps supporting the useless, supporting them when they have loadsa kids . . . well. Stands to reason, as a race, we're going down."

Incensed, Gem leaned across towards him. "So what you're saying is – babies should be left to die if their parents aren't up to supporting them?"

Jack shrugged. "Maybe not *die*. Maybe taken into care. . ."

"Oh, nice. So the kid suffers twice over. Poor, and taken from its parents."

"I haven't worked out the fucking details yet, have I? I just know all this softness and *weakness* – it's gonna finish us off. The Spartans – maybe they had it right. Leaving babies out on the mountainside to see if they deserved to live – they sifted out the weak from the strong."

"Which is why *Sparta* is still such a thriving country, hmm?"

Jack grinned at her, said nothing.

"Why the Spartans as a race – they're still up there. Ruling the world," she went on, grinning back. "Attending world conferences. Telling America what to do."

"Oh, *ha fucking-ha*. All right. Here's your food."

The plates sailed down on to the table in front of them and, knee to knee, they started to eat. "Tell me you don't really believe all that crap," she said.

"What crap?"

"About Sparta, and letting the weak go to the wall."

"Best place for 'em. Bastards."

"Oh for *God's* sake—"

"OK, OK! I dunno if I mean it. Maybe not all of it. I'm just fed up of the losers getting all the support all the time."

"But if you're strong, you don't need help, do you? You can make it on your own."

"Yeah, but—" Jack was stumped and Gem was enjoying herself. It was some challenge, getting someone as hardboiled as Jack to admit he might not be one hundred per cent right.

"That's why I like rugby," he suddenly announced. "Only the strong survive, no messing, no excuses. Hey – you gonna come and see another game?"

She felt a rush of pleasure and triumph. That was as good as a second date, that was. "Might do," she said.

"Come tomorrow. We're playing Rigsby Town. It's gonna be tough."

"If I come, you'd better not just leave me standing there on the touchline like an idiot again."

"I won't. I swear I won't. There'll be other girls there anyway. We've been getting more of 'em, coming to see us."

Gem smiled to stop a scowl forming. "Bloody hell," she laughed, "rugby groupies?"

"Yeah, why not. We're the business now, Westgate. We're winning everything."

"I might turn up," said Gem, lifting her burger to her mouth, knowing nothing would stop her turning up, "I'll see how I feel."

*

They finished eating, finished their drinks, and Gem insisted on being the one to get up and get the next round in. Then she insisted they stood up to let a couple of girls, who were trying to balance plates of food at the edge of the bar, have their table. Jack was OK about this because it allowed him to press up against Gem in the crush of people round the bar and complain at her. "You're *soft*, you are," he moaned. "We had that table."

"Yeah, and we'd finished eating. Come on – that other couple let us have their seats!"

"You're too nice. There's no survival of the nicest, you know."

"Oh, shut up!"

Jack laughed, and went to get the third round in.

The night went on. They were intoxicated by each other's closeness, and now they were feeling slightly drunk too. Jack was kicking his brain around for something to say, something to let her know how hot he found her. Instead he just let his face get closer and closer as they talked, until they were breathing in each other's breath. If she didn't want this, he thought, she could draw back. But she kept close, her eyes sliding all over his face, like his were over her face. Especially her mouth as it moved, made shapes as she talked. And then in the end he just leant over and kissed her, right in the middle of her talking about how she'd like to be a photographer only the competition was so hard.

Kissing her felt like a jump of faith, a risk, a leap of courage. And right away she was kissing him back, strong as anything, so he knew he'd been right to take that jump.

Chapter 18

After that kiss, they didn't do a lot more talking. Jack slid his hands round her waist, and she put her hands on his arms, keeping them there. Their faces were almost touching. "Shall we go?" he croaked.

She nodded. They finished their beers and dumped the bottles on the bar. Then Jack shouldered his way through the fug of people with a hand stuck out behind him to hold tight on to Gem's hand.

As they pushed through the door, an autumn wind hit them with a skirl of dead leaves, and Gem laughed, squawked, "God, it's *freezing*!" She let go of Jack's hand to button her coat up right up to her chin. Fireworks like artillery fire were hammering away, and a sudden rocket seared the dark with red and blue sparks.

Jack's body and mind were focused together. He knew had to follow up on that kiss, fast, or he'd be back to square one, back to having to cut through the distance between them again. As soon as she'd finished with her coat buttons, he put his arm round her shoulders, hugged her to him, and said, "C'mon."

Gem put her arm round his waist, burrowing her hand in his coat pocket for warmth, and they set off. They fitted well against each other as they walked, they chatted and laughed about this and that and every little thing they said seemed more exciting or funnier than it should have done. Jack was assessing and dismissing this doorway, that side street – where was he going to stop with her? It was all so cold, so bleak, despite the early Christmas lights in the shop windows.

"You getting the H53 bus?" Gem asked. She knew what was going on. She was enjoying Jack looking for somewhere to stop.

"No. I go the other way. I'll see you on it though, yeah?"

"I don't wanna leave it too late."

"We've got ages. Let's just walk for a bit."

They walked on and reached one of the two small stretches of green that broke up the town centre. An old-style street lamp spread rich amber light through the branches of a black, twiggy tree and down across the pavement towards their feet. Gem stopped walking, turning towards him. "Hi," she said. Then she reached up and kissed him.

Jack was knocked back, heart racing with it. Apart from Amy, with girls he'd always called the shots, always made all the moves before. He wrapped his arms round her, tight, and kissed her back. And they ground into each other, kissing hot as anything, accelerating into it, and he thought about manoeuvring her towards one of the benches set around the green, but he didn't want to spoil the momentum. With one hand he started undoing her coat buttons, the top one, then the next down, and the next, and then he was nuzzling into her neck and sliding his hand into the warmth under her coat, seeking out her left breast. *Careful,* he warned himself, *slow this up.* He wanted her so much he was in danger of blowing it.

And then she suddenly drew back, snap, just like that, laughed up at him and said, "Come on, I gotta get my bus. And don't you need an early night, if you've got a match tomorrow?"

Later that night, alone in bed, Gem stretched out as hard as she could, hard until her muscles screamed, then she relaxed back. She was minutely analysing everything that had happened over the evening and she was feeling very, very good about it. Especially the – *self control* she'd shown, at the end. The *power.* "You needn't think *you're* in charge," she said to the picture of Jack hovering inside her head. "I'm the one. I'm the boss." She started moving her hands on her thighs, rocking herself. She thought: You *slept* with those other two guys because you wanted to feel for them what you're feeling right now for Jack. If you feel this turned on right now at the start, how's it gonna be when. . . Her hands moved higher. She was thinking of the amazing kiss they'd had, right at the end, when the bus was stopped and he wouldn't let go of her and they were kissing, kissing, and she only just made it before the bus doors whanged shut.

Over in his bedroom, Jack had been masturbating too, highly pleasurably. He hadn't analysed Gem at all, just thought of the way she looked and felt and smelt and tasted. Just before he fell asleep he downed a pint of water to flush out the three beers he'd had, at least two of which he shouldn't've had, not the night before a match. And now he was face down on the bed, half undressed, fast asleep, snoring.

Chris made himself wait until twenty past ten the next morning, when he finally cracked with curiosity and phoned Gemma's house. As the rings mounted up he prayed it would be Gem who answered and not her mum, because her mum always sounded so friendly and kind it must mean she was sorry for him, which really brought him down. In fact there had been a time – until Gemma mocked him out of it – when he'd ring Gem's mobile and tell her to get to her house phone, cos he was going to call it next.

At the ninth ring, Gem answered, sounding breathless, and squawked, "You got me out of the shower!"

"Sorry! You're up early for someone who had a major date last night—"

"That's cos I'm gonna watch him play rugby. At twelve. So I can't talk, Chris, OK?"

Chris's stomach plunged at these words. Plunged far deeper than he was prepared for. So now he had to keep her talking, just for a bit, he had to try and get her to say something to make him feel better again. "So," he trilled, "it was fantastic, was it?"

"I wouldn't say that. I think he's a complete turn-on and I want to fuck his brains out, but—"

"But?" prompted Chris.

"Oh, you know. He's a fascist. He's all-action man. We're too *different* to make it work. But—"

"But you're gonna give it a go."

"Yeah."

"Well – don't act too keen, sweetie. Turning up for a *second* time to watch him play."

There was a chill down the phone line. Then Gem said, "Chris, I gotta go. I'm dripping."

And Chris put down the receiver, feeling terrible.

Five to twelve at Westgate Rugby grounds; Gem was on the touchline waiting for Jack's team to run out. She was wearing flat-heeled boots and a long coat with a big fake-fur-trimmed hood that made her look like a Russian princess. Just before she'd left her house, shaky with ridiculous nerves, she'd had this brainwave about bringing her camera with her so she could use it as a shield, something to hide behind. But then she thought it would only make her stand out more, so she left it behind.

The day had started out immensely gloomy but now a high, cold sun was breaking through the mist. Around the pitch the floodlights came on, glowed orange for a minute or two, then were extinguished again. Gem, feeling alone and exposed and a bit stupid, retreated further into the fur of her hood and thought about Chris telling her not to act too keen. It still stung. It hadn't occurred to her to baulk at Jack asking her along to another game, although it was a pretty bigheaded thing for him to do. Although to Jack, what was happening to Westgate was so major that questions of bigheadedness didn't come into it. . . *Stop analysing*, she told herself. *Just go with it*. Surreptitiously, she looked round at the other supporters on the touchline. There were quite a few middle-aged men who had to be dads, three brave muffled-up mums, a handful of sporty-looking guys and – just like Jack had said – loads of girls. Two on their own, like her, and evenly spaced out round the pitch, three loud, laughing, huddled-up groups. Gem did a head count, sliding her eyes past. Some of them had to be with the other team, she thought, but even so . . . *fourteen* girls? Last time, she and Holly had been the only ones.

There was a sudden commotion over by the clubhouse, and everyone turned to look as a line of gold-hoop-shirted boys ran out on to the pitch from the left-hand changing room door. And then there was a great group roar from behind the right-hand door, and Jack led his team on to the pitch. The dads were shouting out things like, "Come on Westgate!" and "Get stuck in, Rigsby!" and everyone seemed to be clapping and cheering. Gem banged her mittened hands together a few times so as not to be left out, and Jack, reaching the middle of the pitch, looked over and gave her a knee-trembling grin. She smiled back and waved, then wished she hadn't waved. The whistle went, he looked away and the match started.

That was the last time Jack looked at Gem till the final whistle went, but Gem kept her eyes fixed on Jack. She watched him as he thundered over the muddy grass and disappeared under piles of boys and launched himself at other players and brought them down, and as she watched she was all jumbled up inside. Part of her wanted to burst out laughing at the sheer stupidity of it and part was absolutely thrilled at him, the way he was all intense and tough and warrior-like. It was like how she'd felt last night, when she couldn't decide if he appalled or impressed her. Chris would tell her she was schizophrenic.

The match was brutal from the off. The gold-hoop team rated themselves and had some huge players and they were out to grind Westgate into the ground. After twenty minutes' battle, they bulled their way through the defence and slammed down a try. But there was some problem with it because the dads were yelling at the ref about a *blatant forward pass*, and Jack was shouting at his team to *back off, calm down* – Gem wished she had someone to stand next to, someone to explain the rules a bit.

On the far side of the pitch, a man in a black jacket was pacing the touchline. Boxy, Gem realized. He was shouting, too – abuse at the ref, shouting at Jack and the team to *wake up and focus*! But he kept apart. It was like he had a force field round him, repelling everyone.

The game got going again, harder still, both sides sweating and panting. They scrummed down and vapour rose off them; Gem thought they looked like beasts with their flanks steaming in the cold and wished she had brought her camera, after all. Then suddenly, Jack had the ball and was thundering for the line. The touchline exploded with cheering; Gem screeched: "*Go, go!*" And Jack *went*, passing it to Karl just as the gold-hoops closed in on him. Karl pitched himself full length over the line and whacked the ball down, and the touchline cheering doubled.

By half-time, Gem had lost track of the score, of

everything. Her mouth was dry with tension, with fear for Jack as he hit the ground or crashed into a gold-hoop player. The ref had worked himself into a whistle-blasting rage, all of it directed at Westgate. He kept awarding penalties to the gold-hoops and the blues kept bulling through with tries.

Then, at last, the final whistle went, and it was Westgate who roared with triumph.

She watched, arms wrapped round herself, as the two teams clapped each other off the field and gathered with their coaches for a debriefing. She watched as they dispersed and started shambling towards the changing room, suspended, rigid with anxiety until Jack broke away and jogged over towards her.

"Thirty-two-twenty-nine!" he bellowed, by way of greeting.

"Brilliant!" she called back. "You *won*!"

He drew up right in front of her, panting still, a huge grin on his face. "Aren't you in *pain*?" she demanded.

"Nah. Screwed my shoulder up a bit."

The energy off him – exhilaration, adrenaline, triumph – knocked her back, excited her. And the *smell* off him – it was overpowering, it was mud, and sweat, and blood . . . Gem wanted to wrap herself round him and kiss him. But that would look pretty desperately over-keen, wouldn't it, kissing someone who was covered in mud and sweat and blood.

"You enjoy it then?" Jack demanded.

"Yeah! Well – I didn't understand—"

"We'd've *stuffed* 'em properly if the fucking ref hadn't

blown up for every little thing he imagined he saw! What an arsehole!"

There was a shout from over by the changing rooms. Boxy was there in the doorway, waving his arm like a sabre. "Gotta go," said Jack, turning away. All over the field, boys were leaving groups of girls, heading for the hanging rooms. "You gonna come tonight?"

"*What?* Where?"

"The Fox. To celebrate. It'll be awesome!"

"Where's The Fox?"

Boxy yelled out again, louder, angrier.

"What's your number?" demanded Jack, moving backwards away from her across the pitch. "I'll call – I'll come and get you!"

"968–4521!" Gem shouted.

And Jack grinned, turned, and raced off.

All the way home on the bus, Gem fumed.

What the *hell* did he have to run off so fast for, *why* didn't we swap mobiles last night, *why* couldn't he wait till I'd written my mobile down? He'll never remember my number, he won't phone, I'll be hanging round waiting, I can't contact him, it's all me fitting in with him and his stupid rugby, suppose I don't want to go to the poxy Fox tonight to celebrate, God I can just imagine what Chris would say if he knew about me acting like a stupid rugby groupie – *why am I doing this*?

And then a picture of Jack's face swam into her mind and a sense of him filled her and she knew exactly why she was doing it, and she thought: I'll just play along for a while,

I'll see where it goes, it's an experience I'm consenting to so it's OK, I'm still in charge, God I fancy him so much but I can bow out any time, I'm still in control if I know I can bow out any time. Then she gathered up her woolly mittens and got off the bus.

Chapter 19

Gemma was an only child. She had been accidentally created during the time her parents (unmarried) were vaguely discussing having a child in maybe five years' time. After the extreme experience of Gemma's babyhood, they agreed never to have another.

They adored Gemma; spoilt her. But they left her alone, too, because of their rich and varied busy lives. In many ways it was an ideal existence. She had money and things and support when she asked for it, but lots of space and freedom too. And no brothers and sisters to fight for rights over. It made her self-reliant, and gave her the kind of surety and sense of self that was very appealing to others.

On the kitchen table was a note from her mum, and a twenty-pound note. It read:

Where did you go off to so early?!! Dad back around six – I'm off now till late tonight. Be safe, M xxx

Gem made herself a thick, white-bread bacon sandwich, frying the bacon without cutting the fat off like she usually did, which she felt she deserved after freezing outside for two hours. She ate this with greedy pleasure, swilled down by a big mug of tea.

Then she wandered out to the hall and sat down in front of the computer in the well under the stairs. She often worked here in the quiet empty house. She logged on, played around on the Internet for a while. Displacement activity, she thought, as she picked up the phone, checked it was working, slammed it down again.

In her mind, she could see Jack in the changing room, king of the match, swallowed up by the team, glorying in the victory. Not phoning her. God, I hate this, she thought. This stupid waiting. I hate him.

She switched off the computer, went up to her room, sank down on the bed and flicked through a magazine she'd already pretty much read cover to cover. Then she pulled out a boxfile full of photos she'd taken and started halfheartedly sorting them into good, bad, and possible. There was a phone (in the shape of red lips) on the floor in her room; it remained silent.

I can't stand this, she thought. If he screws me about a second time I'll . . . I'm going out, I'll leave the answer machine on. Only he's probably so thick he'll phone and not leave his number, he'll—

The phone went. Gem snatched it up. "*Hello?*"

"Can I speak to Gemma please?"

Gem felt something sweet and exultant flood into her. It was unmistakably Jack's voice, deep, confident, gorgeous. "Speaking!" she squeaked.

"Hey, *Gem* – it's Jack!"

"*Hi!* God – you remembered it!"

"I didn't actually. Not properly. This is the third place I've called."

"Really?"

"Yeah. Not bad I thought. Third time lucky."

"Right! You OK?"

"Yeah. *Knackered*. Thanks for coming along today."

"Oh, I enjoyed it," Gem breathed. She was starting to relax.

"Yeah, well, we put on a pretty good show for you, didn't we?"

"Yeah. Unbelievable."

"Anyway. You still coming tonight?"

"Yeah – sure."

"It's gonna be a blast. We are so chuffed we beat 'em. Especially with the ref being so fucking picky. Want me to meet up with you first?"

"Er—"

"I'd better. Where d'you live?"

Gem told him her address and he described where The Fox was and said it was the kind of area she wouldn't want to wander round in on her own. They threw up a few suggestions for meeting places but in the end Jack said he might as well knock for her, as it was sort of on the way. "About eight, yeah? Boxy gets pissed off if we don't get there before nine."

"You promise me I won't be the only girl there?"

"Gem – I *told* you – it'll be crowded out with ladies. Half of 'em in love with me. You'd better watch your back."

"Yeah, yeah, ha, ha. See you at eight then."

"I'll be there."

They ended the call and, rolling exultantly across her bed, Gem remembered with an inward wail that once again she'd not got his mobile number. But something told her she wouldn't need it, not tonight.

Chapter 20

Ten to eight, Saturday night. Gemma's dad heard a knock at the front door and, slightly irritated because he'd been watching a riveting French film from the 1960s, went to open it. He gawped at the powerful-looking young man standing all self-assured on the doorstep.

"Hi!" the young man said. "Is Gemma in?"

Normally, Gem's dad would wave her friends genially towards the stairs and tell them to go up to her room, but something stopped him doing this with Jack. "Er – I think so," he said. "Is she – expecting you?"

"Yes!" Jack said, and smiled encouragingly.

"Gem!" shouted Mr Hanrahan, feeling overpowered. He turned to the stairs. "Someone for you!"

Up in her bedroom, Gem jumped. She hadn't heard the knock she had her music up loud. She was also expecting Jack to be late, not early. Anyone else, she thought, grabbing her coat and bag, anyone else would hang about outside rather than knock now, in case they looked too keen, but that wouldn't even cross Jack's mind. . . One last check in the full-length mirror. She'd considered very exhaustively what to wear tonight. She didn't want to overdress because The Fox was just a daggy old pub, but it was still Saturday night and she'd heard these celebratory sessions turned into real parties. She'd ended up in jeans, a tightish top, boots with heels and a strange, striking pendant of a silver unicorn fixed to a black oval. Chris had found it in a junk shop and given it to her, even though he wanted to keep it for himself because he said it might have magic power.

All in all, her reflection looked understated but sensational. Satisfied, she scooted downstairs, calling, "Hi Jack!"

"Hi!" he grinned back, thinking, *Christ*, she looks classy. "Ready?"

Gem headed for the door and before her dad could wonder if she was going to introduce the confident boy, the front door closed behind them and they were off down the street.

They jumped on a bus to the centre of town; then it was only a ten-minute walk to the pub. They held hands and hurried along, both talking lots to cover up how nervous they felt, how desperate they were for it to work out. Gem was tight with anxiety about meeting the team, however much she told herself they were mostly just boys she'd been at school with for years. Jack was on edge, too; not that this translated into thought. As they drew up outside The Fox, his mobile went and he railed into it, "Yeah, I'm coming – I'm in the door, you dickhead!"

And they walked through the shabby pub, into a side bar. Immediately, there was a roar of greeting and jeering.

The team, with a handful of girls on the outer fringes, filled the small bar. Gem felt herself freeze. "I thought you said there'd be *loads* of girls?" she hissed.

"They'll be along later," Jack muttered, "it's just the girlfriends here now," and before Gem could process the weirdness of this, he gripped her hand and towed her over. Gem felt like she was being given marks out of ten by fifteen pairs of eyes, which made her pull back her shoulders and lift her chin and do her damnedest to stare back.

And then Boxy was standing right in front of her, like he had an absolute right to be there. "So," he leered, "aren't you gonna introduce us, Jack?"

"This is Gem," said Jack. He didn't introduce Boxy.

"And is she?" asked Boxy. "A gem I mean."

Jack laughed, even though it wasn't remotely funny. "What's she drinking?" Boxy demanded.

"Gem?" said Jack.

"White wine, please," she said. "Dry."

"*Very* sophisticated," Boxy sneered, and turned to the bar. The moment he stepped away, Big Mac, Rory and Karl headed for Jack, crowding him, jostling him, joshing, trading insults. Close to, they didn't look at Gem, didn't even acknowledge her, which gave her, she felt, a kind of breathing space. Close to, they weren't anything like so formidable; they were just boys she'd known by sight for years. Jack kept hold of her hand and bantered back at them, and the boys rehashed the game, swore about the ref, relived the tries and the brilliance of winning. Then Boxy broke through with their two drinks, and bellowed into the crowd, "Is everybody here? Who's missing?"

"How can he afford to buy everyone drinks?" Gem hissed at Jack.

"Dunno," Jack hissed back. "He always does. They're the only drinks he ever buys, but—"

"OK, so we're all here!" boomed Boxy. "Except for that tosser *Mark* who said he had a *party* to go to and if he's not here he clearly don't count, right?"

"Right!" the team yelled back.

"So – are we celebrating?"

Another roar of affirmation. "We stuck it to them *pretty thoroughly* today, boys," Boxy crowed. "We showed 'em who was in charge. We're premier league. They're fourth division." Another roar. Behind them, one of the boys had put the jukebox on – loud, crude, rhythmic music. Over it, Boxy shouted, "You played well. You were *committed*. The score line shoulda been better – we gave away too many penalties. Look lads – what do I keep telling you? If you want to sort someone out, don't do it in front of the ref. Wait till you're at the bottom of a ruck and then *kick the crap out of them!*"

Yet another roar from the boys. Some of them slung their arms round each other's necks and started to jump to the music, shouting the words of the song. And then as if on cue, as if they'd been standing outside waiting for their signal, the door opened, and the girls came in.

Gemma felt her jaw drop. There were about ten of them – she recognized some from the touchline earlier – and they were dressed like they were going clubbing. Short skirts, high heels, lots of skin showing. They were smiling, full of bravado, laughing at the jumping boys as though it was a cabaret laid on for their pleasure. They watched till the song ended and the team broke up, then they waved and called out, and shimmied across to the bar.

Several of the boys peeled away from the team, heading determinedly over to this girl or that. Jack was with a few others crowded round the jukebox, laughing and demanding more sounds. And Gem was tingling with nosiness. She headed over to the bar too, and pushed in next to a skinny blonde who she recognized from the year below her at school. "Hey," Gem said, "hey – it's Sam, isn't it?"

"Yeah?" said Sam, suspiciously.

"Are you – why are you – oh shit. I'm just wondering – *well*. Why you're all here."

"Why're *you* here?" Sam threw back, narrowing her eyes.

"I came with Jack Slade."

"Well – good for you. We're just here for fun, OK?" She turned back to the bar.

"But you all look so gorgeous," said Gem, trying flattery. "Like you're seriously off out on the town – you're too good for most of this lot. I mean – look at that fat bastard," she said, waving in Big Mac's direction. "He could be the twin of Fungus the Bogeyman."

Despite herself, Sam snorted with laughter, then she turned back to Gem, smiling. "You ever been clubbing with a group of boys?"

"Yeah – well, once or twice. They're not that into it, are they."

"Exactly. They're inhibited and uptight . . . well, they are unless they're gay. We really like the way these guys are around each other. We like how they've got something going on together. We like their confidence, OK – their *dominance*. Don't look like that. It's just fun, OK? No mystery."

Across by the jukebox, Jamie had stripped his shirt off and was flexing his muscles while the others roared in derision. "See?" went on Sam. "They're a laugh. Sometimes it's fun to be around guys when it's not just one-on-one and trying to pull."

"But you pull them too."

Sam laughed. "*Yeah!* They're all so full of themselves after a good match – it's a challenge. Trying to distract them. It's a laugh. It's – it's like going after a band. 'Cept there are more of them and they're in much better shape."

Jack appeared at Gem's side, and threw his arm round her shoulders. Sam smirked, and disappeared with a beer bottle in either hand. "Want another drink?" he said.

"I'll get them."

"Are you hating this?"

"No. It's fascinating."

"Hey – barman's free – get the drinks in if you're getting them."

The night went on, loud and anarchic. Jack kept ricocheting away from Gem to join his mates, then coming back to her side again. Gem decided she'd better get pissed to deal with it all and around her fourth glass of wine decided she could see why Sam and her mates liked being around the team. They were the centre to the evening, the reason for everyone to be there. The triumphant energy

122

they all gave off was like nothing she'd ever come across, it fired up the night. And as it got later, just as Sam had said, it got sexual. Girls were joining in with the tribal dancing, changing it. Couples were peeling off from the group, leaning up against the wall, flirting, necking. Jack towed her over to an old padded bench in the corner, turfed off Iz, who was drunkenly slumped across it, and they sat down and folded into each other.

Then ten minutes later, like a slash of cold water in the face, all the overhead lights came on and the barman was shrieking, "OK, come on now, drink up, time to get out!"

"Did you hear last orders?" grumbled Jack.

"No," mumbled Gem. "But I think I've had enough. Drink. Not you."

"Good. Glad not me."

They stood up, hand in hand, blinking in the sour harsh light. "We got to find ourselves somewhere new to go," announced Boxy, loudly, as everyone headed for the pub doors. "That bastard likes our beer money but he can't stand us. All right, lads. Tuesday training. As usual. Don't be late." And he disappeared off into the night.

As the group outside The Fox gradually dispersed, saying goodbye, shouting *see you*, Gem and Jack wrapped their arms round each other and lurched off towards the bus stop. They were both too drunk to make much sense as they talked, and they found just about everything the other one said hysterically funny. "I'll see you home," he slurred. "You're not safe. Too pissed. You'll get adjudicated."

"Abducted!" Gem squawked.

"Yeah, that. Abducticated. You will. I'll see you all the way home."

"No. I'm fine, I'll be fine. I'm not so pissed as you are. Just see me on my bus."

They staggered up to the bus stop and leaned sideways on against the smeary scratched unbreakable glass of the shelter, looking at each other. "You're beautiful," Jack said suddenly. "I wish I wasn't so pissed then I could kiss you properly."

Gem flared with pleasure, muttered, "God, *why* did we drink so much?"

"Dunno. We just did. I am . . . *completely* wiped out. I'm gonna sleep for a week."

In the distance, the H53 turned the corner and rumbled towards them. Gem, spotting it, reached out urgently and took hold of his jacket collar with both hands. "Swap mobiles!" she breathed.

"Christ, *yes*!" Jack fumbled in his pocket and pulled out his phone and then they were both telling their numbers at once until Gem squawked, "Stop, *stop*! What's yours?" and she punched it in, carefully, using all her willpower to concentrate and get it right. Then the H53 stopped beside them and she hugged him and he kissed her half on and half off her mouth, and she scrambled on the bus calling back, "I'll call you!"

"Tomorrow!" he shouted. The bus drew away.

Gemma felt she had sobered up quite considerably by the time she got home. She let herself in and crept upstairs to the chic little shower room that was only used by her unless there were guests in the house. She stared at herself in the mirror as she slowly smeared cleanser all over her face, then wiped it off with damp cotton wool. Sometimes she only did this once but tonight she did it twice. She felt excited, delighted, scared, thrilled, everything. It was overpowering, how much she wanted to be with Jack. Talk with him, look at him, touch him, sleep with him. She thought how different he was to her, how mad and not-her-thing the whole evening had been, how they were probably heading for disaster, but she knew she couldn't stop heading wherever they were going, not now.

This bit is so weird, she mused. This stage where you're still checking each other out, wondering if you're going to make it as a couple. Waiting to see if you're going to make changes in your life to take in the life of the one you want. You act like not a lot has changed, you're just dating a few nights a week, but inside . . . everything's changed. Inside you're waiting.

She unscrewed the top off her moisturizer, and smoothed it into her skin, eyes locked into her eyes.

For his part, Jack was exuberant as he lurched off the bus and weaved his way up to his front door. His desire to get with Gemma had been through some kind of trial and come out the other side, passed and approved. She'd seen a rugby match. She'd been to the booze-up afterwards. She was OK with Boxy and the boys. They were OK with her. Her was going to sleep with her, and he wasn't gonna get screwed about his time, because this time, he knew better. He'd learned.

God, his life was good.

Chapter 21

Last January, Gem's mum's resolution to get fit had led to her taking out a year's family membership at a local gym, one posh enough to have sunbeds and Jacuzzis and saunas in it. Gem made much better use of it than her parents did. That was where she headed the next morning, setting off almost as soon as she woke up.

She was buzzing. She felt great that it was her with Jack's mobile number and not the other way round, but she also felt the burden of deciding when to call him. Too early would seem too keen, but she knew she'd be on edge till she'd called. She jogged on the running machine for fifteen minutes, then she messed about on the big machines shifting light weights with her legs and her arms for twenty minutes, then she headed with a clear conscience to the showers. After forty minutes split between the sauna and the hot tub, Gem was feeling brilliant. Outside in the heavy late-November air, she took a deep breath and phoned Jack.

"Where are you?" he asked.

"Just been to the gym," she said smugly. "I'm outside it now. Where are you?"

"Home. Still in bed. I told you I was knackered."

"I was wondering – you want to get some lunch or something?"

"What, out? But it's Sunday. I have to be here for Sunday lunch."

"*Wow*," said Gem, disappointed. "Traditional."

"Yeah, we are. Aren't you?"

"Nope. Not sure if I'll even get fed today."

"*Aaaaw*. Little Orphan Gemmy. I'd ask you to mine only Mum hates last-minute guests."

"Don't worry. Not really into meat and three veg."

"You're mad. It's coming up the stairs at me now and it smells fucking brilliant, I can tell you."

"Well – OK then," said Gem, beginning to feel needled. "You'd better get up, hadn't you? Unless you're gonna eat it in your jimjams. And I'll get off home and get myself a salad."

"Well, can we meet up after that?"

Gem's irritation vanished. "Yeah. What you wanna do?"

There was a pause, then Jack said, "What about a walk?"

Gem's eyes widened. Walking was one of her things – her solo, private things. Ever since she'd been small she'd taken off on her own and walked for the sheer pleasure of it while thoughts and ideas formed in her mind. It was her way of meditating; she'd never thought of it as the sort of thing to do with another person.

And now it seemed Jack liked walking too.

"Only I'm being forced to take the sodding dog out," Jack announced. "Did I tell you I got a dog?"

*

Jack's dog was brilliant. A minky-coloured, silky-furred lurcher called Mimi who took to Gemma on sight and pressed her soft, sensitive nose trustingly into her hand. Gem, who had set out to meet Jack feeling a bit put out, feeling she was just fitting into what he was doing – *again* – melted immediately.

They'd met at the gate of the big local country park at three o'clock, both of them coming to it from different directions. It was cold and gloomy, with a fret of water in the air and the low sun shrouded. They kissed, a bit awkwardly, almost formally, then they took hold of each other's hand and went through the gates. Jack stooped down and let Mimi off her lead and they watched as she bounded off, radiating dog pleasure. "What I thought we could do," said Jack, "is walk for a bit, head towards that woody bit over there – and the other side, there's a café. It stays open till about four-thirty on a Sunday. We can get a cuppa tea. We'll need it, in this cold."

"Sounds great," said Gem. "What about Mimi though?"

"Oh, we can sneak her in. Or tie her up outside."

"We can't leave her outside, not in this weather! She needs a little coat."

"Don't you start. She's got a little fucking coat. It's *red* and *fur-lined*. I refuse to take her out in it."

"Poor *Mimi*!"

"It's bad enough calling her by her stupid name. *She's* bad enough. I wanted a Staffordshire bull terrier."

"You'd look like a right thug with one of those."

"Don't care. They're the business."

"She's gorgeous!"

"She's a pain! Look at her."

Mimi was turning in circles on the tussocky grass for the sheer fun of it, before prancing off towards the trees. "She's *gorgeous*," Gem repeated. "How did she get her name?"

"I got two little sisters – they chose it. I'm always outvoted about things like that."

Gem laughed. "You're lucky, having little sisters . . . I always wanted a sister."

"You can have mine. You got any brothers?"

"No. I'm on my own."

"No kidding? So you're spoilt, right? A brat?"

Gem dug her thumbnail into his hand and he laughed and they strode on into the woods, talking, talking, telling each other all about their families and their friends and their lives, filling in the gaps between the facts they already knew about each other. It was easier to talk side by side than facing each other, it was less intense. Although the closeness, the excitement between them, as they listened and answered and agreed and argued, was palpable.

They went into the wood. Mimi was ahead of them, snuffling and butting into a mound of earth beside the path. "Foxes!" said Jack. "Go get 'em, Mi!" Mimi yapped and darted off. A mist was hovering between the trees, forming strange shapes in the last of the filtering sun. Jack pointed to it. "Creepy," he said.

"Dryads," breathed Gem, then kind of wished she hadn't. Dryads were things you talked about with Christian, not Jack.

But Jack took it in his stride. "Those are girls who live inside trees, right?" he said.

"Yes. Well, like the spirits of trees."

"It's cos it's twilight. I've got a theory about twilight. I was here not so long ago, down by the lake – and I saw this bloke in among the trees, taking a piss. I swear to you, I saw his woolly hat and his trousers tucked into his welly boots, and I headed towards him cos I wanted to embarrass him—"

"Nice of you!"

"—and when I got closer he turned into a broken tree."

"*Wha-at?*"

"Well – OK – he'd been a tree all along. But somehow my brain had seen it as a man, and the thing that got me was – it had supplied all these details. Like the hat and the boots, the fact that he was pissing. It really freaked me, Gem. I mean – I was *so sure* it was this bloke, taking a leak. It got me thinking about reports of ghosts, you know – and trolls, dwarves, stuff people used to believe in."

"Fairies," said Gem.

"Yeah, and your dryads. Always stuff people talk about seeing at *dusk*. I reckon they just see a bit of old wood like I did, or a weird-shaped boulder, but the light makes it look like a ghost or a goblin and their brains supply all the details."

"And when the thing disappears – when they get closer – they think it's vanished."

"Or turned back into a tree."

Gem shuddered happily. She loved what Jack was saying, she loved it that there was this side to him. She was almost scared to take it further in case it wasn't really there, like the creatures they were talking about. "Where's the café?" she said. "I'm getting spooked."

Chapter 22

The light and the warmth of the café was deliciously cosy after the bleakness of the park. Nearly all the tables were full, mostly with tired-looking parents and noisy children who'd been taken out for a late walk in the hope that they'd fall asleep early that night. There was a festive kind of hubbub of noise. Behind the counter a cheerful-looking man stood cutting up chocolate cake. He glanced up as Gem and Jack came in, and when Jack nodded down to Mimi and gave a questioning thumbs-up sign, he grimaced, then smiled and pointed towards the table nearest the door that nobody wanted because of the draught when the door opened.

"Great," said Jack, as they peeled off their coats and put them on their chair backs. "I thought he'd be OK about it. What d'you want? I'm having some of that cake."

"Oh my God, I thought you'd just put away a big Sunday lunch?"

"So? You burn calories breathing when you're as fit as I am. You want some too?"

"I'll have a bit of yours. And – I dunno – a scone or something. Please."

"OK. Here, take Mimi." He handed her the lead, and headed to the counter while Gem sat down and ogled after him. She loved the way he moved, the way he looked so sure of himself. She loved his broad shoulders, muscled arms, strong legs. *He's with me*, she thought, blissfully, then looked down to see Mimi gazing quizzically up at her. "You should understand," she whispered. "It's an animal thing. Now sit! Sit!"

Mimi was curled up comfortably next to the radiator by the time Jack got back with the loaded tray. Gem picked up a mug of tea and took a sip, watching Jack through the steam. He cut up the fudgy cake slice and handed her a chunk. She silently offered him a bit of her scone, and he shook his head.

Neither of them could think of a thing to say. After the talking and the closeness of the walk, this face-to-face intimacy across the café table was almost too much to deal with. They were both aroused, and waiting. Then Jack blurted out, "You been out with lots of guys then?"

Gem smiled. "Two or three."

"Two or three? That's not what I heard."

"Yeah?" she bridled. "What've you been hearing, then?"

"I dunno. That you go out with lots of people. Well you would do, wouldn't you. Looking as good as you do."

"Well *thank you*. But that doesn't have to mean you've got a bell and saddle."

There was a pause while Jack processed this; then he grinned. "I'm not saying that! Christ! Just – you know. I'm wondering how long I got before you ditch me for someone new."

Gem loved this. Loved him talking as though they were definitely an item now, loved him saying that it would be her ditching him and not the other way round. "*Sure* you're wondering," she scoffed. "So the arrogance is just an act, then?"

"Arrogance? What arrogance?"

"Oh – just a few things I'd noticed. About the way you behave."

"All that's just an act, babe. Inside I'm shaking." They were leaning closer and closer across the table as they talked. "Come on, I'm interested," he went on. "How many guys you been out with?"

"Dunno. Quite a few when I was younger. Only two that count."

"Yeah? And why do they count?"

"I dunno, they seemed more serious."

"Because you slept with them?" The words were out before he could check them.

Gem looked straight at him and said, "Sort of."

He was prepared for it, he knew there was no way she was a virgin, he didn't expect her or want her to be, but even so it hit him hard, this news that she'd had two boys before him. "Who were they?" he demanded.

"You wouldn't know them. They weren't from school."

"Right. So you're slumming it with me, yeah?"

"Too right I am. Really lowering my standards."

"So come on. Tell me."

"*God*. It's really not that interesting. The first was this guy I met clubbing, he was really smooth, he was older, it was like this first-love thing, but it didn't last."

"Who finished it?"

"Mutual. We were just arguing all the time. Well – him really."

What Jack wanted to do now was cross-examine her about what the sex was like, but he knew he couldn't, not yet. So he asked, "And what about Number Two?"

"That was Jason. I met him on holiday in Spain and when we got back he used to get on his motorbike and drive a hundred and twenty miles to come and see me."

"Blimey. He must've been smitten."

"He was. And I liked him too, loads, it was dead romantic, but somehow back in England. . ."

"The sex was better in Spain."

"We never actually slept together. We were going to, but with the distance and everything . . . it fizzled out."

Jack sat back, pleased. "And that's it, is it? No one nighters?"

"What *is* this? Some kind of a morality quiz?"

"Just interested."

"OK. But I want to hear about you next. And the answer is, no. No one-nighters. The only other thing was this guy I slept with twice. . ."

"A two-nighter."

"*No!* I was going out with him! I liked him! But then I slept with him and he was useless so I gave him a second chance and he was even worse so I finished with him."

"Bloody hell. Poor bastard."

"I was nice about it. I mean – I didn't tell him that's why I was ending it."

"He must've known."

"No. He thought the sex was fantastic. He thought I was ending it cos I was scared of getting too deep in. That's what I told him."

Jack laughed, feeling shaken, shaking his head. "Jesus Christ. And they say blokes are callous."

"I wasn't *callous*! I was protecting his feelings! And anyway – don't you come on all moral-majority."

"*What?*"

"I mean morally superior. I bet you've had loads of one-nighters."

"Yeah well."

"Yeah well *what*? You have, haven't you? God, I can tell from your face that you have. And any minute now you'll tell me it's *different for a bloke*."

There was a long pause, during which Jack looked steadily at Gem. He was so turned on by all this talk about sex he was in physical pain. Underneath the table, while Mimi slept peacefully, Gem crossed her legs tighter and hoped the heat wasn't showing in her face.

"It *is* different for a bloke," he said at last.

Gem shrieked scathingly. Jack laughed, grabbed her hand and said, "Calm down, you'll get us kicked out. Say what you like, I still reckon it is. Anyway I haven't had *loads*. Just a few. And they don't mean much."

"OK, what about girlfriends?"

"I dunno. I had a really serious one when I was fifteen. God, I was all gooey over that one, it lasted six months. Then I got bored and she went psycho when I dumped her and then I kind of avoided all that *relationship* stuff. I mean, I *saw* girls, yeah, but—"

"What about that girl over the summer?"

"Amy? What about her?"

"Jack – you were *seen*. Practically shagging each other in the park, that kind of stuff."

Jack grinned. "I loved that. I loved making all the other guys sick with wanting to be me."

"Oh, *mature*."

"Sod off," Jack laughed, and then his face kind of closed down. The mention of Amy had sent him into reverse.

"Want another cup?" said Gem. She couldn't bear to leave the café. She wanted to get back to where they'd been before Amy had come up. Outside the windows, the light was fading fast and a wind had got up, keening round the walls, making the door rattle, making it seem even more intimate inside.

"Yeah, why not," answered Jack. "If he'll serve you. I reckon he's waiting to close up."

Gem stood up and headed for the counter. Jack let his eyes gorge on her as she moved. God, she was hot. Why couldn't they go outside now, go into some shrubs somewhere in the dark, lie down together. . .

She bought two more mugs of tea and came back to the table. "What're you thinking about?" she demanded. "You've gone all quiet."

"I was thinking," said Jack, "that we've both been round the block a few times. Haven't we?"

"What the hell is that supposed to mean?"

"Just – we're not beginners. At this."

Gem glared at him. It was obvious what he was getting

at. He didn't want to hang about, he wanted to get down to it. His functionality chilled her.

"Don't look at me like that," Jack said. "I can't help it if I fancy you this much, can I?"

Gem stopped feeling chilled, and covered it by spitting out, "You can help being so *crass* about it."

"Sorry. Sorry. I don't mean to be crass. What is crass, anyway?"

Gem laughed. "It's crude, rude, stupid, clumsy. . ."

"OK, OK, I get the message. I just want to be honest. I just think this is amazing, what's going on here, and I just think we should . . . go with it."

There was another silence, only the wind moaning round the dark windows. They were the last customers in the café now. Jack looked at her face and thought she was saying yes. And then his mobile blurted out, from somewhere in the creases of his coat. "*What?*" he snarled into it. "No, of course I haven't. She's here now, we're in a café . . . no . . . I *know* . . . that's none of your business, OK?"

He rammed the mobile back in his pocket, saying, "Mum thought I'd lost the stupid dog."

Gem smiled, said, "We'd better go", and they stood up, Jack picking up Mimi's lead, and walked out of the door. It was as if a decision had been made. What was hanging in the air between them was that Jack was right and there was very little point in waiting, for either of them.

Chapter 23

When Gemma got home that evening, vibrating with excitement, the house was still empty and there was no note telling her where anyone was. She went up to her bedroom, stripped down to her bra and pants, lay flat on the bedroom floor and did thirty-five sit-ups. Then she swivelled in front of the long pier glass she'd inherited from a great-aunt. It was oval-shaped, painted white with carved apples and leaves at the top, and Gem loved it, loved her reflection in it. She never wasted time wishing bits of her were different, like Holly did, always moaning that she wanted longer legs and even bigger breasts. Gem liked what she saw, what she *was*. But today, she looked at herself and thought how fit and tonked-up Jack had looked, pounding about the rugby pitch. She thought she might try and do a bit more exercise herself, squeeze in another visit to the gym each week maybe. And actually *do* stuff there, rather than just lie about in the hot tub and the sauna. And she'd drink more water, and eat more fruit, and get another of those face packs with sea minerals in that had made her skin *glow.* . .

Then she bundled herself into her dressing gown, flopped down on the bed, and sat rocking and swooning over everything that had happened over the weekend. Jack was inside her head, talking, walking beside her, touching her. . . This is major lust, she thought, on a whole different level to anything I've felt before. It's distorting everything, I'm letting it get too important. What I need to do – is sleep with him, get it over with, let all this pressure out!

She burst into slightly hysterical laughter. "I'm giving myself *permission*," she sang, scrambling off the bed. "I'm saying it's *OK*!"

She needed to talk to someone, earth the electricity racing through her. Chris, she needed to talk to Chris. Their last conversation, yesterday morning – only it felt like weeks ago now – had been prickly and awkward and she hated things being like that with Chris. She owed it to him, she told herself, to put things straight between them, to tell him how things really were with Jack – how it was brilliant lust, and she was going to let herself go completely mad with it for a while. She picked up the phone and punched in Chris's number. She'd invite him over, she decided, and cook him some supper.

Meanwhile, Jack was slumped down at the kitchen table while his oldest little sister cooked him beans on toast. She'd just started food technology at school and had got into basic cooking and Jack was happy for her to practise on him as often as she liked. He was buzzing too, just like Gem was, but he didn't feel the need to analyse it all. He just wished she was here now. He wished she was here and no one else was, so they could get on his bed together.

A little over an hour later, Christian, sitting opposite Gem in her kitchen over a plate of pasta, courgettes, peppers and grated Parmesan, was feeling almost unbearably betrayed. He could cope with hearing about the rugby match and the pub celebration – it was crude, alien, and he could tell Gem sort of felt this too. But she'd just got to the bit where Jack had taken her into the woods and they'd had this conversation about *dryads*. Chris knew that Gem was hoping this would make him warm to Jack, but he hated it. He couldn't bear it that she'd shared the sort of thing that was special to them with that *meathead*.

Chris sat on his hurt, though. He didn't want her to pick up on it in case she censored anything else she might say. He wanted to hear it all, however upsetting it was. He smiled and chewed and listened, pretending he was just a good loyal mate, and as soon as he could he steered the conversation back to the night at the pub.

"*Really* doesn't sound like your scene, precious one," he said campily. "I mean – is this going to be your Saturday night scene from now on?"

As he'd hoped, Gem's face fell. "God, I dunno," she said. "I haven't thought that far."

"Well, it could be worse. I mean – at least there are other girls there."

Gem grimaced. "Yeah. *The groupies*. That's what Boxy calls them."

"And does he include you in that category?"

"*No*. Don't know. Don't care. God, it's weird though."

"Why is it weird? Rugby's pretty cool nowadays – it's the new football. The papers are always full of glam girls hanging out with footballers."

"*Chris* – they're *famous* footballers. Celebrities. They've got money, and big cars, and they get into the best clubs . . . they're not a crew of seventeen year olds who can barely afford a pint."

"Well, we're back to Darwin again then, aren't we, darling."

"I might've known we would be."

"Survival of the strongest. Lure of the most macho. They like the sheer *energy* that comes off a gang of guys who've just beaten up another gang of guys. Some primitive race memory in those girls wants to breed with the strongest tribe."

"Chris, you really are chock-full of shit."

"I'm also right, darling, and you know it. Why else are they hanging about?"

"I don't know. They say it's just for fun and to pull them, but—"

"Same reason you're hanging about," he spat out. "They haven't *evolved*. And I bet Boxy does call you a groupie."

Gem glared at him. Chris looked back and thought he could actually see her pupils contracting, shutting him out. He knew he'd have his work cut out to bring her round, now.

He began by smiling, wide and apologetic. Interesting, he thought, how you can be this lacerated inside and still smile.

Chapter 24

Tuesday night training. Jack was on his way across the muddy field to join his team, thinking about the disastrous phone conversation he'd had with Gem the night before. If you could call it a conversation – it was more like a fencing match. He'd pretty soon got the feeling she was pulling back from the closeness they'd felt in the café, regretting their silent decision to sleep together, and this put him straight on the defensive. Finally they'd just hung up, saying, "See you at school." Which was a terrible arrangement, as the school was so vast and shifting you could never be sure you'd bump into anyone.

Jack had no way of knowing, of course, that it was Christian's subtle hard work that had caused the shift in Gem's attitude. Under the guise of discussing whether you could start seeing someone profoundly different to you and keep it on a fun, sexy level that didn't in any way compromise or lessen you, he'd filled her with doubt and confusion, the sort that had hung around and swollen up and mutated all Monday, so that when Jack phoned she could barely talk straight to him.

Sod it, Jack thought, as he stomped onward towards the goal posts, I'd phone her now if I hadn't run out of fucking credit, well I'll phone her when I get back tonight and I won't get into chatting, you can never talk on a bloody phone anyway, things always come out wrong, I'll just get her to meet me tomorrow, and once we're together again it'll be the same, it'll heat up, it'll. . . Jack only noticed the new guy when he practically ran into him. Instantly, he squared up. This new guy was taller, broader, looked older than Jack. He felt like a threat. Who the hell was he?

"Decided to join us, Jack?" Boxy said. "You're the last."

Defensively, Jack glanced about him. He didn't like being last. The other members of the team looked back at him, subdued, waiting. They didn't seem to like the presence of the new guy either. Boxy had said he wasn't taking on anyone else.

"No need to count heads, mate, I've already done that," boomed Boxy. "OK – we'd better start, but before we do – you've probably all noticed this ugly tosser here."

The new guy grinned nastily. He wasn't ugly. Just mean looking, broad-faced with hard flint eyes.

"This," Boxy went on, "is Stev Kroege. He's joining us, as from today. He used to play for the Leighton Turks. Then he had to leave. Maybe you heard about it?"

There was a grumble of assent. Of course they'd heard. "Didn't you kick someone's eye out?" demanded Jamie.

Stev smirked. "Nah, he kept the eye. After a bit of surgery."

"Shit," muttered Karl. "And didn't you—"

"Look," said Boxy, "he was involved in some *incidents*,

OK? Someone's arm got broken – someone else needed stitches in his face. Bad luck. The kind of shit that can happen to any of us out on the field, right?"

"Right," said a few of the team, automatically.

"And the last time – with the eye – there was an official complaint," Boxy went on. "And the Turks decided they didn't want that kind of mud sticking to them – also they're a load of bureaucratic wankers – so they gave Stev the boot. Which – believe me, lads – is our good fortune. I've seen him play. He's awesome. He's a tank."

Stev grinned again, looking round at his new team. Then Iz said, "What does Len say?"

Boxy rounded on him, eyes lasering. "About what?"

"Well – you know. If he's been banned from another team an' all."

"Since when've you cared what *Len* says, ay, Iz, you fairy?"

"I just wondered—"

"You don't wanna do that. You wanna keep all your energy for your game. Cos you've been pretty weak these last few sessions and if you don't up your game pretty smart you'll be a permanent fixture on the bench, OK?"

There was a silence. Iz was smiling like he hoped it was all a joke, but no one else smiled. Or even looked at him.

"We're gonna need Stev this Saturday," barked Boxy. "We gotta tough match coming up. Newtown Tigers. We gotta show them who's the boss if we're gonna move up the league and start playing teams that're really worth playing." He paused, glared round at everyone. "OK, can we get down to some work here? Laps. Fast."

*

For the whole of that session, Boxy was focused on Stev, giving advice, shouting encouragement. Which Jack guessed was OK – he was the newcomer, after all; he had to be made to feel part of the team. For his part, Jack worked harder than he'd ever done before. He watched Stev and made sure he matched him, speed, strength, everything. Stev was achieving it all but hardly sweating. Maybe he's only in second gear, thought Jack, panicking; maybe he's got a lot more to come.

He didn't know what was going on inside him about Stev. Jealousy and admiration and disapproval and fear, all mashed up together.

Everyone kept their heads down as they trained; there was hardly any banter or messing about. Jack knew that something had shifted in the team. It was partly Stev being there and it was partly the way Boxy had singled Iz out like that, set him apart, ridiculed him. He'd never done that kind of thing before. Sure he'd had serious goes at them all, but it was good humoured, it was all part of being the trainer, being their mate, wanting the best for them. He'd never been that vicious before. Jack felt this niggling sense of shame that he hadn't stuck up for Iz but what was he supposed to do? Boxy was the skipper.

When they moved on to ball-handling skills, Stev was opposite Jack. And Jack thought: He's good, but the way he chucks the ball – too hard, like he wants to knock my block off – he's not with me like a teammate; he's up against me.

And he thought: He wants to be top dog. He means to take over as captain, that's what.

Chapter 25

The session ended, and they all trooped off satisfied and weary to the changing room to get showered. "OK, boys," shouted Boxy above the noise of pounding water, "hurry it up, get your gear on, we're gonna head to The Fox for a bonding session. Welcome in our new teammate, Stev, with a few jars, yeah?"

"I been banned from The Fox," said Stev.

Dosh snickered, and Big Mac demanded, "Yeah? What the fuck for?"

"Never mind what for," broke in Boxy. "What for is we got a problem now. Half of you boys look like you should still be drinking milkshakes. The Fox was nice and relaxed about that. Where the hell can we go now—"

"We can go to my pub," said Jamie.

There was a kind of thrumming silence. Then Boxy said, "Jamie, are you telling me you got a pub?"

"You knew that," said Jamie. "My mum runs it."

"I did not know that, Jamie. Or me and the team would have been round before now, partaking of free beer."

"Yeah, well, she won't let us upstairs. She's big on the

over-eighteen rule. But there's a cellar we hang out in—"

"Yeah, but she won't let all of us down there," broke in Dosh. "Not after that party we had for Iz's seventeenth. When she said she had to sandblast the bogs."

"Yeah, well you're wrong. We was talking, last night. She said she used to be worried but she's not now, she was all positive about the team, saying how impressed she was with the way I've shaped up – *shut the fuck up!*" he howled over the hoots of derision. "All right, forget it then!"

"Jamie, Jamie," soothed Boxy. "Don't get in a strop now. Go on with what you was saying."

"She said – we could go down to the cellar. And if we had something to celebrate – you know – like a good win next Saturday – she said she'd fix us up with some drink."

"And you didn't think to mention this before?"

Jamie hovered. He'd thought it sounded a bit too keen, he didn't want his mum coming on all keen. "No chance to, before," he muttered.

"Well, it's a brilliant offer," said Boxy. "Let's get going. Sharpish."

"She said Saturday," said Iz. "Not after training."

"She said when we got something to celebrate," snapped Boxy, rounding on Iz. "And we're celebrating our new team member, right?" There was a pause, during which everyone – especially Iz – remembered what Boxy had said about kicking Iz out. "Now come on. I am *thirsty.*"

Jack felt very weird watching Boxy with Jamie's mum. He didn't treat her like a mum. He was charming, confident, in control – practically flirting with her. "This is seriously good of you, Mrs Cooper," he was saying, all smooth, as she pulled pint after free pint for them at the bar. "It's great to have a place where the boys can hang out for a bit, after a match."

"No problem," Jamie's mum beamed. "I've told Jamie – you can use the cellar any time you want a get-together. I'd sooner they were down there than out on the streets getting into trouble."

"You're right there."

"I talked to Len at the Club a while back. I suggested the Rugby Club might have a room the Under 17s could use once in a while. He said there was absolutely no way. I know for a fact he didn't even bother to put it before the committee."

"That doesn't surprise me." Boxy leaned in towards her across the bar, and Jack glanced across at Jamie, but Jamie's face didn't move. "To be honest, the boys aren't really welcome there. I had a real fight to get them permission to use the gym equipment."

"Ridiculous. After all, who're going to be the players of tomorrow?"

"Our lads, if I have anything to do with it," smoothed Boxy, and Mrs Cooper twinkled back, "Well, you've made a real difference to the team, Alan. I hope those idiots on the *committee* appreciate it." Then she paused in her pint-pulling and called out, "Hey lads – pick up your beer and get down there! I don't want it obvious we've got underage drinking going on!"

"Yeah," rapped out Boxy, "anyone who's got a pint – disappear, OK?"

Pretty soon just Boxy, Jamie, Jack and Stev were left at the bar, and Boxy was whisking out a wallet Jack thought he had no intention of opening and saying, "You gotta let me pay for these beers, Mrs Cooper."

"Absolutely not!" she smiled. "On the house. Oh – and I was thinking – I got some leftover shepherd's pie from lunch – perfectly good, but I can't re-serve it. Health and Safety regulations. You want me to pop it in the microwave? There's enough to go round."

"Mrs Cooper – you're a star. That'd be ace. We're all starving."

"I bet you are, after all that hard training," said Mrs Cooper. "There – that's the last pint. Jamie – give me a hand." And Jamie went off with her, fighting to look nonchalant.

Jack picked up the last pint and followed Boxy and Stev down the wooden stairs to the cellar. As he turned to shut the door to the pub behind them he overheard Boxy muttering, "Got her eating out of my hand, mate. We can come here any time." He looked up, saw Stev's sneering grin, and felt this feeling that he didn't really understand grip hold of him. There was anger in it, but excitement too, and fear, and he half wanted to stick up for Mrs Cooper, to protect her, but he half wanted to join in, laugh with them – have Stev give him that sneering grin, too.

Boxy seemed to take possession of the huge old cellar as soon as he walked through the door. He looked all around, grinning, and pronounced, "This is the *business*." Back in the 1970s, the cellar had been briefly opened up as a small, live-music club, which had meant the installation of toilets, a bar at one end, and a small wooden stage, now covered in empty beer crates, at the other. Jamie's sofa and telly floated like two abandoned rafts in the centre.

Boxy paced the floor and jumped up on the stage, kicking aside a couple of crates. "This is fantastic," he crowed. "This is gonna be our team headquarters, yeah?"

"*Headquarters?*" said Jack. "What – we turned into the SAS or something?"

"Yup. The SAS of the field. And it's good to have somewhere to get together."

"Yeah. Well. If Stev's been banned from The Fox we need somewhere, don't we."

Abruptly, Jack felt the full force of Boxy's laser-eyes on him. "You got a problem with something, Jack?"

Jack was shaking his head before he'd even processed the question. The desire to placate Boxy was suddenly overpowering. "No," he muttered. "Not at all."

"Good. Here's little Jamie with the grub. Everybody say thank you to Jamie!"

"Thank you Jamie!" they all echoed, jeering.

Up to the elbows in red-striped oven-gloves, Jamie headed self-consciously across the floor and plonked a large china dish full of steaming, meaty-smelling potato-topped pie on the bar. The boys cheered at the sight of it. Behind Jamie was his mum with an armful of plates and cutlery. "Mac," Boxy barked, "take those off Mrs Cooper!"

Big Mac complied, and Boxy said, "Mrs Cooper, you're terrific. A round of applause for Mrs Cooper!"

As the boys clapped and cheered again, Boxy took hold

of the huge serving spoon and started dolloping out the pie, and everyone elbowed their way in to get a place standing at the bar.

Mrs Cooper retraced her way up the cellar steps, shaking her head and smiling. Her boy hadn't mucked in with a group of lads like this since . . . well, since Boy Scouts. Alan's got them in the palm of his hand, she thought. Well, Jamie could do a lot worse for a role model.

"Nutrition," Boxy was saying, mouth full. "You wanna be a good athlete, you gotta have good nutrition. Protein to build your muscles; carbohydrates for energy."

"What about vegetables?" demanded Karl.

"Yeah, vegetables too, Karl, you lettuce-chomping weasel."

"Weasels eat meat!" squawked Dosh.

"*And* you gotta eat fruit," added Boxy, casually cuffing Dosh. "*Now* boys. Down to business. We gotta discuss the game plan for Saturday. Now we've got—" and he grinned at Stev – "extra arsenal."

There was a shift round the bar. "You gonna play him right away?" Dosh asked.

"Yes. Hit 'em hard right from the start. I want you to play at number 6, Stev. I know you were 8 before but I've gotta hunch this is gonna work. And Iz – I want you to move to 7. OK?"

There was a silence. That left Leo off the field. Leo waited for Boxy to say something, something along the lines of, "Don't worry, you'll be back on again soon," but he didn't.

He just dropped him and left it at that.

*

Walking home, Jack suddenly remembered he'd totally forgotten about Gem, forgotten about their stupid phone conversation and his resolution to call her that night. Since the first sight of Stev, he hadn't given her a thought. He speeded up into a dog-trot.

Chapter 26

When he got home, there was a message waiting for him laboriously penned by his youngest little sister.

Phown Gem 07798 824900

Gem had woken up Tuesday morning full of longing for Jack, furious with herself for screwing up her phone call with him, for letting Christian influence her. She resolved never to listen to Christian and his weak talk about Darwin ever again. She'd phoned Jack but his mobile was off, and it stayed off throughout the day. She'd hunted for him at school, her longing for him growing with every hour she failed to find him, then tracked down his house number (from an awed and monosyllabic Big Mac) and phoned him at home when she knew he'd be back from training.

Jack, of course, was dead pleased with the message. He felt it was a distinct one-up to him, and rang back straight away. Gem exuded warmth and enthusiasm even when he was giving her his lame excuse about running out of credit and he got roused up just listening to her. It couldn't have been more different from the fractured, stilted conversation of the night before. Jack didn't worry about it though. He just put the change down to female moodiness.

They met up the next night in a quiet pub ten minutes' walk from Gem's house, and sat opposite each other at a tiny round table with their knees touching underneath. Jack talked about Stev Kroege, the new player at Westgate, and Gem, looking across at him, wanted him so much she felt like her face was swimming into his. Jack was really turned on to her, and delighted she seemed so interested in what he was saying. She drew out of him stuff he'd barely begun to process, like the heady mixture of admiration and dislike Stev inspired in him, the threat he felt from him.

"He sounds *adorable*," sneered Gem, supportively. "I mean – being kicked out of your old club for ultra violence – it's hardly a recommendation, is it?"

"Boxy reckons he had bad luck – he reckons the authorities overreacted."

"No smoke without fire."

"Maybe. I mean – *we're* an aggressive team. Boxy's always cranking us up, it's how we play, but this guy. . ."

Gem reached across the table and put her hand on his.

"I bet you're a better player," she said. "If he had to half-kill people on the field, it's probably cos he's got no skill."

Jack grinned. He loved the feeling of her hand. And he loved talking with her like this – kind of working things out, seeing them through to the end. It was different to the way you talked to your mates; they'd think you were going soft if you talked like this. He left it a few moments, just enjoying the touch, then he laced his fingers in hers. "We'll see on Saturday, I suppose. Boxy's put him at number 6, and switched Iz to 7 . . . which means poor old Leo is on the bench. You gonna come and watch?" He trailed off, suddenly wondering if he wanted Gem to see that match, where Stev might stand out more than he did.

"Sure I'll come," she said.

They ran out of conversation. Gem racked her brains for something to say but no topic seemed interesting enough – not beside the physical fact of Jack sitting opposite her. Then Jack announced he was starving and wanted some chips. "Come back to mine," said Gem. "I'll make you a sandwich. Cheaper. And *healthier* – I thought you were an athlete?"

On the way back to Gem's house, they held hands and made the odd comment on things they saw – a manky-looking cat, a noisy car with its exhaust shot – but they didn't talk. They were so aware of each other, every physical fibre of each other, that talking was impossible. Gemma's mind was in overdrive, plotting, planning. She was wondering if the house would be empty, wondering how far to take things if it was. The attraction she felt for Jack was like a great leaping beast, it wouldn't let her think straight, and part of her just wanted to get into bed with him and get it over with, get things in perspective again. She was beginning to think like that, of taming it, getting it over with.

After all, she brooded, as her house got closer, no one need know. I wouldn't tell Chris. I wouldn't tell Holly. She thinks it's the depths of slagginess to sleep with a boy until he tells you he loves you . . .

Gem didn't trust that word, "love". People used it like syrup, some kind of sticky glue to keep a couple together. Her first "lover" had used the word all the time like a mantra and still it had all fizzled out and they'd split up after only a couple of months. Her second "lover" had been obsessed by getting her to say it to him and in the end she had but she hadn't meant it, not at all.

Gem decided she liked it that she couldn't imagine "love" as part of Jack's vocabulary.

They reached her house.

Chapter 27

Gem's house seemed very silent as they pushed the front door shut behind them. "Aren't your parents in?" asked Jack. His parents were always in.

"Dad's away," Gem said. "In Brussels. Not sure about Mum. . ." She walked through to the dark kitchen, Jack following. There was a phone on a low shelf on the far side of the kitchen with its answer machine light flashing. Gemma went over to it and pressed the play button. The message that came out was loud and clear enough for them both to hear.

"Hi, darling! I've got held up here . . . bloody spreadsheets again – realistically it's going to be ten-thirty at the earliest before I'm back. I'm *so* sorry, Gem – I know I promised you chicken stir-fry! I'll do it tomorrow. There's lasagne in the freezer. Lots of love!"

There was a silence. The large round silver clock on the wall said ten to nine.

"Your mum sounds nice," Jack said.

"She is," said Gem. Then she walked over and put her arms round his neck.

*

Slowly, undressing each other as they went, they made it up to Gem's room. Jack was careful to pick up his shirt, dropped on the stairs. They didn't want to stop kissing, they didn't want to draw back or let go in case the feeling changed, in case one of them said something. Gem felt like she was heading over the top of a waterfall. She loved the inevitability, the way it drove all the thoughts out; she loved the violence of what she was feeling. She had her fingers hooked into the waistband of his jeans, her thumbs easing the stud undone. He was circling one hand on her breast and the other was on the back of her neck, keeping their faces crushed together.

Then suddenly he swore and pulled back, muttering, "My coat . . . I've got . . . I need my coat."

"S'OK," she muttered back. "I've got some upstairs." She grabbed his hand and they blundered up the last few stairs and into her room. By the bed, she dropped his hand and, standing apart, they stripped off the last of their clothes, scrambled under her swirly purple duvet, and seized hold of each other.

To his absolute horror, Jack found himself trembling. The shock of being like this, the *perfection* of it, like it used to be with Amy, naked and delicious with all the time in the world, it was too much, it brought it all back . . . He brought his mouth down, too hard, round her nipple, and pushed his hand between her legs.

And she hissed, "*Don't.*"

He drew back, shocked. Their eyes locked into each other, unbearably close and intimate. Gem hadn't meant to say that. She'd blurted it out because it seemed like he was going through some tried and much-practised routine, his "technique", and she didn't want that. Now she was full of remorse in case she'd ruined everything.

She seized hold of him, kissed him, started kissing down his neck, and his chest, lower, lower . . . but she felt clumsy, hopeless, so she reared up again and leaned over to her little bedside cupboard, pulling open the drawer at the top. She rummaged for a couple of seconds then came out with a silvery-packaged condom, which she chucked at him, gracelessly. He caught it, then grabbed hold of her again, buried his face in her hair. They could barely look at each other. They kept kissing and kissing because that was like hiding and meant they didn't have to look at each other.

Jack had a sudden memory of how it used to be with Amy. The playfulness, the confidence she'd had, the way she'd teased and managed him. The way she'd talked to him, admiring him, encouraging him. In this silence he felt a bit desperate. He sat up, turned his back on Gem, put on the condom. Then he turned back to her and they took hold of each other and as she guided him inside her they both let out a groan, of relief, of finality, and then they moved together and far too soon, Jack came. He collapsed on top of her, quaking with pleasure and disappointment. And he wanted to apologize but instead he heard himself say, "That ain't a patch on how it's gonna be," and his heart gave a panicky jump because it sounded like commitment, like a promise.

Gem held on to him, tight, while he dealt with the condom. She was full of a kind of triumphant joy that it had happened at last, that all the fencing and wondering and *what-if*-ing was over. Her body felt like it was convulsed with greed, with wanting more. Swivelling her eyes, she could see her pink bedside clock with its bikini-clad bathing beauty, hands just coming up to twenty past nine. They had an hour, they had at least an hour. She wrapped her arms round his neck, wound her legs round his legs, started kissing along his shoulder, ended up on his face. Then they were locked in the safeness of a long kiss. His hands were exploring again, meeting her hands doing their work. He was hard again, she could feel him against her stomach. She pushed him back, climbed on top of him, and he reached for another condom and laughed, and the sound of his laugh lifted both of them, they were both suddenly flooded with confidence because here they were, doing it twice, and it was working for them, working so well.

Afterwards they showered together, in the tiny shower room with the trendy glass bricks in the wall and the clever lighting and all the silvery chrome fittings. "Is this just for you to use?" demanded Jack.

"Yup," said Gem, soaping his back. "Unless we've got people staying over, then they get to use it too."

"Well, poor you!" he said, half impressed and half incensed. "I bet that's a real pain for you."

"Doesn't happen very often, or it would be. Hey – can I use a scrub on your back?"

"A *what*?"

"A scrub. Tea-tree and sea salt. To exfoliate. You got quite a few blackheads."

"Well *thank you,* babe!"

"Oh, go on."

"Sure. Feel free. Whack it on. Attack me. *Again.*"

She sniggered, and dolloped some scrub on his back, working it in with swift, skilful fingers. It was wonderful to have jumped to this closeness, this ownership of him. The tangy smell of tea-tree mixed with the steam and filled the little room, and they breathed it in happily. "This is so much easier on someone else's back," she said.

"Mmmm, that feels good. *Ouch.* That didn't."

"My *God*, you gotta let me get rid of these – they're gross!"

"So how come you're enjoying yourself so much if they're gross?"

"Dunno. I'm sick. I love *grooming*. I reckon the apes have got it right. You know – sorting through each other's hair, scraping off ticks, picking off bugs. . ."

"Very attractive, Gem. You can be quite a turn-on when you put your mind to it."

"I'm not *trying* to turn you on, I'm knackered," she giggled, and he laughed and turned to face her and they kissed, quickly, then she swivelled round and handed him the tub of tea-tree cream.

The ease, the intimacy, it was delightful, intoxicating, it was there in the shower room like the steam and the tea-tree smell and it felt like it would be there between them for ever. "This is why we ran out of conversation in the pub," she said, feeling brave.

"What?"

"In the pub. We went all silent because we just wanted to . . . you know. . ."

"Yup. I do know." He smoothed in the cream across her back, then slid his hands round to her breasts, and she laughed and turned the shower on again, full blast.

"What the *fuck*—" he squawked, through the pummelling water.

"I was getting *cold*," she laughed. "Come on, we better get dressed."

They hurried through to Gem's bedroom, aware the time was moving on, aware Gem's mum might get back earlier than she'd predicted in the phone message. Gem rummaged in the top drawer of her dressing table for her new turquoise bra and pants set, and pulled them on. She knew they looked gorgeous on her. She'd bought them last week, thinking she'd wear them when she made the decision to sleep with Jack. She turned to face him now.

But he wasn't looking at her – he was scrambling into the clothes he'd left strewn about the bedroom floor. "God, how can you bear to put your old dirty clothes back on?" she demanded.

"I haven't got a choice, have I? Anyway, what you talking about? These clothes are *clean*."

"I s'pose to a rugby player, clean is a relative term."

"Yeah, well, we're not all princesses with our own bloody bathrooms, are we?" Then he did up the button on his jeans, and looked up. And grinned. "Nice," he said.

"You like them?"

"Very much. I look forward to tearing them off you sometime soon."

"Don't be corny," Gem said, feeling herself go slightly hot. She turned quickly and pulled a crisp clean shirt out of her wardrobe. She was embarrassed, like she'd been blatantly parading for him. Possibly, she thought, because she *had* been blatantly parading for him. She put on her shirt, picked up her jeans from the floor and stepped into them, while Jack shook the mangled duvet evenly over the bed.

"You're gonna make Mum suspicious, doing that," she said. "I never do that."

"Would she go ape?"

Gem shrugged. "Not her business."

There was a silence. It seemed different, somehow, now they'd got their clothes on again – slightly awkward. Like what had happened between them was so massive, so all-encompassing, that they couldn't see a way to fit it into ordinary everyday conversation, into ordinary everyday life.

And they wanted each other to speak but they didn't know what they wanted each other to say.

"You gonna make me a sandwich?" Jack demanded. "You promised me a sandwich. I was hungry then, and I'm *starving* now."

"OK, OK, don't whine!" she laughed. "Come on."

"You can see your bra straps through that shirt."

"So? You really don't know anything about fashion, do you, Jack?"

"Nope."

"Come on, let's go down."

He put his arm round her as they left the bedroom and she, loving the contact, thought, God, this is *us* now. This is how things are gonna *be*.

In the kitchen, Jack sat at the long granite-topped counter that divided the cooking area from the eating area, and watched Gem make three doorstep-sized sandwiches, two for him and one for her. "What happens when you stop burning all this off?" she asked. "You gonna get all porky and fat?"

"Probably."

"You want tomato in this? Or lettuce?"

"Just lettuce, please. And more of that mayo, yeah?"

Gem pulled a face at him, then screwed off the top of the mayonnaise jar and dolloped some more out. She felt fantastic. She thought: This must be the afterglow you're always hearing about, this must be *it*. She'd never felt like this after sex with anyone else. It was almost like she was . . . *grateful*. Jesus, she had to hide that from Jack. Like she had to hide the fact she was loving feeding him, loving the whole thing of him sitting there watching her making him food.

For his part, Jack was dazed and amazed by what had happened. He looked at Gem and his mind went glorious flashback to her on top of him in bed. But he was also so hungry now that he couldn't think beyond sinking his teeth into one of the sandwiches taking shape in front of him. As soon as she pushed a towering plate towards him, he grabbed one and rammed it in his mouth. "Steady!" she laughed.

"You got a pint of milk I can have?"

"*Milk?*"

"Yeah. You know – cow juice."

"Yuch. Yeah, I guess so." She fetched one from the fridge and came and sat beside him, and there was silence apart from the noise of chewing. That tiny, creeping distance that had started when they put their clothes on was still growing between them, like coming down after being high. They both felt it; neither of them knew what to do about it.

When he'd cleared his plate, Jack said, "I guess I'd better go."

"You just want to avoid meeting my mum."

"No I don't. Well – OK, yes, it could be embarrassing. But I've got this sports science project I gotta hand in tomorrow. . ."

"You're never gonna work tonight!"

He grinned. "No. No way. I just want to *sleep*. But I s'pose I'll set my alarm and get it done in the morning." He leant towards her, put his arm around her neck and kissed the side of her face. "When can I see you again?" he murmured. "Tomorrow?"

Too soon, she thought, immediately. She wanted time to absorb all this – to process it. "I got my gym class tomorrow, eight till nine," she said, "and stacks of work to hand in for Friday."

"Oh. OK."

"Let's make it Friday night, yeah?"

Jack got down from his stool. He was thinking about the match on Saturday, the first time Stev would be playing.

He needed an early night, no beer, pasta for dinner for the energy it unpacked . . . "Friday nights are never good for me," he said. "Not with a match the next day."

Gem felt like she'd suddenly telescoped up miles and miles and miles away from him. *Fridays are never good for me?* What kind of a relationship was this going to be?

She slid down from her stool and he put an arm round her as they headed towards the front door. "Look – you wanna come and watch the game?" he said.

"I dunno," she answered, feebly.

"Well – text me. Or gimme a ring. But I'll see you Saturday night, yeah?" And he grabbed her and kissed her, and she kissed back automatically, then he left, and she shut the door behind him.

Chapter 28

Gem ran up to her room to deal with what had just happened. She felt she'd skidded somewhere, skidded insanely – one minute they were making love, flying, floating, *fusing* . . . and the next they were quibbling and not connecting and it was all down to tedious little arrangements they couldn't agree on and him pushing her aside cos of some *rugby* match. . .

Gem reminded herself she'd pushed him aside too, because she'd said "not Thursday". But that was different. Wasn't it? That was just time to draw breath, cos of *him*, cos he'd made her so breathless. But *he* – he'd put her second. Definitely second. And she was hurt because she'd made all these assumptions because of the amazing sex they'd had, assumptions to do with being together all the time, or at least all the time she wanted to be. . .

Why do things have to do this? she thought. Why can't they be good all the time?

The team talk that Boxy gave before the match that Saturday was even more fierce than usual. In training in the week they'd worked on their new moves, how they were going to make best use of Stev. Now it was time for the inspiration.

"The Newtown Tigers are big bastards," Boxy said. "They got a stone on each one of you. And they use that weight, trust me. But that's not gonna matter, right? Because you're not afraid of them." He paused, looked around, letting his eyes rest on each one of them. "You're gonna make them afraid of you."

Stev grinned, like a crocodile. He was rocking himself slightly as he listened. Jack watched him and was seized by the feeling that Stev was going to change things, crank everything up a gear, infect the whole team with whatever drove him.

And right now, listening, Jack wanted that too. He stopped thinking about Gem, whether she'd be there or not on the touchline, whether he should've phoned her last night just for a chat. He stopped feeling sorry for Leo, supplanted by Stev, sitting there as a sub with a crushed kind of look on his face. He focused on what was coming; he focused on running out on to the pitch.

"It's down to the forwards," Boxy growled. "It's always down to the forwards. You think – you do the hard work, you do the dog, and no one sees it, you're not the ones running in the tries, getting the glory. But we know it, we know we're getting the glory off your hard work. We're a team. No one does it on his own. The team does it. And you're gonna show Newtown that they don't even deserve to be on the same pitch as us, OK? *OK! On your feet! Grab a shirt!*"

Jack was standing next to Stev as they formed a circle and gripped each other's shirts. Stev had hold of him so tight it was like an attack. He was radiating ferocious energy. Jack couldn't see his face but Iz, opposite, was staring at him transfixed. Jack could feel everything in him coming together, coalescing, like a red haze, a force. His team. *His team.*

Jack talked. The team chanted; they shouted. Then they ran out.

It wasn't until the game was over and Westgate were roaring with triumph at their 14-11 victory that Jack remembered to look for Gemma. He scanned the touchline, but she wasn't there. He felt a brief stab of angry disappointment that she hadn't made it, she hadn't seen him tackling like a maniac, working in punishing partnership with Stev, running in the second try. Then Jamie jumped joyfully on his back, and he forgot about her. "Line up, lads!" he yelled. "C'mon! See 'em off the field!"

Westgate formed a grinning, jeering line either side of the dejected losers as they trooped to the edge of the pitch. They clapped each other but there was no good feeling between the teams now the match was over, not like there should be. There'd been too much trouble in the game. Two fights had broken out, quelled immediately by the ref. Stev had played as dirty as he could get away with. He'd been warned twice, but not actually sent off. He'd goaded and barbed his opposite number mercilessly throughout. Now he reached out and jeeringly ruffled his hair. The

Newtown number 6 swiped at his hand, swore, his voice savage with hatred. Stev crowed with laughter.

When Boxy called them to him, he was practically shaking with triumph. "It worked," he said. "I knew it would work. Jack, Stev – you got some partnership shaping up there. You got into your stride towards the end of the first half, then there was no stopping you."

Jack grinned, and flashed a glance at Stev. Who was staring back at him, grinning too, but there was still something closed off in his face.

Boxy carried on with his match debrief, praising everyone, telling them today's win was just the start of how it was going to be, then he wound up with, "So. Tonight. Serious celebrations on the agenda." The boys cheered agreement, and he added, "Jamie – your place? Still OK?"

"Yeah, fine," said Jamie, importantly. "Ma said – if we put together a kitty, she'll let us have a couple of crates at cost price."

"Your mother, Jamie," announced Boxy, "is a queen among women. A fucking empress. OK, lads – you heard him. Seven-thirty latest, and I mean latest, downstairs at The Crown. Which is a suitable place for us, lads, cos today we're all fucking wearing one."

Chapter 29

"Hey, Gem."

"Hi."

"You weren't there."

"No. Well – I had a late night last night. I didn't wake up till about twelve o'clock."

Jack wondered with a stab of pure jealousy what Gem had been doing Friday night. She waited for him to ask her, and he waited for her to ask him about the match. He broke the silence saying, "Well, we won. *If* you're interested."

"Course I am – well done."

"Great match. Fourteen-eleven. I got a brilliant try."

"Yeah? Great. Did the psycho play? The one you were telling me about?"

"Yeah," said Jack, defensively. "He was good."

"And was he psychotic?"

"Well – he sailed a bit close to the wind a coupla times. But he got away with it. He's good. We're good together."

Another pause. What Gem had done last night was go out drinking with Holly and a few of the other girls and (during her third glass of white wine) tell them about sleeping with Jack. Shrieks and queries followed; she regretted telling them, wanted to escape. So she left with the excuse (to knowing shrieks) of being knackered, and left.

She planned to pretend she'd gone on to a club with them, when Jack asked her.

But Jack didn't ask her. He said: "So. You gonna come tonight?"

Gem felt needled. She wanted to say something dead childish like *Oh let's just do everything you want to do, shall we?* Instead, to make her point, she asked in a pettish voice, "Do we have to stay to the end?"

"Not if you don't want to. But we got somewhere new to go – Jamie's pub – The Crown. His mum's letting us have the cellar."

"Letting you *have* it—?"

"Letting us have a party there. We're all really up for it. It's gonna be great."

There was a pause. Then Jack muttered, "Look, I know it's all rugby, Gem. But I gotta go tonight and . . . and I really want you to be there."

Suddenly, because of the way he said this, Wednesday night was there between them, hot and amazing. Suddenly Gem wanted very, very much to see him. "Why didn't you call me?" she asked. "Or at least *text?*"

"Why didn't you?" he said. "I looked for you in school."

"Me too."

"Come on, say you'll come tonight."

"OK, I'll come," she said. "You gonna call for me?"

*

Nine o'clock Saturday night, and the cellar was packed and heaving. The sounds from the decks Dosh had set up were pounding out through the high, barred windows on a level with people's legs going by in the street. The party had already far outstripped the best night the team had ever spent in The Fox. Excitement pumped through every conversation, sparked like electricity through the air. This wasn't just a meaningless social gathering – this was celebration. The team had triumphed, they were the focus, and this was their place.

Jamie had been as nervous as a stray cat as the evening kicked off, wondering if his vague mutterings about "maybe a few other friends and girls coming too" was such a massive understatement that his mum would freak at the stream of people coming in, more and more as the texts went out. But Jamie's mum, standing upstairs in the main bar pulling pints, was fine about it. She believed in the right of teenagers to have somewhere safe to gather. And also, the floor was thick and the pub was full and she could hardly hear a thing.

Gem was forcing Jack to dance with her. "Move," she laughed. "*Move!*" She felt comfortable, luxurious with him, now she was pressed up against him again, head to toe. She felt sure.

"Look – I told you – I don't dance. C'mon, lets give it a break. . ." He started to manoeuvre Gem towards the corner by the bar, kissing her as he went. To be interrupted by Boxy, bounding up on to the little stage next to Dosh, shouting, "*Who's the boys, then? WHO'S THE BOYS?*"

A great roar came back at him. Dosh at his decks

responded with loud, heavy beat music, and Boxy shouted out: "RULE NUMBER ONE?"

And the boys yelled back, "YOU DON'T TALK ABOUT WHAT GOES ON DURING TRAINING!"

"RULE NUMBER TWO?"

"YOU DON'T TALK ABOUT WHAT GOES ON DURING TRAINING!!"

"Oh – my – *God*," Gem wailed silently, ears ringing, as Jack let go of her hand. "Beam me up to the mother ship!"

"RULE NUMBER THREE?"

"YOU DON'T TALK ABOUT WHAT GOES ON DURING TRAINING!!"

"Rule number four – *Don't ever question me!* RULE NUMBER FIVE!?"

"*ONE IN, ALL IN!!!*"

And the team swarmed together, arms round each other's shoulders like before a match, jumping in time to Dosh's music, yelling out the words of the song into each other's faces. They were fired up with triumph, bonded on a high of belonging, and everyone else was drawn into their sheer power, circling them, laughing and singing along too. The noise shook the room, rattled the bars at the high windows. Slicked with condensation, the walls of the cellar shone.

The song ended, and the jumping stopped. The boys broke away, cheering and laughing, and the room shifted again as the music changed and they were absorbed back in among the girls and the others.

Jack made it back to Gemma's side. "You OK?" he demanded.

"Sure," she said.

There was a pause, during which both of them wondered if she was going to take the piss out of what had just happened; then she laughed and he nuzzled his face into hers.

"What was that chanting stuff about?" she asked. "You don't ever talk about what goes on during training?"

"Oh – it's a joke. It's like a joke ritual we got going now. It was from an old DVD Boxy got us to watch once – *Fight Club*. He brought it in and set it up in the clubhouse and we watched it after training. It was brilliant. These guys with this kind of secret society of beating the shit out of each other."

"So you're saying the *team* . . . is like a secret society."

"*No!* Well – only so far as Len and the alackadoos at the Club wouldn't approve of Boxy's training methods, if they ever found out what they were. It's just – it was all about what men are really about, how we're not really about jobs and cars and money and shit. Boxy reckons that's like us."

Gem looked at him. She wanted to ask him more; she was drawn to what he'd said about men not being about jobs and cars and money. Jack put his arm round her and started to steer her towards the sofa shoved up against the far wall when Boxy, left arm round Stev's shoulders, lurched towards them and blocked their way. "How's my captain?" he roared. "You done great today! The two of you – the way you ran it in, round that lardy-arsed full-back. . ." He lunged forward, got hold of Jack, slung his right arm round his shoulders, and Jack felt like he was in a kind of triumvirate of power, he and Stev, Boxy in the middle. He was exultant, head clear, no doubts, no hopes, not wanting anything else than this. He looked across at Stev, who grinned at him, and grinned back. There was a link between them now, he couldn't deny it, a connection that the other boys weren't part of. Nothing you could ever talk about, but it was there – something in them that was the same.

Ignored, Gem tottered back and leant up against the bar, ogling Jack, and couldn't believe that she didn't mind about what was happening.

At eleven-fifteen Boxy jumped up on the stage beside Dosh, got him to kill the music. Then he shouted, "OK, time to finish up! We're not going to abuse Mrs Cooper's hospitality by staying later than the punters upstairs. Or by leaving a mess. Cos we wanna come back, don't we?" The team roared *yes*, and someone flicked the lights on. "I want all the bottles and cans picked up," Boxy bellowed. "I want spilt beer mopped up. Iz and Dosh – you check out the bogs. I want this place pristine!"

And everyone got to it. Jack wouldn't meet Gem's eyes as he stooped for a bottle by her feet and came back up beside her. "Bloody hell," she sneered, "I don't believe this!"

He ignored her. "Anywhere else this would be considered a real downer," she persisted.

"I know that," he hissed back. "But it's not here, OK?"

Chapter 30

Five minutes later everyone was trooping up the cellar steps, Iz carrying a bulging bin bag. They left the pub with the last of the punters. Boxy thanked Mrs Cooper profusely and charmingly on the way out, and she replied that they were welcome there any time, Jamie knew that. And Boxy grinned with a mission-accomplished grin and his team and its followers surged out on to the pavement and swaggered along the high street, like an army high on victory. Bit by bit it splintered and split; Boxy going off alone first, then Sam and her mates, then Karl and Rory and a load of others who lived on the east side of town, and soon only Big Mac, Iz, Dosh and Stev were walking with Jack and Gemma. Everywhere, Christmas lights were twinkling in shop windows sparkling against the dark.

At the turning for Gem's bus stop, the four boys insisted on coming along too. They all reached the bus stop and Jack said, "OK, guys. You can fuck off now."

"Oh that's *nice!*" slurred Dosh. "Telling your teammates to fuck off!"

"We'll see Gem on the bus too," said Iz.

"Oh no you won't," laughed Jack. "Now *fuck off.*"

Laughing, pushing each other about, the four shouted goodbye and ambled back towards the main road. "God," Gem murmured, pushing her face against Jack's chest, "I thought they'd never go."

"Yeah, well, they have now."

"The psycho seemed OK, at the party."

"Yeah. Quite mellow." He kissed her hair, inhaling its coconut smell. The road was deserted now. She craned her mouth up to his, and they kissed. "I'll get the bus with you," he said. "You're not going home on your own, not this late."

"Aw, my *hero.* You'll never get a bus back." They kissed again, folding into each other. "You gonna get a cab?"

"No money. I'll walk." A longer kiss.

"Stay with me. Mum'd let you kip in the spare room."

"Yeah?"

"Course she would, if you saw me back."

"And then I could creep across the landing and get in bed with you . . . God, Gem, Wednesday was. . ."

"I know."

"I didn't plan it, I never thought. . ."

"*Aw!*" a harsh voice shouted. "What a *sweet* little lovey-dovey *scene.*"

Gem and Jack spun round. Five drunk, aggressive-looking men – late teens, early twenties – were loping across the road towards them. Jack and Gem, all absorbed in each other, hadn't noticed them turning the corner into the street, hadn't noticed them watching. They ambled forward, sneering, chewing, and formed a half-circle round the lovers, trapping them against scarred perspex of the bus-shelter stand.

"Got a lovely arse, in't she?" leered one of them.

"Take it up the arse, does she?" said another.

Jack wanted to punch that one who'd said that straight in the mouth so hard his fist smashed out the other side, but he didn't. He pushed Gem behind him, so he was between her and the gang. He could feel her breathing, taut with fear and anger.

"Love to go up 'er I would. Front or back."

"Yeah, me first."

"Fuck off. I ain't 'avin your seconds."

Jack stared expressionlessly at the faces surrounding him, each one of them blurred and mean with drink. Envy and viciousness and a kind of sick anticipation was coming off them in waves. They wanted to end their evening with a thrill, a high, and he and Gem were going to be that high.

They were scraggy-looking, unfit – a couple of them had bellies. Jack could do them, no problem. If he was on his own, he'd take on all five, fight his way through, leg it. But not with Gem here. Three could be on to him, two grabbing her.

"Look like she could do with a good fuck, don't it."

"And all he was doing was *talking* to her."

"Wiv a little kiss now and then. *Aw*. Kissy-*kissy*."

Gem was the reason he wanted to smash their heads in, and Gem was the reason he couldn't. He could feel her trembling behind him. The humiliation, the rage, were doing for him. He knew he'd lose it in a minute.

Why wasn't anyone around? Looking out of their windows? Phoning the police?

Phoning – Jack remembered something. He remembered the last call he'd made, to Dosh, at the start of the evening, checking the time they were all meeting up at the cellar. Dosh, who, with the others, couldn't be more than five minutes away right now.

He slipped his fingers in his pocket and they closed round his phone. He pressed redial. Felt it ring.

"Show us your tits, doll."

Answer it Dosh you bastard!

"I could fuck her brains out. Right now."

He sensed rather than heard Dosh answer. He palmed his phone, draw it to the mouth of his pocket, and said loudly, "Hey, come on. Leave it, OK?"

This provoked a triumphant malevolent chorus from the men, because they thought at last they'd cracked him.

"Yeah? Why should we?"

"She's dying for it. He's not giving her any, is he?"

"Shift it, mate. Out the way."

"Or we'll shift you, OK?"

"*Leave us alone!*" wailed Gem.

"Aw, don't get upset, sweetheart. What you upset about?"

"Give 'er a cuddle. Somebody give 'er a fucking cuddle."

They pressed in closer to Jack, smirking with pleasure, waiting for him to react, waiting for him to crack. One move, one word, and that'd be all the trigger they needed and they'd be on him. One man shoved his face in so close

180

to Jack's that he could smell his sour beer breath. Jack stared back at him unblinking. "You gonna move or are we gonna make you move, ay?" he slurred.

And then, in the distance, Jack heard drumming. Four pairs of feet, running in time, like when they ran on to the rugby pitch. He didn't stop staring but his eyes narrowed and he let a smile spread slow and wide across his face.

"Got somethin' to smile about, mate?" snarled the man, and shoved Jack hard, back into Gem. And at last, Jack reacted. He slammed his right fist straight into the man's jaw. The man gasped, sagged, collapsed.

The gang was swarming on to Jack just as Stev and the others raced round the corner.

Stev's whole face was alight with battle-lust. He didn't stop running, just ploughed straight into the gang like a truck out of control. Big Mac, Iz and Dosh were right behind, mowing in too. "They got knives?" Dosh bellowed.

"Dunno!" Jack yelled back. He kept his back to Gem and smashed his fist into heads, stomachs, chests.

The gang didn't have knives, not ones they could get to anyway. The fight, if it can be called that, was over in thirty seconds. The team mopped them up and threw them down and they cowered on the ground, curled up like fetuses, arms wound protectively round their heads. Stev grinned, aimed a hard boot at the back closest to him. "Outnumbered, ay, Jacky boy?"

"Could have taken 'em if I hadn't had Gem here." He reached behind, took hold of her hand, but kept his eyes on the five sprawling men.

Stev leered his shark grin at Gem, still half-collapsed

against the glass wall of the bus shelter. "Women, see? Like Boxy says, they make you weak."

"Fuck off, mate. And thanks for coming back."

"We wondered what was up," panted Iz. "Dosh kept shouting into his phone. . ."

"*I* twigged on something was up," put in Big Mac. "Told him to shut up and listen."

"And then we legged it back."

"What we gonna do with this lot?" demanded Stev, and he kicked out again, this time at a hunched shoulder.

"Leave it, mate," said Iz.

"Leave it? They gotta be shown a lesson. Let's take them down the canal. Chuck 'em in. Can you swim, scum?" He kicked again, at a shielding forearm. "Gonna learn, ay?" One of the gang rolled over on to his side, groaning horribly, and spewed out a stream of yellow vomit.

"Charming!" sneered Dosh.

"Can we get out of here?" wailed Gem. Jack turned to her and put his arms round her.

The man he'd landed his first punch on started to scramble to his feet. Stev gathered him up in a crunching tackle, crowing with laughter. "Going somewhere are you?" The headbutt that followed was so fast Gem wasn't entirely sure she'd seen it. But the man collapsed like a puppet, so it must've happened. "Get 'em up," ordered Stev, grinning, the man all-but dangling from his right fist. "Get 'em on their feet."

"Jack, I mean it, can we get out of here?" muttered Gem. And then a police siren broke into the night, getting louder, closer.

"We gonna run?" hissed Big Mac.

"No," said Jack. "Why should we?"

"OK," agreed Stev. "Right. Citizen's arrest, right?"

"Let me do the talking, OK?" snapped Jack.

The police van careened round the corner and slammed to a halt beside them. The four men on the ground uncurled, scrambled to their feet, snarling and spitting, demanding arrests and justice. Two weary officers clambered out of the van. "*Quiet!*" yelled one of them. "What's been going on?"

Stev let go of the man he was holding, who collapsed back on to the ground. The officer turned to Gem. "You all right, miss?"

Gem nodded. "I was at the bus stop with my boyfriend," she croaked, "and those five came up and started threatening us. . ."

"It was disgusting," said Jack, looking the officer straight in the eye, "what they were saying."

"They wanted to rape me," said Gem.

"I wanted to kill 'em," said Jack, "but there were five of them. So I phoned my mates. . ."

"We were just round the corner," put in Dosh.

"I did last-dial. In my pocket."

The officer, looking straight back at Jack, asked, "Who started the fight? Who landed the first punch?"

"*He* did," broke in Gemma, pointing at the gang leader on the ground. "He shoved Jack back against me, I went into the glass—"

The officer looked down at the gang leader and said, "Well, well. Look who it is. Micky Waller. In trouble again, eh?"

The gang, sensing it was going against them, broke out afresh with howls of rage and protest. "Look at my face, it's all over blood!" "He's broken my fucking ribs!" "That one –" pointing at Stev – "he's a psycho, you wanna put him away. . ."

The second officer turned to face them. "Well, lads, you certainly look in a bad way compared to this lot. But it was five on five, right? Maybe you're just lousy fighters." Then he said to Gem, "You want to press charges, miss? For attempted rape?"

Amid a fresh outburst of rage from the gang, she shook her head. "They never touched me. They were just. . ."

"Horrible. Well, don't worry. We'll get everyone's names down and take this lot into the station for a bit, put the fear of God into them. Although –" looking round at Jack and the others – "looks like you've already done that." And he smiled at them, almost approvingly. He was thinking that they were the sort of lads they could do with recruiting on to the force.

Chapter 31

"Don't get me wrong. I'm glad Stev was there – *Christ*, I'm glad. I'm glad he was on my side. It's just. . ."

"Just what?"

"He didn't feel all that different, that's all. To them, how they acted. The way he wanted to make them crawl and everything."

"Gem – *I* wanted to make them crawl. The things they said to you. I wanted to fucking kill 'em."

"You didn't though. You . . . *stopped*. When it was over, you stopped. He wanted to carry on."

Gem and Jack were wound round each other on the back seat of the bus, headed towards her house, talking over what had happened. The way Jack had saved her – the way he'd fought for her – she was dazed with it. "That was such a brilliant idea," she said, for about the fifth time. "You doing last-dial on your phone."

"I know it. I'm full of 'em."

"D'you reckon – if the police hadn't come – d'you reckon Stev really would've dragged 'em down the canal?"

"Hey, come on, let it drop now," Jack murmured.

"C'mon, we're nearly at your place. Try and put it out of your mind." He hugged her, and they fell silent. He was thinking: If Gem hadn't been there, maybe I'd've laid into them harder too. Kicked them right into the fucking ground for what they said to her, for the way they had me over a barrel, the cowards . . . maybe I'm not so different from Stev.

Then he grinned. God, but that'd been satisfying, he thought. That'd been *good*.

Both Gem's parents were up when they got back to her house. Jack had assumed she'd keep quiet about what had happened, like he always did when he was involved in a ruckus on the streets. But Gem went through the front door with a kind of high-pitched wail and fell into her mother's arms.

Soon, the whole story was out and he and Gem were being given hot chocolate with a dash of brandy and buttered toast and Gem's dad was chatting to him all man-to-man and telling him what a good thing it was he played rugby because it made him able to cope with the type of vile thugs you came up against on the streets nowadays. And Gem's mum kept saying, "Thank goodness you were there – what would've happened if you hadn't been there!", not quite getting the point that Gem had just been an excuse, a goad, he'd been the one the gang had really been after. Still, Jack was enjoying all the gratitude too much to enlighten her. He sat there, smiling and modest, and ate the toast and drank the chocolate, while Gem's dad went off to make up the spare-room bed for him.

*

Everyone went up to bed more or less together, and by midnight the house was silent. Jack lay awake in the strange double bed, thinking back over the fight, thinking about Gem in her bed only a few feet away from him.

Then there was the softest of noises, the door moving open across the carpet, and he looked up and saw her outlined against the glow of the landing light. She was wearing baggy pyjamas but Jack could see the shape of her through them, and it made him instantly hot. "I can't sleep," she whispered, speeding across the room and sliding under the duvet beside him. "I'm too traumatized."

"*Traumatized?*" he repeated, delightedly, getting hold of her. "Bollocks – I was the one doing the work – you were hiding behind me!"

"Yeah, but I was terrified."

"Look – you shouldn't be here."

"They're asleep. I heard Dad snoring, and if Mum's awake she jabs him one if he snores, so she must be asleep too." She launched herself on him, kissed him hard.

"Gem," groaned Jack, "this isn't *fair*."

"Why not?"

"Cos I wanna *do it* with you!"

"So go ahead."

"What if they wake up?"

"They wouldn't care. They think you're a total hero who can do no wrong. And for the moment – so do I. So you better make the most of it, hadn't you? Hey – got you a present." She fumbled in her pyjama pocket, and produced a single silver condom packet.

If Jack had been turned on before, now he was insane

with it. That she could be so direct, it was amazing, it was. . . He pulled her pyjama top off her. "You just better be quiet," he hissed.

"Me?" she hissed back. "It's you I'm worried about." And she fastened her mouth on his.

Chapter 32

Tuesday night, after training, Boxy and the boys headed back to The Crown and found Mrs Cooper waiting for them with seventeen pints already lined up, a wide smile across her face, and an open copy of the local paper, which she waved at them excitedly. "Read this!" she crowed. "Go on!"

Boxy took it, and read aloud. The article was called "Our Police Can't Be Everywhere" and it was about people taking a stand against street crime. Boxy skipped through two threatened shopkeepers "having a go" and a "plucky pensioner" before raising his voice gleefully to describe how five brave members of the Westgate Under 17s rugby team stopped a group sex attack on a girl at a bus stop.

"*Mum!*" erupted Jamie, delighted.

"I don't *care*!" Mrs Cooper bubbled back at him.

"It was *her*!" Jamie said, pointing. "Her mate Maggie works for the paper!"

"Jamie, it was meant to be! Iz and Dosh are here Sunday morning, telling us all about the attack, and Maggie walks in Sunday lunch time! Moaning about this piece she was doing about people standing up to street crime, saying she was two-hundred-odd words short and the deadline was last week . . . well, what was I supposed to do?"

"Help her out, of course," beamed Boxy. "With the words all fresh in your mind. Well, this is brilliant, boys. I'll show 'em this at the Club. Stop the crap about me leading you astray and you being thugs on the pitch. You know what I heard someone call you the other day? Boxy's Bastards." He paused, savouring the name, as the lads laughed. "Well, you might be bastards, but you're not thugs, are you, boys? You're heroes."

"I didn't give names," said Mrs Cooper. "No time to ask the boys' permission, and anyway—"

"It's probably just as well. No need to get personal, is there? Now drink up, lads. You're celebrities!"

The story of the bus-stop attack speedily circulated in the community. Jack's head teacher called all the Westgate Under 17s who attended his school into his office and congratulated them on the newspaper article. Then he lectured them on always dialling 999 first if possible, because knives could be involved, and asked them to keep an eye out because in the last few weeks there'd been a spate of muggings on younger years after school hours.

At the end of the week, Big Mac and Rory Knight were nearly knocked off their feet by two hysterical Year Eights cannoning out of a side street on the way home. "You gotta come, you gotta come!" they shrieked. "He's got Tommy, he's gonna kill 'im!"

Mac and Rory raced down the side street, followed by the Year Eights, and saw a stocky, dark-haired boy, late teens, straddling a bike, pinioning a younger boy against some metal gates. He had the boy in one hand and in the other he raised a steel truncheon. "You want me to use this?" he was yelling, and the kid was screaming he didn't have anything else, he swore, he'd given it all to him, he *swore*. . .

Mac and Rory raced forward and Mac tackled the mugger in a massive broadside just as he was spinning round. He crashed on to the pavement with his bike wrapped round him, and as he scrambled up, swearing, Mac grabbed him, pinioning his arms. "Drop that weapon, filth," spat Mac, bear-hugging hard.

"You're fucking *breaking* my *rib*—!"

"*Drop it!*"

Smack! Rory cracked his fist into the side of the mugger's face. The steel bar clattered to the ground.

"It's him!" one of the Year Eights was squealing, as another one dived on the truncheon. "It was him wot got Mike, and Arnold Baker from year nine last week—"

Mac increased his grip in one last death squeeze, then threw the mugger back down on to the ground. "So you're the one who's been feeding off little kids, are you?" And he slammed a boot into his back.

"You can't do this!" the mugger howled.

"No?" said Rory. "We can't do this but you can go around terrorizing little kids?" Then he landed a kick on him, too. The mugger wailed in pain, started scrambling away across the ground.

"Don't move," said Mac. The mugger froze. "Don't even think about it. Rory – you got your phone? Get the police."

"Oh, come *on!*" howled the mugger. "Look – gimme my bike back. You can have this – look—" He pulled a wad of notes out of his pocket, and three phones. "You can have this. Just let me go."

Mac shook his head. "We don't want your stuff."

Rory was giving directions into his phone.

"For fuck's sake!" screamed the mugger. "Look – you can have the bike. Just let me go. Come with me to my bank, I'll clear out my account, you can 'ave it. . ."

Mac shook his head again. "You just don't get it, do you mate. We don't want your stuff." He paused. "We're not like you."

"They're coming," Rory said. "They're on their way."

"They'll be interested to see this illegal weapon you've been totin' about," said Mac.

"Can I get my phone back?" squeaked Tommy, the mugged Year Eight. "I didn't have any money, he made me jump and down to see what I had in my pockets, but I din' have any. . ."

"Yeah?" Mac turned to glare at the mugger. "Show us what you made 'im do." He grabbed a fistful of his hair and pulled him to his feet.

"Oh for *fuck's* sake—"

"*Show us!*"

The mugger flinched, then jumped halfheartedly, limp with humiliation. "Higher!" roared Mac, and he jumped higher.

The three small boys stood and watched, in an ecstasy of revenge.

*

The next day, giving his victim's statement, Tommy asked the policeman if Mac and Rory would get a medal for what they did. The policeman laughed and said he'd have to see about that. He also laughed when the mugger told his brief that he wanted to prosecute Mac and Rory for assault. The brief, who didn't laugh, advised him against it, on account of the illegal weapon he'd been carrying.

That weekend, Mrs Cooper officially turned the cellar over to the Westgate Under 17s. Over two dynamic days, and with her full approval, it underwent a stunning transformation. All the rubbish was cleared out; crates and barrels were stacked neatly by the door. Two more ancient sofas, eight assorted battered chairs and a large rickety pine table were appropriated and moved in. Posters of rugby stars and two enlarged copies of the "local heroes" newspaper article were pinned up. A sign in Roman-style script saying "Vomitorium" was attached to the gents' toilets. Another saying "Treacle Tin" was attached to the ladies'.

The cellar was theirs, and not just for Saturday nights. You could turn up anytime and be sure that at least a few of the team would be there, chatting, watching TV, messing around, blagging free food from Mrs Cooper. Boxy took to turning up there too, hanging out with the boys more and more, not just after training and matches. He'd run through new ideas he had for game plans, give them pep talks on fitness and working out. And then he'd talk about attitude and mindset. And the thing with Boxy was, sometimes you weren't sure he was just talking about rugby when he did this. Sometimes what he was saying seemed to spread much wider than that, right into the rest of life.

The atmosphere was very different when he was there. He was the undisputed ruler, and everyone was subsumed by this. You felt good if he talked to you, brilliant if you made him laugh, and terrible if he was short with you or ignored you. If he took the piss out of you, everyone laughed, no one stuck up for you, but it was OK because mockery was how the boys showed each other they belonged.

And they did belong, all of them – they folded round each other like barricades. Will's arm got broken by a really hard tackle, and he was told to rest for three months, minimum. Any fears he had that he'd be cast out from the team were evaporated by Boxy insisting he still turn up to training and be on the touchline for every match. In the cellar, he was awarded first claim on the comfiest sofa.

The boys were constantly jockeying for position in the hierarchy, which depended on who was in Boxy's good books and who had been demoted to a sub that week. Only Jack and Stev were immune from this, and even Jack sometimes felt edgy. He wondered whether he was safe as captain; whether Stev might get the job. He was pretty sure Stev was too much of a lone wolf to be captain, but he couldn't ask Boxy about it, not directly. It would have been showing weakness.

Chapter 33

As November gave way to December, Jack and Gem became lovers in the real sense. At school, they ate lunch together, hung out together, went off together at the end of the day. Bathed in the glamour of the meteoric rise of the Westgate Under 17s, they were the school's new golden couple, the ones everyone talked about and wanted to be. With their looks, their confidence, Gem's sense of style and Jack's power, they were a potent couple. Envy lapped at their heels, making everything sweeter still.

Very soon after the bus-stop attack, Gem's parents had gone away for twenty-four hours, over Thursday night, and Jack had moved in. He and Gem had made love right away in her bedroom, slowly, taking their time, deliciously uninhibited. They'd wandered naked through to the shower, then they'd ordered pizza and made love again later on the sofa as they watched a film. They went to sleep in each other's arms in Gem's wide bed, skipped school, and made love again in the morning.

It was like a seal on what they had, and it made the next two times they had sex (in the woods walking Mimi, and in a locked bathroom at a mid-week impromptu party thrown by a girl Gem knew) maybe fast, Gem thought, but not sordid.

She went to all the Saturday matches, home and away, and along to the cellar at The Crown for the party afterwards, although she wouldn't have dreamt of going there at any other time. She felt the team accepted her as Jack's girlfriend now. And she felt that's what she was, almost all she was – Jack's girlfriend.

Instinctively, she avoided Christian. She knew if she talked to him she'd have to justify the way her life had been swallowed up by Jack's life. And as for Christian, he knew without listening to the gossip that Gem and Jack were sleeping together. He dealt with this by avoiding Gem as much as he could and being impossibly breezy and jolly when he couldn't. They had no serious conversation together at all.

It was something Gem didn't want to look at, not yet – the way she'd been swamped by everything that had happened over the last few weeks. After all, it was so amazing, this thing that was happening – her and Jack, the *team*. . . She told herself she was living in the moment. They were both in a cycle of desire, sex, afterglow, desire again. It was physically overwhelming. It was enough to just let it happen.

One Wednesday they bunked off school and took a trip to a town nearby. They tumbled on to the train like a pair of manic puppies, crazy with pleasure in each other, unable to stop touching and teasing and kissing each other. The carriage was practically full, but Gem put her hands on

Jack's waist and together they jostled through to the back and a two-seater that had just been vacated, and sat down, so close together they only took up two-thirds of it.

The stale air of the carriage, the claustrophobia of all the other people pressing round them in their various states of sourness, tiredness and boredom – it struck the lovers as hysterically funny. It was hilarious, the contrast between how the carriage felt, and how they felt. Gem rocked in her seat, dug her fingers into Jack's hand to stop herself giggling.

Directly opposite them sat an old couple, seventy-five at least, probably older. They looked OK – they were dressed like they had a bit of money, and they were fit and well – fit enough to have got on this train and be going somewhere, anyway.

Usually you can ignore the old; they're invisible. But this old couple was sitting opposite, the man opposite Jack and the woman opposite Gem, like some freaky mirror reflection. Gem's giggling dried up in her throat. The man's face had collapsed down into his neck and his nose was sharp with decrepitude; he kept making anxious little pecking glances around him; he looked like an old hen. The woman's eyes were bleary and watering; her skin was like paper that had been screwed up, then smoothed out again.

Jack looked at them from underneath his eyebrows; he felt like a grave had opened up in front of him. He took hold of Gem's hand and squeezed it so hard she winced.

At the next stop, the old couple creaked to their feet and made their way to the exit door. Gem sighed and stretched her legs out, and murmured, "I don't ever want to be that old."

"We're going there," Jack muttered back. "All of us. Like this train."

"Shut up."

"S'true."

"Not for ages."

"No," agreed Jack. What he wanted to say was: *It's all slipping away, minute by minute, like sand, and it's so precious, so sweet. . .* He felt it strongly, he felt as though seeing the old couple had made him wake up to something painful and true and *right*, but he couldn't think how to say this to Gem, he didn't want her to think he'd gone soft.

He sometimes worried that he was getting in too deep with her – the sex was amazing, he couldn't even think of giving it up. But he reckoned the boys kept him real, kept his feet on the ground, because all the time his bond to Gem was growing, his bond to the team was growing too. And the reputation of the team – as rugby players, vigilantes and general all-round hard men – was growing apace with that.

When they were out together, their triumphant, tribal energy would get them challenged by other groups of young men, especially if it was Friday or Saturday night and everyone had been drinking. Jack would stand his ground and leave the challengers in no doubt what would happen if they took them on; then he'd tell his team to *leave it* and they'd walk away. But if the other lot were too tanked up and aggressive, Stev would lose it and start laying into them, and then all the others would follow, because you don't leave a mate to fight on his own.

They began to feel they could start on who they liked; no one could stand up to them. Plus they had, as Boxy said, "establishment backing": they were known and approved of by the local community and the police. Stev, Max and Ben Worthing, the hooker, had it in for the druggies and dope-heads gathered at the edge of the park, or bumbling their way through town. They'd yell abuse at them; go out of their way to barge into them and knock them to the ground. The druggies never fought back; further proof, to the three boys, of their degeneracy. "They make me sick," Ben said. "They can piss themselves down the drain if they want to, but not where I can see 'em."

"You know what I think?" announced Iz. "It's cos life's not real any more. It's got too safe."

"What the fuck you on about, Iz?" demanded Jack.

"Look – if you nearly died about twenty times a day, like in the old days, avoiding wolves and robbers and stuff – you'd get your high that way, wouldn't you. I was on my bike down by the industrial estate last week, and this *fucking* great guard dog – this *massive* Alsatian the size of an elephant – came outta nowhere and hurled itself at the wire fence, right by me, snarling and barking . . . well, when I'd finished *shitting* myself and it sunk in I wasn't gonna die, I felt fucking elated . . . I felt *great*. And it made me think that our brains are, like, *programmed* to be that way, to need those highs, that's why they do drugs, it's cos everyone's missing life-and-death highs."

There was a pause, while everyone processed this, then Max said, "That's crap," and Jack said, "*We're* not missing it."

"Nah," agreed Jamie. "We get it every week, out on the field."

"Yeah, but they don't. That's what they're looking for, doing drugs."

"You saying that excuses it?" growled Ben.

"No," said Iz. "I'm just . . . *saying*."

On two occasions a local gang sought the team out, wanting to prove itself up against them. The first time, the gang was black, which made it weird for Will and Cory, the only two black boys on the team. They pitched in hard at first, because although numbers were just about even, a couple of the gang were waving knives about. Once these had been sorted – tackled from behind and thrown to the ground – it was clear that Westgate were the victors, and Will and Cory faded back, scourged by abuse from the black gang, reluctant to put the final boot in.

Back at the cellar, they tended their wounds and drank beer and exultantly relived the fight for Boxy. Stev excoriated Cory and Will. "They bottled it – couldn't stick it to the bruvvas, could you? We was wondering whose side you were fighting on!"

"That is just *shit*, man!" exploded Will. "We were in there till it was finished!"

"Oh yeah? Most of 'em were still on their feet when you ponced off!"

"You were kicking 'em when they were down and beaten!"

"Those black bastards had it coming!"

"Hey," said Boxy, putting a restraining hand on Cory,

who'd jumped to his feet, "less of the racist comments, Stev. No need."

"Oh, yeah," snarled Stev, "and what about you the other day, banging on about the immigrants?"

"What I was doing then, Stev, was making a true observation. About people coming into this country and clogging up our schools and our hospitals. True observations aren't racist. Shall I tell you something? When you're in this team, the only colour that matters is the colour of the shirt on your back. *That's* your colour. All right?"

The second time a local gang sought the team out, Jack and his mates were wildly outnumbered, and made a run for it before they were surrounded, heading for the old iron footbridge that spanned the busy main road. Their fitness showed. The huge gang, panting and gasping, reached the bottom of the bridge just as the team raced off the other side of it and began yelling and jeering across the stream of traffic. Incensed, four gang members darted into the road; cars swerved, hooted, and a Corsa went into the back of a Volvo.

The team jogged off victoriously as the sirens came closer.

Both times, Jack and Stev led the fight and flight, working together.

Chapter 34

One night, Karl walked into the cellar with his arms hanging weird and loose, as if his shoulders had been dislocated. From the moment he came through the door, everyone knew something bad had happened to him. The joshing ricocheting between Dosh, Iz and Big Mac petered out; Stev looked up from the tabloid he was reading. At last Karl raised his head; his face had a disintegrated look, as though it had been taken apart and put back together again, but not in the right way.

"Hey, man," said Jack, "where you been?" but Karl didn't respond. He came into the cellar like someone sleep-walking, and collapsed down on the battered sofa that Jack was sprawled on.

"What's up, mate?" Boxy demanded.

Karl's head shook like he was shuddering, like it was involuntary, and he croaked out, "My old man. He's left."

"What – left home?" said Dosh. "Right before Christmas? *Bummer!*"

"Yeh. Just – four days ago. Sunday. Sunday night."

"*Fuck*, man," said Jack. "That's hard. What'd he say?"

Karl's head shook again.

"Did they have a bust-up?" demanded Boxy. "Your parents?"

"He got a new woman?" put in Stev.

"What'd he say?" asked Big Mac.

Another silence. Jack shunted up the sofa towards Karl, thought about putting a hand on his arm, but didn't. "He didn't say anything," Karl muttered. "Sunday night, he drove out to the local garage to get some fags. He was gone ages. My mum was going spare – she couldn't contact him, he'd left his mobile at home. She phoned the garage, she phoned the local where he goes – she phoned round his friends. In the end, midnight, she phoned the police."

"*Fuck.* He'd crashed the car, right?"

Again, that horrible head shaking, like a spasm or a fit. "No. The police – they checked the hospital, they did a tracer on the car. Nothing. No accidents. They got a picture of him on the CCTV at the garage. He filled up, he bought fags like he'd said – then he drove off. The opposite direction to home."

"He's got another woman," said Boxy.

"I dunno – I don't think so. Mum says he's not been acting any different, he's been like he's always been. The policewoman who came round the other day – she said if he's been having an affair, there's always signs. . ."

"Signs?"

"You know. The man smartens up a bit, loses some weight, smells better . . . but Mum said he was the same old guy he'd always been. The policewoman. . ." he trailed off, his hands clenching his legs, everything shaking. And this time Jack did reach out and grip Karl's arm, and Karl gulped and muttered, "The policewoman said how men sometimes just *do* that. Just walk away. Middle-aged men. They go out, just to go to the local for a beer or something . . . and they don't go home. They get a room in a B&B or something, and they don't phone . . . they tell themselves they'll phone the next day. But they don't. They keep going away, moving away. It just kind of . . . *happens* to them. And it gets harder and harder to call home then, and face the music."

Jack let out a long, low whistle. "Shit, man. You must feel gutted. And your mum—?"

"She's weird. She's not cross, she's not crying . . . she's just kind of dazed. Carrying on with the little ones, getting things done. . ."

"She must hate him."

"*You* must hate him," added Dosh.

"Yeah," put in Stev. "Fucking coward. Just pissing off without saying anything."

"Leave it, Stev," said Boxy. "Hey Jamie – you gonna get Karl a beer?"

"A man," went on Stev, loudly, "would *finish* it. He'd tell his wife it was over, then he'd leave."

"Yeah," said Dosh, "or at least write a note. So she'd know."

"Bollocks to a note. He'd tell her, face to face."

"I'm just saying at least a note'd let her know what was happening. . ."

"*Will you two shut up?*" erupted Boxy. Then he stood up, and walked over to lean against the curved bar in the corner. He was standing, and everyone else was sitting. "It's gonna be all right, Karl," he said. "It's tough, but you're gonna be all right."

Karl turned his face up towards Boxy. "It's my mum," he said. "It's her I'm worried for."

"Course you are, mate."

"She thinks he'll just walk back in again at any minute. She scares me. She keeps talking like he's coming back—'We'll sort that out when your dad gets back, we'll think about that when your dad gets back.' It's like him leaving is a just a glitch, you know, a blip, and soon it'll all be back to normal. . ."

"Maybe it will be," said Jack. "Maybe he will just come back."

"No. Not now. It was like that policewoman . . . it was like she *knew*."

"Yeah, but she can't, can she, mate. She can't know."

"She said . . . the longer they're away, the harder it is to come home. The less likely it is that they'll come home."

"Yeah, but it's not a week yet. It's only—"

"What about you, Karl?" interrupted Boxy. "D'you reckon he'll be back?"

Karl shook his head violently.

"Why not, mate?"

"Cos . . . cos things have been crap for ages. He's seemed so . . . *bored*. Like he's only half there most of the time, half alive. If I was him I'd leave. I dunno."

"Yeah, you do know," said Boxy. "You know you'd leave. Cos you expect more out of life. When you think about the existence of the average middle-aged man you see around you today, it's kind of amazing more of 'em don't walk out." He paused. Everyone in the room was looking at him, and he looked straight back at them. "Tied down to a crap, boring job, to pay off a big mortgage, with kids who don't respect you, a wife who despises you, uses you . . . why wouldn't you walk out? What you gotta do is *use* this. I know it's hard, I know it hurts, but you can use it to make something a whole lot better for yourself. You're not gonna be like your old man, are you? You're gonna make fucking sure you're not."

Karl took to sleeping over in the cellar for the odd night after that, on one of the battered sofas, with a coat over him. He said he needed to escape from "all the crap" at home. Pretty soon, at Boxy's suggestion, he was joined in his overnighters by Max, whose dad had a problem with drink and whose mum alternately leant on him and turned on him.

Max had got into rugby because it was a good place to let rip and get out of his skull. Off the pitch, though, he kept his head down; no one could talk to him. But over the last couple of months, Max had been like a chain uncoiling. He looked people in the eye; he talked about the future.

Big Mac was another player who'd been transformed. He strode out now, instead of bumbling along. No one called him fat any more; if they said anything, they said he was a tank, and they meant it admiringly. He'd started to wear better clothes and he got his hair cut properly. A bubbly brown-haired girl called Nina kept turning up at the cellar on Saturday night and getting off with him until finally they became an item.

Watching Nina becoming Mac's girlfriend, watching her being absorbed into the way the team worked, gave Gem pause for thought. She was starting to get resentful about Boxy and the team and the cellar getting more and more important in Jack's life.

Chapter 35

Westgate's long winning streak ended on the second Saturday in December with a 12-9 loss to a highly drilled team and a ref who was a stickler for the rules. During the last ten minutes, with both Stev and Dosh in the sin bin and the ref pulling them up for each and every transgression, half the team lost heart and gave up. After the match, Boxy harangued them, long and hard, and it was a subdued set of boys who gathered in the cellar that night. The girls who turned up couldn't understand it. "What's going on?" they muttered. "I mean – it's just a match – has somebody *died* or what?" Jack pulled away from Gem when she tried to put her arms round his neck, and answered her questions in monosyllables. Then Boxy, who'd kept them all dangling for twenty minutes or so, stood up and said, "There are too many people in this room who're not afraid of losing. If there weren't, we wouldn't've lost today. You can't always have it the way you want, you can't always have it easy. If you want an easy life and you wanna play easy rugby – piss off out of it. Find yourself another team." Then he downed the last of his pint and said, "OK, we're gonna put this behind us. But I never want to see you beaten again, OK? I don't mean you can't lose. You can be two men down and lose a game, and still not be beaten. OK? *OK?*"

And like a lever had been pulled, the mood in the cellar switched. The noise level cranked up and Boxy and the team went for the beer like it might run dry at any moment. Jack focused on Gem again, fetching her a drink and saying he was sorry he'd been so off with her; she was just thawing to him when Boxy came over and, ignoring her, slung his arm round Jack's neck and towed him away.

Boxy stood in the middle of the cellar with Jack, looking round at all the boys. "Look at 'em," he slurred. "Look what I've done with 'em."

"What you mean?" Jack muttered.

"This lot. They were nothing till I came along. I gave 'em the guts to change."

Jack laughed uneasily.

"They believe they can do it, now. Anywhere, anytime. They won't put up with second best ever again. In their lives, their work, from women, anything. That's what I've given them. This lot – they can get whatever they want."

When Jack got back to her side, Gem indignantly demanded to know what Boxy had wanted. Jack shrugged and said, "Nothing much."

Something in her snapped, and she went on the attack. She thought she was just telling him about an invitation they'd had, but really it was an attack. "Hey – something's happening!" she carolled. "Louisa's having a party next

Saturday. Her parents are away, it's gonna be great – she's got this big kitchen with a conservatory off it, with a fantastic sound system cos her dad's into jazz. . ."

"Great – we can go along when we're through here."

"Oh – *what*? I don't wanna turn up at midnight!"

"Parties don't get going till midnight!"

"Louisa's do. She can't keep the music on too late or the neighbours complain. She says we can come round anytime after eight . . . what're you looking at me like that for? Surely we can give the cellar a miss for *once*, can't we?"

"Yeah, of course – if we *have* to. But we don't have to, do we?"

"I want to get there early, Jack. Her parties are the best."

"Fine. You go, and I'll join you later."

"Oh, fuck off! You saying you can't give it a miss just *once*? I'm always here with you!"

"No one's making you."

"Oh, *nice*—" Gem exploded and Jack broke it with, "Look – I'll leave early. Ten, latest. But I can't not show up, not unless it's a wedding or a funeral or something. You know that – you know how it works here. I thought you *understood*."

"Understood what? That you're not supposed to have a life apart from the bloody rugby team?"

"That's crap and you know it."

They both drew in a breath. They were on the verge of their first real row. Gem felt scared to take it any further. She muttered grumpily that it would be OK to turn up to the party late as long as it wasn't any later than ten-thirty.

And Jack, pleased and grateful and just a tiny bit triumphant, promised her it wouldn't be.

The Christmas holidays came, and rugby matches stopped for a few weeks, but training didn't. Boxy made the boys work extra hard to counteract, he said, "the tide of mince pies and booze and *selection boxes* you're all gonna be porking back over the festive season."

The Westgate Rugby Football Club Youth Section Christmas Party was held on the fifteenth of December, but it was not a success, mainly because as soon as the subsidized meal and speeches had finished, Boxy led the boys and their girlfriends off to the cellar.

Gem had expectations about Christmas. She thought there would be time to get closer to Jack, now that the demands of school and rugby had stopped for a while. But she had reckoned without the demands of Jack's family. There always seemed to be an aunt he had to visit, a grandparent he had to stay in and see. And he was impatient with her moaning about it because, as he said, she wasn't the one who had to sit there getting bored off her face. And as he still had training, and still went to the cellar, it didn't feel all that different at all.

Out of the blue, Christian turned up on her doorstep on the night before Christmas Eve with a present. They hadn't talked properly in weeks, and she hadn't bought him anything, so it was pretty awkward and embarrassing, although they acted like it wasn't, kissing each other and laughing. He came through into the kitchen with her and she decapped them both a beer, then he watched her unwrap the present. "I got it for you back in *August*," he confessed. "In an antique shop. Well, OK, a kind of junk shop. But isn't it perfect?"

It was a strange and exquisite trinket box on claw feet with a worn green velvet lining that she could easily replace. She loved it; she flew at Christian and hugged him, then she went and got her ragbag and together they found a gorgeous magenta-coloured strip of silk that would be perfect as a new lining. When they'd run out of chat about that, though, things grew more and more awkward. They skirted round the subject of Jack, and the rift that had grown up between the two of them. Chris left after half an hour and they both vaguely promised to "meet up soon".

After a long, complicated and bad-tempered phone-discussion, Jack came round on Christmas Eve to collect Gem for the party in the cellar that night an hour and a half early (Gem had wanted longer) so they could exchange presents. Gem felt upset when she opened his present to her because it was so clearly chosen by one of his little sisters – it was a glittery girly bracelet, perfect for a twelve year old, but not for her – but she said how pretty it was. Jack said he liked the fashionable T-shirt she bought him but he wouldn't try it on because her parents were out and all that mattered was to go up to her room and have sex. It was rushed and not brilliant and afterwards, they almost had a row when he told her to hurry up getting dressed again.

The party was noisy and riotous; Gem felt tired and disoriented, and as if Jack was continually being torn from her by a surge of boys. At the end of it Jack said he had "no hope" of seeing her till the twenty-seventh, earliest.

On Boxing Day, she put the bracelet in the trinket box that Chris had given her and immediately took it out again because the contrast was too awful.

As the holidays drew to a close, Gem had to acknowledge to herself that they'd been a disappointment. It was almost a relief to get back to the routine again, when school started.

Chapter 36

It was a Friday night at the beginning of January and Gem was walking along the dark streets heading for the Green Man pub feeling good. Jack agreed to meet her for a bite to eat although he insisted he couldn't stay out too late and he wasn't going to drink because of the match next day. Gem intuitively felt this was a bit of a triumph. It was the first, tiniest chink in Jack's armour, the first sign that he might be prepared to put her before the team.

Recently, she'd been thinking more and more about wanting to be put before the team.

Passion can't stay at high-tide for ever – it's just not possible to sustain it. There has to be an ebb, a slowing; a time to step back, take stock. And now, after the disappointment of Christmas, Gemma was starting to take stock.

Her mobile went. It was Jack, but she could hardly make out what he was saying. The team was in the background, braying, shouting, crowing. It sounded like the end of a match, a match where they'd had a huge victory.

"*Whaat?*" she screeched, irritated. "*What* you on about?"

"I can't make it, Gem! I got held up!" More shouting from the team.

"*What?*" squawked Gem.

"Come to the cellar! You gotta *see* this!" The line went dead.

Gem was beside herself with anger and intense curiosity. She jabbed *call* on her phone.

And got Jack's voicemail, which she huffed at.

Standing there on the street, she knew she had a clear choice. Storm back home and wait for him to phone her again and grovel. Or go along to the cellar.

She decided to combine the two: go to the cellar, and make him grovel there.

She opened the door to the cellar on to a striking scene. Three of the team had spray cans in their hands and were jigging about, graffiting on the walls. The rest of the team were egging them on, swigging beer. Amid squiggled runes and jagged lines she read "Hardwired to be violent" and "Boxy's Bastards Rule!!" and "Give it Up 100%".

"Hey, Jacky boy," shouted Stev, leering over at Gem, "the wife's here."

"Fuck off," Jack rapped back, and he came towards her, all cocky and kind of indifferent, not really focused on her at all. He claimed her with an arm round her shoulders.

Which she straightaway shrugged off. "Oooooh!" mocked Stev. "Lover's tiff! What you *done*, Jacky—"

"What's up?" demanded Jack, face up against hers, all indignant. Then without waiting for a reply he put his arm round her again and hugged her to him and said, "It was *amazing*, Gem! It was such a fucking laugh! We had this extra training session, going over tactics for tomorrow – and just as we were winding up—"

"—heading for the clubhouse," put in Big Mac.

"—we saw these six skinny street rats legging it away across the far pitch. We just yelled at them, but when we got to the clubhouse we saw they'd done a *real job* on the back wall of the building."

"Graffiti. Everywhere. Three colours," said Mac.

"All their shitty little tag lines," said Jamie, joining them.

"Like we care who they are!"

"Like we were gonna stand for their *crap* on our clubhouse!"

"And Stev yelled, 'Let's get 'em – we're gonna wipe that off with their *blood*!'"

The team was surrounding Gem now, falling about laughing as they remembered Stev's clarion call to action. Gem was overwhelmed by their focus, and weirdly flattered, even though she knew she was just a function, she could've been anyone – Jamie's mum, the cleaner, anyone. What they wanted was an excuse to relive it all again together.

"So we went *after* them," said Jack. "We knew they was heading for the main gate, so we legged it across to the side gate, climbed over—"

"Iz fell," guffawed Mac. "The *prat*."

"Yeah, well, I got up again didn't I?"

"—and headed them off just as they were coming through on to the road. *Christ* you shoulda *seen* their faces!"

"They were *shitting* themselves!"

"Pranging it! We were like – two to one—"

"At least—"

"We just rammed into 'em, knocked 'em all arse over tit—"

"And then Boxy came up, through the main gate—"

"And he yelled out, 'OK, boys – weight training – one between two – take 'em back to the wall they just *defiled*.'"

"I thought they were gonna *die* of fear, I swear it. We picked 'em up—"

"The one I got with Karl kicked out so we just dropped him – *blam!* – and he didn't try that again—"

Boxy, lounging against the bar, grinned, and his eyes were fixed on Gemma. She saw this, knew he was waiting for her reaction. She kept her face blank as everyone's words roared over her.

"And we got 'em back to the clubhouse, and Mac got hold of one of 'em and started *rubbing* him up against the wall, like he was a rag—"

"I thought I was gonna *pass out*, laughing. All this red paint was on his hair and stuff—"

"Anyway, what with the noise, one of the Club alackadoos came out. Which is when Mr Box took over. He said we'd *apprehended* these *hooligans*. . ."

". . .and we were gonna make 'em clean up the paint. The alackadoo was so fucking impressed he nearly fell at Boxy's feet. He got us the keys to the maintenance shed, we got out all the gear—"

"—scrapers and stuff, and white spirit—"

"—and we made them clean it all off. Didn't take long, it was still wet. Then we *confiscated* their spray cans—"

"—and then we made 'em *crawl*."

"*What?*" croaked Gemma. Jack's arm was still round her shoulders, and he squeezed it now, but whether it was for comfort or in warning she couldn't tell.

"Boxy told them to get on the ground, and not get up till they were sure we couldn't catch 'em again. Because once they were on their feet, we'd be on to 'em. They crawled halfway across the field—"

"*God*, we were proper pissin' ourselves!"

"Then they *legged* it—"

"—like a fucking *tank* was after them—"

"—you shoulda *seen* them!"

"*Yeah?*" snapped Gem. "Well, I'm glad I didn't."

And Stev was on her. "Yeah? Why's that then?"

Gem didn't answer.

"Come on, Miss Bleedin' Heart, why's that?"

"Shut up, Stev," barked Jack.

"What d'you think we shoulda done, Gemma, ay?" Stev went on. "Patted them on the fucking head?"

"*No*," she spat. "Just – known when to stop."

"But that's the thing about this team," said Boxy, grinning. "We don't know when to stop. That's why we win everything." And he lasered his eyes at Gem, who told herself she'd combust before she showed him any reaction at all. Then at last he looked away and said, "All right, lads, you gonna finish this decoration job or not?"

"*Confiscated goods!*" yelled Dosh, chucking a spray can in the air and catching it again, and most of the team turned and swarmed towards the walls again, filling up the last few blank spaces with red, green and black.

"It's all right," said Boxy, eyes back on Gem, "we got Mrs Cooper's permission. She said we can do what we like down here. She was tickled pink about us dealing with those yobs. Reckons she's gonna phone her friend on the local paper again."

And Gem, heart thudding, said, "Tell her the full story, did you?"

"Most of it, yeah. Stop feeling *sorry* for them, girl! We didn't really hurt them. Anyway, they're losers. Pathetic. We probably gave 'em the best bit of excitement they'd had for years, knocking them about a bit. The thing about lads like that is that graffiting is the only excitement they got in their miserable little uneventful lives. They get a rush out of it – just a tiny bit of the rush my lads get every week on the pitch."

"What if they report you?" she croaked. "For beating them up?"

"To the police, you mean?" guffawed Boxy. "Like they're gonna do that! They was in the wrong, and we were putting them right. I know a few coppers. When you got right on your side, you can use all the might you want to. *Unofficially*, of course."

And he smiled at Gem, as though they understood each other. Gem felt exhausted by standing up to Boxy, standing up against the whole team. At her side, she could feel Jack willing her to smile back at Boxy.

So, just with her mouth, she did.

Chapter 37

"Can we go, Jack?" Gem hissed.

"What? Yeah. Just wanna see what this looks like when it's finished. . ." and he wandered away. Gem stood still, hating him. So much for making him grovel, she thought. It dawned on her that she'd never been in the cellar on her own like this before, just her and the team and Boxy. She felt powerless and unimportant, and she hated it.

The last few lines and blots were being spurted on the walls, and everyone was standing back admiring it when at last Jack said, "OK, d'you wanna go, Gem? We can still get something to eat, go for a drink."

"What's this?" demanded Boxy. "Alcohol the night before a match?"

"I shall stick to Coke, don't worry," said Jack. "Just want some time on my own with Gem, OK?"

"Course you do, mate," leered Boxy. "We understand. Just don't go using up too much energy, all right? Make her do the work." He turned back to the room. "OK lads – time you was off too. Early nights all round!"

*

Walking along the main road, Jack's hand warm and crucial round hers, Gemma felt so churned up and confused she hardly said a word. Jack didn't notice, because he was going on about how great the cellar looked now and how much fun it had been beating up the graffiti kids. What's happening to me? thought Gem. I never used to be this limp.

"There's a bar down here," said Jack, pulling her down one of the trendy side streets leading from the town centre. They passed a restaurant where noise from the open upstairs windows spilled festively out into the night air.

"Private function," Gem said, for something to say. "Think we can blag our way in and get a free drink?"

"Why would you want to? They sound like a right load of idiots." The stagey laughter from the restaurant windows increased. Someone was making a braying, bragging speech, and at every pause, people shouted out and clapped and screamed with laughter. "God, fake it up, why don't you," groused Jack. "He could say anything, he could recite the fucking alphabet, and they'd clap him like that."

"Oh shut up," said Gem. "It's no different to Boxy sounding off in the cellar."

"Yeah? That's where you're wrong. We're real."

"*Real*," she scoffed.

"We *are* real! That lot's just come together cos someone's got engaged or something, and now they're faking it up, so they can say afterwards what fantastic fucking friends they all are. I bet someone's in there taking phony posey photos."

Gem felt something inside her snap. "Christ, you really

believe that, don't you? You really think you've got something special. You think you're better than other people – you think you're more than just a *team*."

There was a pause, then Jack said coldly, "Yeah."

"Well you're not. You're just a team. And how would you feel if I was always putting my friends before you, ay?"

Jack spun round at her, crowing. "So *that's* what all this is all about, ay? You're *jealous*."

"I am *not*!" spat Gem, snatching her hand from his. "I'm just sick of the way I always come second. When you're all together. I feel like I – I feel like I *disappear*! Into the fucking wallpaper. If you *had* any wallpaper. Into the *graffiti* you've just been spraying all over the walls while you kept me hanging about. *OK?*"

It was great, letting the words just hurtle out of her like this. And he was grinning back at her, enjoying it. "Gemmy's jealous!" he chanted, teasing.

"I sodding am not! I'm just . . . I'm outnumbered! I'm fucking shouted down!"

"Come on, you *love* it," he jeered. "You love the whole team thing, when we win, being the captain's girlfriend. . ."

"Oh, *fucking* hell. I'm gonna throw up."

"Throw up all you like, it's true!"

Gem swung a punch at him, and he caught her fist, and there was a beat of time, and then they both burst out laughing.

"Look at me and tell me you don't like it!" he gurgled. "Go on!"

"I'm not saying I don't like it—"

"*HAH!!*"

"I'm just *saying* – when did we last get any proper time on our own, ay?"

"Now? Except you're spoiling it by bitching?"

"Oh, *sod* you – I'm just saying – sometimes I feel like second best!"

Jack put his arm round her shoulders, and pulled her up against him. "It's not a competition, Gem. I mean – the team's completely different to you, isn't it? *Obviously.*"

"Yes, *obviously*—" Gem trailed off. Then she said, "Boxy's got it in for me. He doesn't want me around."

"That's rubbish."

"And Stev – I'm so sick of that fuckhead. He's always picking on me, trying to wind me up. . ."

"So don't let him. Ignore him. . ."

"But—"

"*Gem* – can we not do this? It's fucking boring. It's making problems. There's no problem, with Boxy, or Stev. The only problem's in your head."

Stung and only slightly reassured, Gem shut up. They carried on to the bar, and had just one drink, because it was too late to eat, then Jack said he had to go and get his early night. But on the way back, he pulled her into the grim shadows under the old Victorian railway arches by the station. "You have got to be *joking*," she hissed, grabbing his hand as it started unzipping her jacket.

"Oh, come on, Gem! Don't go all frigid on me!"

"Sod off! If you think I'm doing it in this freezing shithole. . ."

"I'm not cold. Not looking at you, I'm not cold."

"*Jack*. . ."

Gradually, he flattered her, coaxed her, saying it was so good between them they could do it anywhere and it would still be great, and soon she wanted him as much as he wanted her, and he lifted her up and they ended up having hasty sex against the old brick wall.

By the time she got home and was at last alone in bed and able to think, Gem was feeling pretty bad about herself. He thinks he can do what he wants with me, she agonized. He thinks I'll just fit in with him, whatever he wants. He goes on about the amazing sex we have and he thinks that makes everything else all right too.

She clutched her duvet tight in her arms. I thought we were starting to talk then, really talk, but he won't see it from my point of view, he makes out it's my problem . . . it's ages since we had any proper time together. He puts his stupid team first, every time, I just fit round it. Why's he have to make such a big deal of it? It's only sport. Other people do sport without making such a big deal of it.

Gem had never been part of anything like Jack's team. She was a loner, an experimenter, someone who tried out something for a while, then moved on to the next experience. She'd kind of prided herself on this, before Jack. She thought it made her brave, free. But now she thought about what she saw in the cellar every Saturday night, or at the end of a match, or when they were just simply taking on the world like when they beat up the graffiti kids, and she knew she had nothing like that in her life, nothing at all, and she felt alone, afraid and alone.

There was a thought nudging at her, trying to get in;

she didn't want to let it in. She thought about how good it was to be in a couple with Jack, thought about people looking at them, envying them, the golden couple . . . only they didn't really know them, they didn't know what was going on. She thought about Christian, and was suddenly stabbed with a strong, lonely, hungry wish to get together with Christian again, tell him everything, mull it over with him. There was such a rift between them now, though – he'd think she was just using him.

Then at last the thought she'd been keeping at bay nudged its way into her consciousness: Jack's more important to me than I am to him. He's the centre of my life, I'm just on the outskirts of his.

She wouldn't let it take a hold, she wouldn't let it win. She told herself it wasn't true and they just needed space, time together, if they didn't always have to fit round the stupid team they'd be all right . . . There were two sides to the problem, she reckoned. The first side was Jack putting the team before her all the time. The second was her getting swallowed up by Jack and putting her own life on hold. Somehow, she had to tackle them both.

Gem sat up in bed, and pushed the duvet back, rigid with determination, feeling like she'd made a serious new year's resolution for once, even if it was a bit late, not just one about eating less chocolate and watching less crap telly.

She'd made up her mind to do something about her and Jack. Something definite.

Chapter 38

Saturday followed its usual course. Gem went to the match and took her camera with her. This was part of her scheme to reclaim her old life and her old interests; it was also to signal that she wasn't just a spectator at Jack's life. As she focused on Jack through the viewfinder she felt her anger at him dwindle away. She loved him running, shouting; she loved his courage and his energy. She felt full of wanting him and took shot after shot, just of him. At half-time Boxy walked over to her and told her he'd like to see the pictures she'd taken. She felt flattered, then immediately annoyed that she was flattered. Her annoyance didn't stop her taking a lot more action shots in the second half of the game, though.

Ten minutes from the end, with Westgate only three points ahead, a fight kicked off. The opposition number seven scrambled out from a ruck with his hands clutched to his head, raging that Stev had gouged his eye; Stev laughed; two of the opposition squared up to him; Stev threw a punch. In the mayhem that followed the opposition trainer yelled at Boxy; Boxy told him to eff off; and the game was abandoned. Len and a couple of the other Westgate alackadoos remonstrated with Boxy for his unprofessional behaviour; he turned his back on them and walked away. This, of course, only added to the excitement for the team.

At the start of the party in the cellar that night Boxy gave a wild, crowing speech, claiming they'd won the match fair and square. "It's not our problem if other teams can't take how we play!" he bellowed. "If they don't wanna play with the big boys they should keep off the pitch!"

At the peak of the party, the music was suddenly killed. Shouting their annoyance, everyone looked over to the decks, to see Boxy making his way purposefully towards a tall, brown-haired girl with so much mascara on that her eyelashes looked like spider's legs. She had her arms round Will's neck and she was nuzzling into his neck.

"*You*," Boxy said to her. "I want you out of here."

"*What?*" she squawked. "What's going on?"

"I don't like the way you been messing around with two of my team, playing them off one against the other," said Boxy, evenly. "Last week you're supposed to be going out with Leo, now it's Will. It's causing bad feeling. We don't need it. So you can get out, and I don't want to see you here again, or at the matches, or having anything to do with my boys. OK?"

The girl erupted into mocking laughter. "Who the fuck d'you think you are, telling me what to do?" She turned to Will. "Who is he – your nursemaid? You gonna let him push you around like this?" Will wouldn't look at her. He was staring at the floor, hard. Leo was behind Boxy's shoulder, looking straight at the girl. She turned on him. "What's this about, Leo? Sour grapes? You so pathetic you got to get your trainer to stick up for you?"

"OK, OK," said Boxy, "so you got a crowd round you and you're making the best of it, hamming it up, but at the end of the day you can make all the fuss you like and the end result's gonna be the same. You – going through that door and not coming back. So why not do yourself – and us – a favour, and make it now, so we can all get back to the party."

"Who the *hell* d'you think you are?" she screeched at him. "Some kind of fucking dictator?"

"Come on, love," said Boxy. "You're getting *really* tedious." He got hold of her arm. She wrenched it violently, but he held on hard, so hard that her eyes went kind of glassy and afraid, and she allowed herself to be propelled across the floor and up the steps. Will and Leo looked after them and didn't move. Then Boxy pulled open the door, shoved her through it, shut it again, and came back down the steps grinning. "Come on," he shouted, "ain't you got the music back on yet?"

"*Bloody* hell," hissed Gem to Jack, "I don't believe I just saw that!"

"What?" snapped Jack. "She had it coming."

"What – from *Boxy*? What is he – the relationship police? Look at Will – what's wrong with him? I can't believe he just stood by just then! They were eating each others' faces off ten minutes ago—"

"She's been messing him around. Two-timing the pair of them. He's well off out of it."

"That's not the *point*, Jack! *He* should be the one to tell her to clear out, not Boxy—"

Jack shrugged. "Reckon he's done both of them a favour. She's a bitch."

"That is not the *point*. It's none of his fucking business – it's *their* business. He's got no right to—"

"Oh, for Christ's sake. If Will and Leo are OK with her being kicked out – why should you worry?"

"OK. So if Boxy suddenly gets it in his head that I'm bad news, and kicks me out – you're gonna stand by and let him, are you?"

"Don't be stupid. That wouldn't happen. She's a nasty little dirtbag, and you're not."

Gem was silent. The almost-compliment was sweet to her, because compliments were pretty rare from Jack. She felt treacherous, like she should carry on defending the girl who'd been thrown out, but instead she leant her forearms against Jack's chest and said, "*So* glad you think so."

"I know so," he said, and kissed her on the neck, by her ear.

"I just think. . ."

"What?"

"I think it's weird. I mean – he seems to spend all his free time with you, he's here every Saturday night with you. Hasn't he got any friends his age?"

"Course he has. But he likes being with us. We're the business."

"Maybe he's gay."

"Oh for fuck's sake, Gem, if you're gonna get—"

"OK, OK – just a joke! But he doesn't ever date *women*, does he?"

"Sure he does. Sometimes. He said he was engaged, once, but it went wrong."

"So now he hates women."

"Oh, *Jesus Christ*. Are you gonna be like this all night? What's this sudden obsession with Boxy all of a sudden? You fancy him or something?"

Gem felt battered, unable to fight back. Slightly hating herself, somehow feeling she'd failed, she wound her arms round Jack's neck and set out to seduce him.

The next morning, Sunday, Gem woke up determined to resume her battle to take charge over Jack. She offered to cook eggs and bacon for her parents, and as they were sitting gratefully and a little surprised round the kitchen table, she asked them outright if they'd mind if Jack stayed over some nights. As in – stayed in her room.

Immediately, the atmosphere set like cement. "In your *room?*" grated out Mr Hanrahan. "You've only just met him."

"I haven't, Dad. *You've* only just met him. I've known him for ages."

"Oh, come on, Gemma, you know what I mean. It's one thing for a serious boyfriend to stay the night . . . eventually . . . but quite another for—"

"He is serious, Dad. Really serious."

"Well it's got serious pretty quickly, then, hasn't it."

"Are you calling me a slut?"

"*Don't* be ridiculous, Gemma, there's no need for that sort of talk!"

There was an angry silence. Gem's mum had said nothing throughout, which Gem knew was a good sign –

it meant she didn't necessarily agree with the line Gem's dad was taking. So Gem went in for the attack. "OK, Dad, fine. If it makes you that uncomfortable, fine, he won't stay. We'll have to find somewhere else. Like round the back of a bus shelter or something."

"*Gemma!*"

"*What?* Don't be such a hypocrite, Dad! I thought one of the things you and Mum valued was – not being a *hypocrite!*"

There was a pause. Then Carrie Hanrahan murmured, "She's got you there, Mick."

He turned on her, relieved to look at his wife and not his daughter, relieved to let his anger out somewhere less risky. "*Fine. Thank you* for your support. I can see you're going to gang up on me over this, aren't you?"

"Oh, Mick, don't be such a child. It's not a matter of ganging up and you know it. Oh, *come on*! Aren't you glad she's this open with us? You want her to be one of those poor little kids sneaking around behind our backs, making herself sick with the morning-after pill?"

Mick Hanrahan knew he was beaten. He plunged his face into his hands and groaned.

"Jack isn't the first boy I've slept with," Gem went on, brutally. "Mum knows so I bet you know too cos she tells you everything, doesn't she? But this is the first one I've felt really seriously about. So."

"Oh, darling," murmured Carrie, "do you?" and Gem said, "I'm *seventeen*, Dad!"

Another pause. Then from behind his hands Mick came out with his last defence. "But we've only met him once!"

"Well, that can be put right," said Carrie, briskly. "He can come to supper next Saturday. We should be going to the Jones's for drinks, but—"

"Not Saturday," said Gem. "Saturday night they always have this big rave, at The Crown."

"Well can't you go on to The Crown after we've eaten?"

"He has to get there early. He's the captain."

"O-*kay*," said Carrie, carefully. "And you go to it too, do you?"

"Yes."

"Every Saturday? Suppose there's something else on – a party or something?"

"Well – we'd go to both, probably. *Look*, Mum—"

"All right, what about Friday?"

"*No*. Not the night before a match. He can't drink, and he has to get an early night. . ."

"*Thursday*, then!"

"Yes," said Gem, stiffly, "that should be fine."

"Unless he has training or something," put in Mick.

"Oh, shut up, Dad," snapped Gem. "He takes rugby seriously. I thought you'd approve. What – you'd sooner he was out on the street, graffiting?"

"*What?* Where did that come from? Of course I approve. As long as he's taking you seriously, too."

"Well he is."

"Good, that's terrific. I can't wait to meet him properly."

"This Thursday, then," said Carrie, hastily. "I'll do a casserole or something, we can open some wine."

"And he can stay over afterwards," said Gem.

Chapter 39

Wednesday evening. Gem had towed Jack home from school, promising that her parents wouldn't be back till seven at the earliest cos they'd told her to start the evening meal. After they'd had sex on the sitting-room floor they put the few clothes they'd shed back on again and sat on the settee and turned on the television. And during the advert break she'd taken the remote off him to stop him channel-hopping and told him of her plan for him to start sleeping over.

"They *agreed*?" demanded Jack. "I don't believe it. What – you just told 'em we were shaggin' each other?"

"D'you *have* to call it shagging?"

"Making love. Gaining carnal knowledge of. Whatever. Did you?"

"Well – I kind of left them to work that out for themselves," said Gem, patronizingly. "When I asked if you could stay over."

"And they didn't say – yes, but only in the spare room, with electrified tripwires stretched across the landing?" Gem laughed. "Fucking hell," he went on. "I just – I dunno. I've always kept my sex life private. It just feels a bit dodgy, having a chat about it with your folks."

"So didn't your dad ever sit you down and—"

"No. NO! I'd've walked out if he had done. None of his bloody business."

"I mean sex education. When you were younger."

"He knew we got it at school."

"Well," said Gem, "my mum and dad have always gone on about openness, *you can tell me anything, darling*, that kind of thing. So that I'd go to them if I got pregnant or into drugs or anything. So I just took them at their word."

Jack shook his head. "There is no way I could have a girl in my room. There was one time – I was doing it on the floor of the living room with this slag Jenny Harker, late at night, and the old man came down. . ."

"Oh my God. What happened?"

"He came in, and switched the light *on*, then *off*, wham wham, just like that, as he clocked what was happening. Then he just went up to bed again. Spoilt the mood, I can tell you."

"Did he bollock you the next day?"

"Na. Didn't say a word. Too embarrassed – he couldn't even look at me. Took him about a *month*, just to get round to talking to me again. Kept glaring just past me, like I disgusted him so much he might throw up if he actually laid eyes on me . . . he's good at the silent treatment, my old man. There was no way I was gonna try that again after the way he was about it, not in the house, not unless I was a hundred per cent sure they were far away and not gonna come back suddenly."

"Well, I think that's all wrong. Old-fashioned and stupid. Although you have got little sisters. . ."

"Yeah, and I can just imagine what he'd say if one of *them* starts asking to have a boyfriend to stay! No way. Not ever. Not if she was twenty-five and engaged to him. We're just not *like* that."

Gemma sighed. She felt they were getting off the subject. "Anyway," she said, "it's OK, isn't it? You'll stay, Thursday? Mum wants you to eat with us first, and—"

"*What!?* No way."

"What d'you *mean* – no way?"

"Sit across from your old man and him knowing I'm gonna be doing it with you in a couple of hours?"

"Oh, for God's sake! You can't stay and avoid him altogether! You'd see him in the morning, wouldn't you?"

"No. No, I would not. I'd get up at five a.m. and sneak out."

"Oh, bloody hell, Jack! This is all so stupid! It's *primitive*!"

Predictably, Jack smirked.

"Don't smile like that, you *prat*!" railed Gem. "Honestly, the way you talk – it's like two hundred years ago, girls being *owned* by their dads, who have to protect their virtue until they're handed over in *marriage* to some male. . ."

"Bollocks to all that, Gem. It's just embarrassing.

"But *why*?"

"I told you. Because he'd know."

"Oh for *Christ's* sake – so *what* that he'd know? It doesn't have to be there in the *room* with us. He knows you shit too, right? You saying you can't look him straight in the face cos he knows you take a daily dump?"

Jack was still smirking. "God, Gemma," he drawled, all superior, "I'm sorry to hear you equating sex with shitting."

"Oh, *fuck* you—!"

"*Ha!* Got you there, Ms Superior-Analysis Smarty-Pants Hanrahan!"

Gem shrieked with frustration and rage and launched herself at Jack, hard, knocking him right back on to the settee. "*Aaaaagh!*" he squawked, and grabbed hold of her, choking with laughter as she slapped and pummelled him. "OK, OK," he gasped, "pack it in, look, I'm sorry, I'll be there, I'll be modern about it, I'll ask your dad to lend me a condom—"

Slap!!

"*Haaaaargh!* Gem, stoppit, stoppit, *please. . .*"

They writhed, shifted and slid and then with an almighty thump, they landed on the floor. To Jack, used to crashing down all over the rugby field, this was nothing. But Gem was shocked and slightly winded and this gave Jack all the advantage he needed to heft himself up and pinion her underneath. "Now I'm gonna dribble on your face!" he crowed.

"*JACK!!* Jack, you *dare,* you fucking *pervert*!"

She reached up and pinched him, hard, under the arm, and he collapsed down on top of her, both of them laughing, and then they grabbed each other and cuddled. Gem kissed his neck, his ear, kissed the scar above his eyebrow. She was starting to feel turned on again. She pulled his head down to hers, pushed her tongue between his lips. He kissed her back, then suddenly looked at his watch and pulled away from her, scrambling to his feet, saying, "It's six-thirty already! Didn't you say they'd be back around seven?"

"Yeah, but it doesn't matter. . ." she wailed.

"Yes it does! I'm off – I'm not bumping into your old man. S'gonna be bad enough tomorrow!"

But despite all the effortful planning, Thursday night was a bit of a failure. Mr and Mrs Hanrahan were determined to be relaxed, modern and open as they all ate dinner together. Their full-on cool parents act – complete with jokes and the occasional swear word – froze Jack into a rigor mortis of embarrassment and he found himself hardly able to utter a word. He covered this by finishing his food before the other three had barely started on theirs, which Gem covered by scraping the last of the mashed potato on to his plate. Dessert (a creamy gooseberry fool, made with the last of Carrie Hanrahan's precious gooseberries frozen from last summer) was eaten in near silence. Then Mick Hanrahan brightly told everyone he'd do the clearing up ("No, I don't want any help – no, you three clear off") so Gem and Jack sat side by side on the sofa and watched TV.

The question of *going to bed* hung like one of those swinging blades of medieval torture over the rest of the evening. Although normally Gem would have had no problem in taking him up to her room to listen to music, now it seemed like a too-obvious statement of intent. Mrs Hanrahan made decaffeinated coffee ("Or would you prefer hot chocolate – it's no trouble, honestly") for everyone at around ten o'clock, and an hour or so later she and Mr Hanrahan went noisily upstairs, calling out, "Night!" Jack tried to call goodnight back but his voice came out like a duck being throttled.

Gem turned on him. "*What* are you so *uptight* for?"

"I just fucking *am*, OK? And don't have a go at me – everyone's uptight, OK?"

"You're the worst!"

"No I'm not! What about your dad – trying so hard it's fucking agony!"

"At least he's *trying*!"

"*I'm* trying! I told you it wouldn't work! It's too fucking weird!"

They hissed at each other a bit more, then they crept up to her bedroom and went to sleep back to back (Jack hiding with his head under the duvet) without making love first. Jack woke in a panic at six-thirty a.m. and shuffled silently out of the house to go back home to shower and change for the day.

Gem wasn't too depressed about it though. She reckoned they'd set a precedent, and it would be bound to get easier with time. She planned to tow him back pissed at the end of that Saturday night.

She was also determined to carry on with her plan to get her old life back. She decided she'd take her courage in both hands, and phone Christian. The rift between them had gone on far too long.

Chapter 40

Christian was over the moon to get a phone call from Gem. He'd promised himself she had to come to him – and now she had. For the first five minutes they lied warmly about how they'd just somehow not ever had time to talk when they'd bumped into each other at school, and told each other they'd *meant* to phone, they really had. She said how good it was to catch up at last and he announced as casually as he could that he'd booked the darkroom for after school Friday and if she had anything to develop she was welcome to share it with him. Gem agreed immediately, delighted, then after they'd said goodbye she remembered that all she really had to develop were photos of Jack and the team.

Well, tough, she thought. Too late to pull out now, that was just how it was, Jack was a big part of her life now – face it, he practically *was* her life now. Maybe the photos would be a good way to start them talking about that and how to put it right.

In the darkroom, they covered any awkwardness by getting straight down to work. First they did the contact sheets; then they developed a whole series Chris had done for a project on urban decay – lots of burnt-out cars and artistic graffiti and rubbish piled high. Then they stood side by side watching Jack's face swim slowly together in the developing tray in front of them. "Symmetrical features," said Chris gloomily. "That's why he'd be considered good-looking."

Gem didn't answer. She found the sight of Jack kind of . . . *coalescing* in front of her so erotic that she didn't trust her voice. It was like a bewitched mirror, a magic picture in the sand . . . she stared at him, took in a long, shaky, passionate breath.

"You said you got some action shots as well?" barked Chris.

"Action—?!"

"*Rugby*, Gem – I'm not suggesting you had the sodding camera set up at the foot of the bed. . ."

"*Right* – yes I have. Quite a few. I think they'll be a bit confused but some of them should come out . . . look, Chris – do you *mind* doing this?"

There was a long silence. Jack's face continued to form itself in front of them. Gem slid her eyes sideways to look at Chris, but his profile was just a mask in the dark. "All I mind is if I don't get to see you any more," he said gruffly. "Spend time with you any more. You'd better get lover boy out of the tray. He's done."

Gem got the tongs, hooked Jack out and dumped him in the sealing tray, then she pegged him on the line of photos. "I've missed you too," she said.

"Really? I thought you wouldn't have time to miss me. With your new life and everything."

"Oh, *Chris.* It's not a new life. It's just a new boyfriend."

"Is it all working out?"

"Kind of. He's – I'm a bit gone on him, Chris."

"I gathered."

"But it's like – I'm – I—"

Chris slid another square of paper in the developing tray. "What?" he prompted.

"I dunno. I'm too swallowed up by it all. I need some of my old life back. Like seeing you – I've *really missed* seeing you, Chris!"

Chris was so intensely moved by this he didn't speak for a minute; then he said, "Well, like I said, me too. But won't your old man get jealous?"

Gem didn't know how to tell Chris that it wouldn't even cross Jack's mind to be jealous. She just leant her shoulder against his for a second, then said, "D'you wanna come into town with me sometime?"

"You know I want to. When?"

"Next week? I haven't trawled round the shops for ages—"

"Clearly."

"What d'you *mean*, clearly?"

"Well, I don't want to be rude, Gemmy, but you've been looking a bit, well. . ."

"*What?*"

"Restrained, clothes-wise. Mainstream."

"Oh, *God.* You think?"

"Just a bit. Lacking your usual original ideas."

Gemma gripped the side of a developing tray in sudden anguish. "You're right. I've gone safe. It's Jack's fault."

"Oh, God. Please don't say you let him tell you what to wear."

"Of course not. Just—"

"What?"

"Well – the only times he tells me I look good is when I'm dressed really simply. Well, a bit tarty, but simple. His big compliment is to say, 'That shows your shape off.' He doesn't like anything too weird, or different. You know? He likes kind of – tarty sporty."

Christian had closed his eyes. "Tarty sporty," he groaned. "Too much information, Gem."

"Sorry. Anyway, you're right. I've got to stop letting him influence me like that. It's ridiculous. I've gotta get back to *me*, my taste. So – major shopping, next Thursday?"

"Sure. I'd love to."

They peered companionably into the first developing tray, all the chill and awkwardness between them gone. "That's shaping up," said Gem. "I thought it'd come out blurred, but—"

"Not blurred enough, in my opinion. What ugly bastards! Look at Mac, what a troglodyte! What are they up to here?"

"That's – I think that's a maul."

"That figures. They look like they're mauling each other. Jesus, what a stupid game!"

"I know."

"Do you really enjoy watching it? I mean – *really*?"

Gem took in a deep breath. "Sometimes. Sometimes not."

"And when it's not – it's because it's a crap game?"

"No. It's when I'm pissed off with Jack."

"*Ah*."

"When I'm – you know – *into* him, it's just brilliant, watching. He's an amazing player, it's so exciting to watch him, even though I feel sick half the time in case he gets hurt, and afterwards they're all so full of themselves, it's great, there's such a fantastic buzz when they've won. And they have the best parties. It's just—"

"Just?"

"I guess it's beginning to pall. A bit. It's like – where do I fit into all this? I'm beginning to feel like an onlooker."

"Or a groupie," gloated Chris, leaning over the developing tray. What Gem was saying was better than he'd dared to hope for and he didn't want to risk breaking the spell by asking any questions. "This one's done," he murmured. "God – he looks a mean shit."

"That's Stev," said Gem. The picture showed Stev half on top of another guy, his hands gripping his head, his thumb gouging into his eye.

"Is that *normal* for rugby? Blinding the opposition?"

"No," said Gem. She scooped it out of the tray with the tongs and peered at it closely. "God, that didn't show up on the contact sheet, did it? This was what all the trouble was about, last week! This was why the game was abandoned. Stev got accused of gouging but everyone said it was an accident. . ."

"An *accident*? No way."

"It could have been!"

"No, Gem. Look at the direction of his eyes – he's looking straight at what he's doing. He means it all right."

*

Meanwhile, outside, it was snowing steadily, and Boxy was leading the boys on to the training pitch for an extra session. Next day's match was top-league stuff, against a team that really fancied itself, with rumours circulating that the Midlands Selector might turn up to talent-spot.

"You have got to be *joking*!" groused Big Mac, as snow settled on his shoulders, melted on his face. "I ain't running around in this!"

"I think you'll find you are!" jeered Boxy, and carried on walking on to the pitch. The floodlights were on, and the snow-filled pitch was a square of light in the blackness all round it. "OK," yelled Boxy. "Start your laps. Then we'll train. And we won't stop till we've fucked up every inch of this *lovely* white field!"

They ran, they did press-ups (Boxy pushing their faces into the snow if they weren't working hard enough), and some serious tackling training. Then Boxy yelled, "No one else is mad enough to train in six inches of snow! That's why we are – who we are! And your reward is coming, boys. I'm gonna let you make – snow angels!" The team looked at him, some of them laughing, some of them confused, then they all raced after him to the far side of the pitch where the snow was still virgin. There they fell flat on to their backs, arcing their arms up and down to make angels' wings in the snow, stars showing like laser points above them in the freezing sky. "This is *amazing*," breathed Jack.

"Yeah," said Stev. "It is."

Jack turned to look at him; he hadn't realized he was within earshot. But Stev's eyes were fixed on the night sky.

"All right, on your feet," shouted Boxy, "can't have my

lads freezing solid, can I?" They all scrambled up to admire the shapes they'd made.

"We got a whole heavenly choir here," said Boxy. For a moment, the boys looked around at each other, grinning, enjoying the whiteness, the spiritual power of it all, then Boxy stooped, gathered snow, and chucked a snowball, hard, at the back of Jamie's head.

The snow fight lasted fifteen minutes; then they headed back to the changing room talking about tomorrow's match. "I heard Southchurch thinks we're a bunch of pussy-boys," said Iz. "With a bit of skill."

"Yeah?" said Boxy. "Well tomorrow you can prove them wrong, can't you?"

"Yeah," said Stev. "Don't settle for anything less than abject humiliation."

"Right. You heard what they said – you know what they think – you know what you gotta do. Warm up, switch on, and put it together. Front up to them – I want two big hits, then spin it wide – I want *big* yardage – their forwards are gonna come off broken. When we've broken the defence we can release the backs. Make sure they know what's going on. Humiliate. Dominate. OK, boys? OK."

In the changing room, Jamie found he'd got a missed call on his mobile from his mum, saying she hoped he hadn't got pneumonia and telling them all to go to the cellar, where she'd got hot leftover vegetable soup waiting.

"Look, OK, no one wants a really fat bird," Stev was saying, as, showered and changed, the team hurried along the main street to The Crown, talking about girls. "But these skinny ones you see in magazines and adverts – they're disgusting. They look like they wouldn't be able to *breed*."

"Well, that's good, innit?" chuckled Dosh. "If they can't get pregnant?"

Stev turned the full force of his superior crocodile smile on Dosh. "You, mate," he sneered, "have got a lot to learn."

"I'm just saying—"

"Yeah, and you're saying shit. You wanna make it with a *woman*. Not some stick doll."

"Well, granted, they gotta have *tits*—"

"It's not about that."

"So you're saying," said Jack, "that you like the thought she might get pregnant. You like the risk. It adds a thrill."

"Maybe," said Stev. "But that's not it. Fuck me, it's not that complicated. You're a man – you need a woman. One who can breed."

Another silence. If anyone else in the team had come out with stuff like this, this man/woman breeding stuff, they'd have all been falling about laughing and making *ug-ug* Neanderthal noises. But because it was Stev saying it, they didn't.

Dosh took in a breath. "Yeah, but – if you're not gonna have a kid and everything, what the hell does it matter?"

"It matters, you prat. It matters cos it's what the girl *is*."

What she is, thought Jack. *What* she is. Not who she is. And he decided not to say anything else, to let the whole topic drop. But he'd felt that weird, dark kinship once again, that sense that underneath everything, all the stuff on top, he and Stev understood each other. About what mattered and about what they were.

Chapter 41

Just as they reached the pub, Gem phoned Jack. "I got the pictures!" she said. "They're brilliant! Where are you?"

"Just going down the cellar."

"Shall I bring them along? I'm on the bus, I can get off at the high street. . ."

Jack was silent. Within the team, an unwritten, unspoken rule had evolved that said the cellar was only for the boys unless it was party-time. And now Gem had challenged that rule, but he didn't know how to tell her not to come to the cellar. So he said, "Go on then," and hung up. He never felt easy talking to Gem in front of the lads; they were too quick to take the piss.

As for Gem, when she walked down into the cellar ten minutes later she knew her sudden act of bravado in suggesting the most logical place to meet had been a mistake. The boys were slurping down great dishes of soup and hunks of bread, some at the bar, some sat at the large battered table, and there was absolutely no space for her at all. Jack was chowing down at the table and he wasn't about to relinquish his seat so he could go over and kiss her hello. He waved at her with his left hand (still spooning in soup with his right) so she sidled over and stood behind him. "Here they are," she hissed coldly, pulling the photos out of her bag.

"Don't give 'em to him, he'll get soup all over them," said Boxy, sitting across the table from Jack. He stretched out his hand, confident that Gem would put the photos into it. Which – after briefly considering telling him to sod off – she did.

Boxy was delighted with the pictures. He crowed over each in turn, mocking the ones he called "love-portraits" of Jack, and passing them one by one to Karl, sat on his right, who passed them on round the table. Once again Gem felt that absurd sense of flattery, like she'd been honoured by the emperor, and once again felt angry with herself for feeling that. As the pile thinned, she watched his face closely. She'd put the photo of Stev eye-gouging at the bottom of the pile.

"Oh, deary me," said Boxy, when he got to it. "Don't like the look of this, Stev. Don't like it at all."

He held it up, swivelling it so the whole table could see in turn, as well as the boys who'd come crowding over from the bar where they'd been eating. "Bloody hell, Stev!" yelped Leo, eyes goggling. "You said it was an accident!"

"Well he's not gonna turn to the ref and own up to it, is he, Leo, you plonker?" sneered Boxy. "Please sir, I did mean it, I'm a very naughty boy?"

Everyone laughed, waiting, wondering what Boxy would say next, whether he'd suddenly go all serious like he sometimes did, and read Stev the riot act for dangerous play.

But what he did was calmly tear the photo into two, then four, then eight little pieces, and put them down in a neat pile beside his plate. "Don't mind, do you, Gemma?" he said, blank-faced. "There's been talk of an official complaint, so we can't have that kind of evidence floating around."

The ripped-up photo caused the first real, serious, no-holds-barred row between Jack and Gem. As soon as they were on their own Gem exploded, accusing Boxy of criminal barbarity. Jack exploded back; accused her of being mad. They railed at each other, maddened by their differences, then she flounced off. She didn't phone him; he didn't phone her.

The next day, Saturday, match day, she woke up not knowing what she was going to do, just sure she was going to do something.

Gem knew about catching the upflow of the day, doing something physical first off. She'd try to get her bike out, run, walk, swim – do something to make her feel good before too many hours had streamed past. She didn't always achieve this, of course. It was too easy to keep drifting back to sleep till midday or later, then stumble down to watch daytime TV with a big bowl of sugary cereal. Feeling as stale and lumpy as the bed she'd just crawled out of.

This morning, though, she didn't need to try. She felt like something was propelling her. All night she'd slept in fits and starts, with lurid dreams, and a feeling of panic underneath it all. And now her need to move, to get out of the house, was like a burning inside her.

She pulled on old clothes, old boots. She cut two thick slices of white bread, spread them with peanut butter, wrapped them in tinfoil and stowed them in her pocket with three pounds sixty in change, a small bottle of water refilled from the tap, and her keys.

And took off. It was still only twenty to nine. She headed straight to the bus stop, jumped on a bus heading to the great sprawling country park on the outskirts of town.

As she jounced along on the back seat of the bus, she thought of Jack. He'd be getting his kit together, eating breakfast, ready for the match. Eleven a.m. kick-off, he'd said. With a guilty jolt she realized she wasn't going to watch him play, not now she was on this bus. Too bad.

Overnight, she'd stopped hating him. But . . . she was *overwhelmed*, that was the trouble. She'd let things – *Jack* – get out of perspective. She was always going to have such a sorted-out, *balanced* life. Love, work, fun, friends. Brain, health, fitness, looks. Everything in harmony. She'd always congratulated herself for the way she'd measured it all out.

But last night, after that stupid row they'd had, she'd dreamt about Jack in dreams so full of yearning and wanting it scared her stupid.

Gem got off the bus and went through the wide, rustic gates of the country park. Then she started to walk, head down, arms moving by her sides as though she were running. She let her thoughts just stream, flow, unchecked. She went over the row, the words they'd said, let all the anger and hurt flow past, and let herself feel it, and after a while, it was like a pattern, a shape, was forming in all her thoughts. She'd done this before. You had to trust the flow, you had to let it all go by you, and after a while, it started to make shapes, it started to resolve itself.

And what she saw was that the hate was linked to the love. That she hated him when he failed her, because the love was so strong. That it was the love that skewed everything else out of balance.

I can't get out of this, she told herself. I can't just stop feeling for him, I don't want to. But I don't have to let it control me. I can stand back, I can look at what's happening, weigh it all up, decide what to do – that way I can be feeling all this, but still be in charge. I can accept that everything's shifted but still be in charge. I can absolutely adore him but still be in charge.

As for Jack, he was furious with Gem for not supporting him, for not being there on the touchline when it was the most major match they'd played yet. She'd let him down. He tackled like he wanted to kill the boys he was pulling down.

The final score was 17-9 to Westgate.

Chapter 42

Monday afternoon, dusk, lights just beginning to come on round the little park that Jamie, Iz and Dosh had stopped in to share some after-school chips. They were still buzzing about Saturday's terrific win and as they ate, they rehashed the best bits yet again, to stoke the good feeling up some more. Then they finished off their chips in contented silence.

"Cannibals," commented Jamie, nodding towards two crows scavenging a KFC box. "Eating another bird."

"They don't know it's another bird, though, do they," said Dosh. "What with being all coated in batter an' all."

"Crows used to hang around battlefields," said Iz. "Pecking out eyes and stuff. It was in a film."

"Yeah," said Dosh. "Feasting on soldiers' guts. When you think about it – the fact that soldiers got slashed to bits was a plus for crows, wasn't it."

"Saved 'em work."

"My dad was telling me about these crows in the Middle East that're so tough they can peck through a corpse's skull."

"Nice."

Suddenly, Jamie stood up, and booted an old lager can at the crows. "Go and find a corpse!" he shouted. The crows took off into the air like lazy witches. "Get some *pride*!"

"Any news about Karl's dad?" asked Iz, as Jamie collapsed back on to the bench once more. "He been back in touch yet?"

"Nah," said Dosh. "Don't think so. Boxy was talking to him, Sat'day night."

"I saw. Karl looked well upset."

"So did Jack," said Jamie. "He and the wife must've had a bust-up – she wasn't at the game."

"Yeah, but eleven o'clock or so she turns up and they practically have it off on the bar."

Dosh shook his head yearningly. "Saw her. What a bitch. I'd never let a girl do that to me."

"Oh – *what*?" erupted Jamie. "What girl, you muppet? You'd let a girl do *anything* to you if you could get hold of one!"

Dosh shoulder-barged Jamie off the end of the bench, and Iz snapped, "*Leave it!*"

"All I was saying," said Dosh, indignantly, "was she's a bitch for playing stupid games on his day of glory!"

"The most *surprising* match that selector'd ever laid eyes on," reminisced Iz dreamily. "That's what he said."

"Yeah," breathed Jamie. "He turns up to watch Southchurch, and sees us kick 'em all around the fucking paddock."

"He was saying there were Westgate players he should've seen in the County Trials. . ."

"No kidding! He said that?"

"Yeah. He picked out Jack, and Cory – said he wanted to see more of them."

"Blimey. So they could be going places?"

"Could be."

"Boxy must be well chuffed."

"Must be," said Dosh, aiming another can at the re-alighting crows. "*Well* chuffed."

But Boxy had not been chuffed. When Mr Mayland the Midlands Selector had called him, Jack and Cory over to congratulate him on the team and state his interest in the two players, Boxy had not been chuffed at all. He listened, with a dry, superior smile on his face, then he said, "Well, thanks for your vote of confidence. But I think for now my boys'll stick with the team they're with. I don't want them diluting their energies with other commitments."

Mr Mayland was thoroughly taken aback. "Now hang on a minute," he bridled, "this isn't just a decision for you, is it? I'm offering these lads a chance, a step up. At the end of the day it has to be their decision."

So Boxy turned to Jack and Cory and said, "OK, lads. Your decision."

His confidence in his power over them was absolute. Jack and Cory had muttered something about "having a think about it" and "getting in touch later". Mr Mayland had frostily handed his card over to Jack, and stalked off.

"Take that as a compliment," Boxy said, as they watched him go, "but don't go letting it go to your heads, OK? You're not that good. You're good in the team, you're good at following my instructions. Take you out of the team, take away the leadership – you'd fall apart pretty quickly." Jack set his face, slid his eyes sideways to Cory, who was looking fixedly ahead. "Anyway," Boxy went on, "think it over. You reckon you can be something on your own – just let me know." Then he too walked off, back to where the rest of the team was grouped by the clubhouse door.

"Why didn't he talk to Stev too?" muttered Cory. "He played a stormer."

"Guess he knows his reputation. Didn't want someone that dirty up at County level."

"But Stev's just about our best player. After you, of course, mate."

There was a silence, while Jack pulled out Mr Mayland's card and looked at it. Then he screwed it up and dropped it on the ground.

The party in the cellar that night was punctuated for Jack by furious mobile calls to Gem. He'd berated her for not being there; she'd almost said she was sorry, tried to get him to come round to her house. He'd refused to leave the party. The battle of wills had lasted for two hours and in the end Gem had cracked and got a cab to the cellar. She'd flown down the stairs and Jack had shoved his way through to her and they'd fallen on each other, kissing and apologizing. . . He'd picked her up, sat her on the bar, she'd wrapped her legs round him. . . "Oi – you two!" Big Mac had yelled indignantly. "Have some fucking *discretion*, can't you?" Gem and Jack held on to each other and kissed like if they stopped they'd drown, they'd die. "Fucking eating each other!" bellowed Mac. "*OI!!*"

Into Gem's mouth Jack breathed, "Let's go, yeah?" and he lifted her down and, arms around each other, they stumbled towards the door. Gem felt like she had her eyes shut. She was seeing but blanking it all out, all the mocking, envious faces around her, the voices demanding to know what Jack thought he was up to, leaving before the party was finished. . . At the door Jack stopped. He couldn't just walk out like this. He made himself put on a false, lecherous face and crowed, "Look, I'm leaving a bit early, OK?"

"Yeah, leave us to clear up!"

"For once, yeah? Fuck off you lot, OK?"

And the team jeered back. Jack was all right. He was on the make, that was all.

Wrapped round each other in the back of another cab, Gem told Jack her parents would be in bed fast asleep by the time they got back. Which they were – the house was breathing silently when they let themselves in the front door.

They crept up to Gem's room and this time they didn't sleep back to back.

Chapter 43

Overall, though, Gem had to admit that her plan to involve Jack more in her life by getting him to sleep over at her house hadn't worked. He'd only come back if he knew the house was empty, or if it was so late her parents were bound to be asleep. And then he got up very early and crept out before they were awake and up.

Gem's new determination to stand back and assess things before she reacted meant she didn't challenge him over this. She just left a space, a silence with enough room in it for him to feel that he'd failed her. That was her way of being in charge. But she couldn't control the fights that caught her unaware, that broke out savagely more and more, often over the most stupid things. Usually she started them, niggling about him always putting the team first, but one time he retaliated by criticizing her for the amount of time she spent with Christian, now they'd made up again. "Your best friend's a *boy*," Jack had said. "It creeps me out."

"*Why*, for God's sake? Anyway I don't have a *best friend*. I'm not that corny. Chris is just a good friend."

"Name someone you like better."

"You."

"Someone you're not shagging."

She laughed, and then there was a silence, as inside her the wish to be honest and the wish to score a point over Jack slugged it out. In the end Jack said, "See? You can't. Which proves he's your best friend."

And it was true of course, he was her best friend. They'd stopped seeing each other for a while, that was all. But now Chris was once more the one she'd phone up if she was upset or sad or confused – he was the listener, he was the giver, which made her (she supposed) the taker – but he didn't seem to mind. He just wanted to spend time with her.

"OK, Jack," she said, "maybe he is my best mate, but so what. You can't be jealous of *Chris*," she added, loving the thought of Jack being jealous. "It's just – it's *insane*."

"I'm not fucking *jealous* of him. I just wanna know why you spend so much *time* with him. Like last Saturday. Your mum said you'd just popped out to the shops, and it was seven o'clock before you got home."

"We were looking for a top. To go with that new skirt I got."

Jack's face screwed up in disgust. "What a faggot."

"You see? *That's* why I go shopping with him and not you. You oughta be grateful to him."

"Most girls go with other girls."

"Yeah, but – you know Holly. She's never gonna steer me towards something that might make me look better than her, is she, but *Chris*—"

"Is a faggot."

"He's *artistic*. He loves style, he loves clothes, he loves it when I. . ." She trailed off.

"What?" demanded Jack.

"Oh, nothing." Chris's face had filled Gem's mind, Chris's face all alight with pride and pleasure when he'd helped her buy something perfect for her, and they'd gone back to her room and she'd put it on again and he was telling her which shoes to wear with it, which jewellery, telling her to do something different with her hair. . .

"Look – can we drop this?" she squawked. "It's so silly."

"I bet you talk about me to him, don't you? God, I hate the thought of you chewing me over with that creep."

"*Whaaat?* Jack – what is this? I wouldn't be jealous of some butch bird you trained with, would I?"

"I'm not jealous. Why d'you keep going on about me being jealous? Anyway – I wouldn't train with a *girl.*"

"Oh – you're just a shit. A horrible *gender fascist.*"

"A *what*?!"

"You heard. Fascist, *fascist!*"

They were laughing now, then they were reaching for each other, and soon they were rolling together on the couch, kissing, and Chris was forgotten.

Jack was sick of how often they rowed, but he liked the way they made up.

Tuesday training was finished, and Jack was pulling on his T-shirt when Gemma called him on his mobile. He saw her name come up and didn't answer it, not wanting stick from the team, but Stev was on to him. "That the wife again?" he demanded.

Jack ignored him.

"God, she can't leave you alone, can she?" jeered Dosh, currying favour with Stev.

"What's the matter, Dosh – jealous?" barked Jack. "Can't find anyone to take your L plates off for you?"

"You may as well answer her," Stev sneered. "You know you're gonna, soon as we're outta the way. She's got you where she wants you, hasn't she."

"Yep," said Jack, leering back. "As often as she wants it, too."

"Yeah, yeah. You wanna play the field a bit, mate."

"I don't wanna play the field. Not any more. I don't need to now I've got Gem." He took a breath, said, "Right now she's all I want, OK?"

The loud conversation on the opposite bench about whose rugby boots were best petered out. "Sure you want *her*," barked Stev, "you want her cos you're doing it together, so there's no messing around, you know you're gonna get it."

The lads grouped around laughed, knowing, lecherous, and Jack shook his head. "S'not just that. It's better with her – every time it's better with her. . ."

"OK. So you're saying practise makes it good. Sure it does. You get with a girl, you play around with her, try out different things . . . but that gets boring, man. Trust me. I'll give it two more months, three maybe – you'll be desperate for something fresh."

Jack looked steadily at Stev. He considered saying: "You arsehole. She's not meat. I don't want *something fresh*. I want *her*. I'm addicted to her. Her skin, the smell of her – it breaks me up. You don't understand. What we have is something you're not even up to *imagining*."

But he didn't say that. He just looked steadily at Stev, who looked sneeringly back, thinking he'd won.

"Aw, Jack," said Jamie, "what's up? You in love or something? Don't go getting all moosh on us, mate."

"He's gone soft, is what," said Stev. "He's forgotten the golden rule: treat 'em mean, keep 'em keen."

Jack refused to be drawn. He knew the way Stev's mind worked about women. You screwed them over before they could do it to you. You took them for as much as you could get. And to be soft on a woman and then have her take you for a fool and cheat on you – well, that was the ultimate weakness.

He kind of agreed with Stev. That was what had happened to him with Amy, after all, but that was all behind him now. The trouble was, he didn't know what was ahead of him. He was unsure, he didn't have the words for it. And however much he tried not to let it affect him, this ribbing from the team, he couldn't help it. It seemed to be the opinion of most of them that his relationship with Gem had gone on far too long. He knew it was the ones who were jealous who gave him the most stick, but it was still stick.

That Saturday night in the cellar he set out to show the others he was in no way in thrall to Gem. He slung his arm round her neck in casual ownership, like he was saying, *Look what I've got, this is where I am, this is status, this hot girl loving me while I ignore her.* . . . Gem hated it, of course. She hated the way he wouldn't focus on her. It was like

261

he'd morphed himself into someone different to fit in with the team, and she was appalled that he could change so completely, because it meant that what was underneath, the side he showed her, ran shallow. . . Or maybe, she thought bitterly, pulling away from him, maybe the bit on show here *was* the real him.

Their relationship – it was like black to white, light to dark. She was in and out of love. She'd be fed up and angry with him and then he'd say something, *be* something, that thrilled her, made her sure they had the same essence. Like the time he'd picked up a copy of *Cosmopolitan*, thrown it back on the bed in disgust, and demanded, "God, Gem, what you buy that shit for?"

"I like it," she'd snapped back. "It's interesting. I like the photos."

"It's shit. It'll mess with your mind. All that advertising kak, making you feel ugly."

"I don't feel ugly. What you on about?"

"I just hate all that stuff, that's all. It's like this slimy, sickly layer over everything, so you can't see what's for real any more. It's what I like about you, you're. . ."

Gem swarmed across the bed and engulfed him with her arms. "I'm what?"

"You're not like most girls, all into show and playing games and . . . remember that programme the other night, the one on plastic surgery?"

Gem grimaced. She wanted him to keep talking about her.

"Remember it?"

"Yes." They'd both mock-retched over the programme,

especially the bit where an elderly man in a white coat had mauled a young girl's tiny breasts, talking about how he was going to improve them with implants.

"It's what we've fucking evolved into," Jack went on, hugging her. "The human race is fucked. We've *degenerated*. You let the twisted get too much power . . . we all go down."

Gem rested her face against his. Then she picked up the magazine, opened it and tore out a page, and another, and another, and dropped them on the floor. Jack laughed, and pulled her backwards on to the bed with him.

It was like . . . she didn't know what it was like. She couldn't begin to understand it; she'd never felt this lost before, this out of control of things before. Like they kept glimpsing something fantastic, getting a little taste of it, a faint delicious sense of it . . . and then it would go and they'd be in some kind of barren hopeless wasteland again with nothing good going on at all. She'd be infatuated with him one minute, ready to love everything he did and hang on his every word, and then the next she was full of disgust and hatred and resentment and she wanted to kill him.

She hated how they'd be fighting over something and she'd be trying to get him to see it from *her* side but he wouldn't, his face would shut off and close down and he'd accuse her of always complicating everything. And she knew he was comparing her to how simple it was with the team, how you always knew where you were with them. He'd go on about how rugby was real. Nothing was as exciting as the feeling the game gave you. Adrenaline before – triumph afterwards. Unless you'd lost, but even then it was OK because of the team feeling, the bond between you. The understanding, the brotherhood – *surpassing the love of women*, Gem thought, but didn't challenge him on it. Afraid of the answer he'd give.

It was crazy to be jealous of rugby, though, jealous of a game. Maybe she was going mad. What had he said the other night, when they'd been rowing? "Get a grip, Gem. You're losing it. Going mental."

Sometimes she thought he was right.

Chapter 44

More and more, Boxy was treated like a renegade outcast at Westgate Rugby Football Club. There'd been an official complaint about the gouging incident, and Boxy had at first laughed it off, saying nothing could be proved, then written a cynical letter of apology – admitting nothing – when it was made clear that the whole team could be banned from play for several months if the complaint was taken further. He'd fallen foul of Stan Head, who managed the Under 18s, by refusing to release some of his stronger players to run out with the older team. When Stan Head had railed at him that he was holding the boys back, and raised again the scandal of him refusing to cooperate with the Midlands Selector, Boxy had simply laughed and walked away.

Everyone involved in the organization of the Club knew it couldn't go on like this, and wondered when the end would come.

It was a Thursday night, late night shopping night. Gem had arranged to meet Jack in town to help him choose his mum's birthday present, and because she wasn't sure exactly what time she'd make it, the obvious place to agree to meet was the cellar. Gem, driven by a desire to keep staking her claim on Jack against the team, had suggested it. Jack, of course, had been against it, but didn't know how to say no without causing a row.

As Gem went down the last three steps to the cellar, she suddenly felt flooded by not wanting to open the door and go in. Suppose Jack hadn't got there yet? Suppose the whole team was there and not Jack?

She stopped for a minute on the last step, pulled her coat tight, flicked her hair back behind her shoulders. She could hear the rumble of the television, but not much else. *Baby*, she cursed herself. Then she made herself take hold of the handle to the door, and turn it.

As she pushed the door open she knew she'd been right in the way she'd felt. Jack wasn't there. About half the team was there, some sprawled in front of the telly, some lounging at the table, mugs in hand, newspapers spread out in front of them, but no Jack. She scanned the room desperately, as though she might be able to conjure him up if she looked hard enough. Which was crazy, because he was so imprinted on her she knew almost before she looked that he wasn't there.

She edged through the door into the room, and all the boys looked up and stared at her. There were several long agonizing beats before Jamie called out, "Hi, Gem."

"Hi," she blustered, "is Jack around?"

"No," said Jamie. Dosh muttered something to him and they both laughed, kind of nastily.

"He told you to meet him here, did he?" demanded Stev. His voice made clear she'd broken the rules, crossed a boundary she should have stayed the other side of.

"Er — yeah. Around six. We're going late night shopping."

A sneer of laughter broke out at this. "There you go then," said Stev, and turned back to his paper.

No one smiled at her. No one invited her to sit down. *Losers!* she railed, silently. *Rude stupid idiots!*

She thought about turning round and going out again but that would be letting them win, wouldn't it, letting them get the better of her, and she was fucked if she was going to do that. She checked her watch. Nearly quarter past six. *I'll kill you for this, Jack*, she thought. Except what exactly would she tell him she was killing him for? It had been her idea to meet here.

She lifted her head and stalked into the room, meaning to sit on one of the wonky old kitchen chairs up against the far wall. As she got closer she realized the three pictures taped above them were naked women in gross submissive poses. She stopped in disgust. "Oh *God*," she hissed.

Stev's head came up like a cobra's. "Oh God *what*? You got a problem with our wall decoration?"

She didn't answer. But she wasn't going to sit underneath those vile pictures that looked like they'd been pulled out of some porn magazine.

She turned, headed back for the door. "What's the matter, Gem?" sneered Stev, as she passed him. "'Fraid Jack won't notice you if you sit under our girls?"

"*Our girls*," she spat back.

"They *are* our girls. We voted which ones we wanted up. So to speak. Didn't we, lads?"

"You're *pathetic*."

Stev grinned like a bully whose goading was getting a good result. "Hey, hey, calm down, Gemmy. It's just a bit of fun. Just a bit of *sex*."

"Yeah, well, you know what, Stev? Those pictures aren't about sex, are they? They're about wanking."

"Well – wanking's kind of about sex, you know, babe. In my experience."

"It's *tossing off*. Not real sex."

"*Real sex*," he gloated. "Hey, guys –" and he turned to the room and raised his voice – "Gem reckons she knows about *real sex*. Seems you lot've just been having the fake sort."

There was a kind of lecherous stir, followed by mocking laughter. All the boys in the room had turned to stare at Gem, who felt the heat spread up her neck and neon-light her face. "Oh, *fuck off*," she hissed.

He let his eyes slide up from her breasts to her mouth and said, "I'm not going anywhere."

And then Jack walked in. He took in Gem's face, and Stev's face, and demanded, "What the fuck's been going on?"

Gem knew if she made a scene, showed how upset she was, she'd lose it. She'd lose whatever fight Stev was waging against her. "Nothing," she snapped. "Can we go?"

"I only just got here," said Jack.

"*Can we go?*" Gem repeated. She felt near to tears. Plus

she was wildly furious with herself for letting Stev get to her. What had happened there? Why had it suddenly kind of – *kicked off* like that?

She turned, and walked through the door, and Jack followed her. As he shut the door behind them there was a burst of jeering laughter and Stev's voice crowing, "*Pussy whipped!*"

"What the *fuck's* up with you?" demanded Jack as they pounded up the stairs.

"Your stupid team is what's up!" she snarled back. "They hate women. Actually I think they're all gay."

"Yeah, yeah. Look, Gem, you—"

"No, really. I mean it. I'm sick of being victimized—"

"*What?*"

"Why were you late?"

"There weren't any buses!"

"Have you seen those foul porno pictures they've stuck up?"

"No. Yes. They're only pictures – what's the matter with you?"

They burst out on to the street, into the cold, metal-tasting air. Gem started to walk fast, wouldn't take his hand.

"They're horrible," she spat. "Your whole attitude to women is horrible."

"Gem – I didn't put them up there. They won't stay."

"I'm sick of it. I'm sick of always being put second. I'm sick of the way you let that psycho Alan Box dictate to you the way you do!"

"He's our fucking *coach* for chrissake!"

"I don't mean about rugby. I mean about everything

else. The way he makes you put training and matches before everything else."

"Well, that's his job."

"Telling you what to do about girlfriends isn't his job. I bet he's had a go at you about me. Hasn't he?" Gem stopped striding on and turned to face Jack. "*Hasn't he?*" she screamed.

Jack was silent. Only the other week, after training, Boxy had taken him aside and talked to him about not getting in too deep with Gem; how if you stayed too long with a girl, they started expecting things, demanding things, things like commitment. "Why don't you just stop yelling at me?" he said, coldly.

"I feel like yelling."

"Well I don't *feel like* listening to it. I'm sick of it, Gem, OK? And if you're so sick of everything with me, maybe we should just call it a day."

"Maybe we should. Maybe we should call it a day for good. Maybe we should end it, now."

She expected him to tell her not to be stupid, pathetic, mental, like he usually did, but this time he didn't. He looked at her in a way that made her go cold.

It was like they were both suddenly standing on the edge of something terrifying, some great void that they could both disappear into. Gem couldn't bear it. She thrust her arms round his neck and sobbed, "I'm sorry."

"Me too," he croaked. "Just stop it, OK?"

Chapter 45

The team continued to train, matches were played every Saturday, and Gem went along to the cellar afterwards. One night, desperate that they did the same thing, week in week out, she told herself she'd take a stand, go clubbing with her mates instead, telling Jack he could come along with her too. Until she realized that of course he wouldn't come. He'd go to the cellar and wonder if she was going to get off with someone at the club, and he'd get drunk, and there'd be someone there flirting with him, and all the other guys who thought she was tying him down egging him on, and. . .

And the upshot was there was no way she could leave him on his own on Saturday night.

She saw lots of Christian, always in the week. By unspoken agreement they hardly ever discussed Jack, or the way the team continued to be set against her. Christian was biding his time, waiting for the end.

February gave way to March, and the end of the rugby season was in sight. When Gem asked Jack if he was going to miss it he wouldn't look her in the eye, and muttered something about Boxy saying they were going to keep their training up over the summer "so next season can be even better". When he said this, she shut off, cut off. She was, she realized, showing things less and less to Jack. She was weighed down by all the things that were wrong in their relationship, but she couldn't stop seeing him. She felt like she was physically addicted to him.

Then, as spring arrived, there was a collision of events.

Boxy went away for the bank holiday weekend – back to see his parents, he said. He cancelled the rugby match for Saturday, causing huge trouble with the alackadoos at the Club. But he held firm. He told Jack: "I'm not there, so the game's off. If Len phones you and tells you it's on again, ignore him."

The weather forecast predicted a freak spell of unseasonably hot weather.

And Gem's youngish aunt asked her to house-sit to look after her cat.

Alone in the tiny, pretty house, with its overgrown courtyard garden, Jack and Gem felt like they'd stepped outside their lives for a while. They dumped their bags in the main bedroom, bed all made up with crisp white sheets. *Just pop them in the washing machine before you go, please*, the note said. Jack tried to wrestle Gem on to the bed as soon as they got there but she told him they had three days all alone and there was absolutely no rush about anything.

What Gem wanted to do was play house. She opened up the door to the tiny courtyard so the sun streamed into the ground floor; she made friends with the cat, then announced she was making a special lunch with all the grown-up food like olives and pancetta and expensive bagged salad that her aunt had left for her. As the sun climbed in the sky, they ate lunch outside at the tiny round wrought-iron table.

It was almost too perfect – it made Jack nervous. He was scared he was enjoying it too much. He told her there was a rugby cup final he had to see and went inside, grumbling about the midget size of the TV. "You gonna come and watch it with me?" he asked.

But Gem was hurt he didn't want to make love after lunch. She said she wanted to get her summer tan started, and got the sunbed out of the shed.

Hovering between them was the question of whether Jack would go to the cellar that night. There'd been no match that day so there'd be nothing to celebrate, but even so most of the team would be gathering there. Gem had made up her mind that it was a test; she wasn't going to say anything, she was just going to wait and see if he passed or failed. Part of Jack's uneasiness was that he'd already pretty much decided not to go and he wasn't sure it was the right decision.

After the match, he loped outside again, to find Gem stretched out on the sunbed with her T-shirt and skirt pulled up for maximum sun-exposure. "What we eating tonight?" he demanded.

"Don't tell me you're hungry already."

"Gettin' that way."

"There's stuff for a stir-fry. Chicken and stuff. Or we could go out. . ."

"Is there any beer in the fridge?"

"Dunno. There's wine."

"I hate wine. I'll go out and get some beer."

Gem opened her eyes, and squinted up at him. He was framed rather gorgeously by some pink and white hanging branches of blossom. "Jack – *relax*," she said. "It's lovely here. Why can't you just enjoy it?"

"I dunno. Cos it's . . . it's very pretty and sweet, but it's not for real, is it."

"What the hell d'you *mean*, it's not for real?"

"It's just your aunt's little hideaway from all the shit going on in the big bad outside world."

"Oh, come *on*, Jack. It's a *house*. And we've got it for three days. Why d'you have to make it all such a battle?"

"Cos it *is* a fucking battle. Budge up."

Gem groaned, stretched her legs out long on the wide wooden sun lounger, and turned on her side. Jack flopped down beside her, propped himself up on one elbow and stared down at her. She didn't look back at him. She knew that if she did, they'd kiss, and go on kissing, and then they'd make love . . . and she wanted to make him talk.

"It doesn't have to be a battle," she said. "Not all the time. You're gonna miss out if you keep *fighting* against everything the whole time."

"Maybe I can't be any other way."

"Oh, bollocks. You just don't *want* to be any other way. You've got a creative side, you just don't let it out. . ."

"Don't I?" he murmured, all joke-lecherous, and his hand went from her arm to the top of her leg.

"Don't be a prat." She held his hand still against her

skin. "I'm not talking about *that*, I'm talking about the things you say sometimes, the way you *think*. . ."

"Oh my God. She reckons I'm intelligent."

Gem laughed. "You *are* intelligent."

"Maybe. But I still wanna kick people's heads in." She crunched his fingers tight and he yelped and said, "Kicking people's heads in is the way forward."

"Yeah, ha ha. I'm *serious*, Jack!"

"Sorry, Gem." He moved in for a kiss but she ignored him. "What you saying?" he murmured, penitent. "Go on, say it."

"I just think – people have got more power over what they do than they admit. You know – over what they do with their *lives*. I'm not talking about jobs and mortgages and stuff, I'm talking about the way we live, what we put time into . . . I dunno. I just think it's in our hands more than people say. I think we can be open to more things than people say. Maybe cos they're scared, or . . . or lazy. We've got the chance to make something *special*."

"Like this garden."

"*No*. I'm not talking about the *garden*. Although – yes, it's part of it. Bev puts a lot of work in it cos it's special to her, in some way it makes her whole life better. . ."

"Aren't *we* making something special, Gem?" He wanted to have sex again so strongly now he couldn't think straight about what she was saying. He liked the sound of it, but that's all it was, a sound. Everything in him was focused on getting her to stop talking and melt and let him in.

Gem knew what was going on inside him. She could feel him hard against her hip; she knew where they were headed. *God* but she wanted to get through to him, though. When had they ever had a better chance – been this close with *words*?

"Your life," she said, "you can decide it. Open up to it. It's like a dance – you got to move, you got to join in!"

"A *dance*?" he scoffed. "You know I can't dance, Gem."

And he moved over on top of her, covering her, but she slithered out, scrambled up, headed inside. "Where you *going*?" he wailed.

She laughed, flicked the music centre up loud, then flicked it back to the start of the slightly jazzy, Spanish-feel CD, which was the best thing her aunt's collection had to offer.

"Come on," she said, and she started to move, mocking at first, like a joke-flamenco, raising her arms above her head, moving across the sunlit tiles of the terrace, laughing at him. Then she turned away from him and moved with the music, making up her own steps, moving down to the end of the garden where the trees made shadows.

Jack got up from the wooden lounger, stood, arms hanging, and watched her. She was so gorgeous with the lovely shape of her body in her thin short clothes he almost couldn't stand it. "Gem!" he croaked, and she turned.

"Come on!" she said, and came halfway to meet him. "Come on, Jack – don't always do things you *can* do."

"OK. Next week I'm gonna make you play rugby."

"Fine." He put his arms round her and she pulled his right arm up in a waltz-hold. "Dance!" she commanded. "C'mon – *dance*!"

And for the first time ever, they slow-danced together.

All around the tiled terrace, in and out of the beams of light, brushing against the big leaves of the exotic plants. It was out of the frame of how they'd been before – it was new to them both. But their bodies were used to moving together so it worked well. They were both laughing, pleased with themselves. And then it was enough and Jack steered them back over to the sun lounger.

They stood together and undressed each other with sure hands. "Can anyone see us here?" he whispered.

"Nope," she breathed. Then she lay back across the wooden slats and he knelt in front of her.

Chapter 46

That night, there was no question of them going along to the cellar – it just didn't come up. They'd gone inside and talked more, and made stir-fry and they opened the wine, and Jack tried some and pronounced it just about bearable, so he didn't bother to go out for some beer. While they were eating Jack talked a bit about Boxy and the team, and how much it all meant to him, and this time she hadn't reacted, she'd listened, so he'd said he could understand how threatened and sidelined she must feel sometimes, and it was like they were crossing a bridge that had previously been absolutely impassable. Gem wanted to say this, she wanted to mark what was happening, but she didn't dare to in case it jinxed it.

They made love again, sleepily, in bed, and it had been like a lovely echo of what had happened in the garden.

The next day, Jack felt like his shag-happy smile was welded to his face. Anyone can *screw*, he thought, anyone can get his end away, but what had happened in the garden with Gem . . . that was something else. She'd curled up next to him afterwards and told him it had been the best ever. Her eyes had been gleaming and glistening so much in the weird spangled garden-light he thought she'd almost been in tears but he hadn't asked her if she was; he was too choked up himself with how fantastic it had been.

He couldn't work out what it was. It wasn't the new position, they'd tried loads of different positions. It had been . . . it had been the way the whole day had been, the way they'd been marooned together in the house, and made love after they talked, the way she'd made him dance, the way it felt like they'd crossed over some kind of boundary, moved something on, he wasn't sure what.

He couldn't wait to make love to her again. It was like they'd been in this sweet space that he loved and then – this vast new space had opened out for them. Unexpected, magic – limitless maybe.

They still hadn't gone out. There was no need to. Jack's restlessness had vanished. They felt completely content where they were. Making love, making food, showering and sleeping was enough.

An article in an old Sunday magazine about Victorian Man, and how he was all pious and moral in public but in private had a taste for child prostitutes, caused a wonderful discussion. "*Men*," Gem had said, starting it. "You're all hypocrites. . ."

"Everyone's a hypocrite," Jack answered, "not just *men*. We're hypocrites because there's a fucking great gap between what we make out life's about – and what it really *is*."

"Yeah, but you can't hush things up nowadays, like you

could in Victorian times. You'd be exposed. By a newspaper – by the media."

"And you don't think the media's the biggest peddler of the whole fake thing? The life it shows – it's beautiful, it's strident, everywhere, all the time, on TV, on billboards, always in your face, in your brain – it's more real than the reality."

They'd talked, they'd explored. They discussed how ads projected an image of life so stunning and seductive that most people just gave up and lived like pale copies of it, wearing the clothes, booking the holidays, getting in debt for the car, hiding from the great gaping gulf between the vivid image and their crap, dreary, failing lives.

And running underneath all this talk like a sweet water stream was the thought that together they'd avoided that gulf. They were real; what they had between them was new, honest, *real*. They could fight against the power of the image. They could hold on to what they were, plug into it inside, struggle to keep living it.

The weather was still hot and they spent all the time they could in the little courtyard garden. On the afternoon of the second day, they'd had lunch, they'd made love again on the sunbed, and fallen asleep. Jack woke and went inside to get a glass of water and, disturbed, Gem opened her eyes to see a chaffinch landed on the rim of the birdbath. Its lovely round breast was the exact colour of the terracotta pots grouped nearby. Gem watched, transfixed by the perfection of the scene, wanting her camera but not wanting to move. "Jack," she hissed, "*Jack!*"

"Whaa?"

"Fetch me my camera. It's on the side there. Please. *Please!*"

He padded over to the kitchen counter to pick up her camera. Still with her eyes glued to the bird, Gem thrust her hand out backwards. "Gently!" she hissed. "Don't scare it!" He put the camera into her hand and she moved fast, focusing, then clicking. Once as it dipped and drunk – once as it peered round – once again as it took flight.

"Oh, they'll be brilliant!" she breathed. "Thank God I had a colour film in! What I'm gonna do . . . I'm gonna play up that gorgeous terracotta colour, I'm gonna make that the focus in the prints, with the green plants all background and blurred. . ."

She broke off. Jack was staring at her with something naked and terrifying in his face. "I love you," he croaked.

And then acted like he hadn't said it, but Gem knew he had.

The next evening, they stripped the bed to put it in the washing machine and Gem got the hoover out, and Jack washed up the cooking stuff from the night before. Neither of them could say much, it felt so tragic that they were going to have to leave the little house and go back into the world again.

When it was time to leave they stood by the front door, not wanting to open it. Jack put his bag down and wrapped his arms round Gem. "We got to do this again," he murmured. "Soon."

"I know," she said back. "When, though?"

"I dunno. A hotel. We'll go away . . . I'll get the money somehow. . ."

And he trailed off. They both knew it was a fantasy.

And then it was back to normal, back to the old routine. Only a few days later they were rowing again, when Gem accused him of "going all shut off after they'd been so close". "You're *scared*, that's what it is!" she railed. "You're scared to . . . to let me in!"

"Oh, for Christ's sake – what do you want? I'm so sick of this, OK?"

Gem looked straight back at his glowering face and knew she wasn't going to back down this time, she wasn't going to be bullied into shutting up. "I know what you lot think," she said. "You think women fuck your life up. I heard some of them talking to Cory the other week. 'Get rid of her, mate. She's eating your soul.' *Eating your soul!* What kind of fucking paranoia is that?"

"One, you shouldn't've been *fucking listening*. And two, Janey Wilson is a manipulative lying little cow who'll nail his balls out on a wall if he'll let her."

There was a silence, then Gem said, "I hate the way you talk sometimes."

"*Why?!* It's true!"

"Stop shouting at me."

"I just don't know what your *fucking problem* is! I never said *you're* like that! You're not! It's bollocks to say I'm scared of you, I'm not, you just make problems, it could all be so good and you just . . . you *screw it up* all the time!"

Another silence, Gem filled with an overwhelming need to appease him, to take his hand, get lost in the physical again. But the need to make him hear was stronger. "I had this thought last night," she muttered, her voice level, "d'you wanna hear it?"

Jack sighed. "Well I s'pose I'm gonna, aren't I?"

"The way you all go on about women . . . if you talked like that about any other part of your life, you'd say what cowards you were. Seriously. It's like you want to avoid risk with women, you want to avoid getting hurt. S'pose you talked like that about rugby – avoiding risk, avoiding getting hurt."

Jack flung himself back in his chair. "That's the biggest load of bollocks I ever *heard*. How can you compare the two?"

"Well I just did," said Gemma. "Didn't I."

She felt she'd scored a point, made a breach. She felt she was on a roll. When she phoned him, wanting to see a film on Thursday night, and he told her he'd already promised to meet up with the boys at the cellar, she spat, "You saw them *Tuesday*. At training."

"Yeah, and I saw you last night."

"Fine, then. If that's how you feel." She was cold at the feeling that he was splitting his favours between her and the team.

"Oh come on, Gem. They haven't forgiven me for not turning up last Saturday yet."

"Oh, for *Jesus Christ's sake*—"

"I'm *joking*."

"No you're not. You mean it. It's like you're in love with them, it's like you got two girlfriends—"

"Oh, don't start this *shit* again, OK?" he snarled, and Gem banged the phone down, and then took it off the hook, and turned her mobile off, so she wouldn't know if he was trying to call her back or not. Then she ran upstairs and burrowed hopelessly into her pillows.

"How can it *be* like this," she wailed, silently, "how can this happen after that weekend we just had, how can it keep changing all the time, just . . . *jump* from dark to light with nothing in between? One day we're close, and everything's right and I *trust*, I trust it all, and I can't see how I'll ever doubt what we've got ever again . . . but then something happens and all the doubt comes in again, and I don't trust, and it's horrible, and I can't keep on like this, something's got to change. . ."

And then she sat up, wrapped her arms round her knees, and let herself be afraid.

Gem had never really been afraid before. There'd been moments of fear – when she hurt herself, when she watched a horror film – but they were all passing, they lasted no time, they could be soothed away. She never had the kind of fear she read about and heard about, the daily, dull dread of being abandoned, or bullied, or of not making the grade. . . She'd never been afraid of people.

What was she afraid of now? Of feeling too much. Of Jack letting her down, leaving her, when she felt this much.

Of being left broken, with less than she had before, of not knowing how to go on.

*

For his part, Jack was in a foul mood till he got to the cellar, and the boys ribbed him about woman trouble. He felt better almost immediately. It was like being out of sorts with Gem made him closer to his mates.

"How much longer you gonna put up with it?" demanded Stev. "I wouldn't put up with anyone who brought me down like she brings you down."

"Shut up, and get me a beer," said Jack. "It'll end when it's ready to, OK?"

Chapter 47

Friday night. Gem and Jack were wandering hand in hand around the frenzied, festive, Friday-night town, with only enough pooled money for one more drink, trying to decide where to go, when Jack got a call from Boxy.

"Jack," he grated out, "get to the cellar. *Now.*"

"What the *hell*—?"

"I'll tell you when you get here. Don't let me down."

Jack turned to Gem, pocketing his phone, and she said, "I heard."

"You coming with me?"

"Oh, so there's no question you're going?"

Jack glared at her. "No."

Gem gagged back all she wanted to say, muttered, "Don't have much choice, do I?" and Jack got hold of her hand and they hurried towards the east side of town, where The Crown was situated.

"Maybe he wants to tell us something about the match tomorrow," said Jack.

"What, and he'd screw up your Friday night for that?" snorted Gem.

"No, you're right. Someone's been in a fight, that's what."

"Someone's always getting in a fight."

"Maybe they're really hurt."

"So they should be down the A & E, not the cellar."

Jack stopped dead in his tracks and snapped, "Look – are you sure you wanna come?"

"Yes," groused Gem, "I wanna know what's happened."

"Nosy cow," he laughed. "Well, stop bitching, and come on."

When they got to the cellar, they found Boxy, Mac, Karl and Iz all grouped round Stev. Who was holding on to his shoulder, bleeding heavily from a cut above his eyebrow, and grinning ferociously. He reminded Gem of her gran's old tomcat, who used to come in triumphant and battle-scarred after a night on the tiles. "Four of 'em!" he panted, as Jack walked over to him. "I took on four of the sad pathetic little shits!"

"Yeah?" said Jack. "What happened?"

"They jumped me. Wanted my money. Fucking *kids*. One of 'em was right in my face, all gobby – he'll be cleaning his teeth up his arse for the foreseeable future." Jack laughed, and the other boys joined in, relishing it all.

"Then the other three thought they could take me on!" Stev jerked his head, smirking, and a fresh stream of blood soaked into his eyebrow, down on to his cheekbone.

"You should get that cut sewn up," said Gem.

"He's all right," snapped Boxy.

"Don't fret, Gemmy," crowed Stev, "my head's a lot harder than the one that did this to me."

"OK, so two down," said Jack. "What about the other two?"

"Pussies," gloated Stev. "Took me five seconds, max, to sort 'em. Three of 'em on the ground – one of 'em tried to run off – didn't bother about his mates nor nothin'. No fucking *honour*. Like the way he jumped me with his three mates. So I thought I'd give him a lesson. Sort him out. Took him on a little walk, didn't I?"

Gem had gone kind of cold and sick. In her imagination she could see Stev bringing his head down like a club into the boy's face, smashing his nose, hauling him like a broken doll to the side of the canal, like he'd threatened to with the gang at the bus stop. . . "What did you do?" she croaked, but no one answered her.

"Oh look," said Boxy, "here's little Jamie with the first-aid box. Well done Jamie, put it down here. Coupla butterflies'll do it."

"So this last kid," said Jack, "just how well did you sort him?"

"I proper pasted him," sneered Stev. "Cowardly little shit. He had it coming."

"That's why I called you, Jack," said Boxy calmly. He dabbed something from a small green bottle on to a pad of cotton wool, and wiped it across the cut on Stev's forehead. "Stev thinks he might've got a bit carried away."

"He threw him in the canal, didn't he?" breathed Gem.

There was a pause. Boxy was good at leaving pauses before he answered Gem, as if he were considering whether or not to bother. "No, he didn't. But he left him – well – Jack, you need to go back and see if he's OK. Maybe get an ambulance."

"Oh, God," squawked Gem, and then, "Why Jack?"

"Are you gonna let her do all the talking for you, Jack, or what?" snapped Boxy. He was fixing one adhesive strip after another to the bloody gape in Stev's skin. "I want Jack cos he's the least likely to fuck up. Also it's the captain's duties. OK? Now. Back of Woolworths, by the dumpsters, you know it?"

"Yeah," said Jack.

"You act like you just discovered him, you call for help on your mobile. OK?"

"OK," said Jack, and headed towards the cellar stairs.

Gem wobbled for a second, then she hurried after him.

Chapter 48

"Slow down!" screeched Gem. "Wait for me, can't you?"

"That kid could be dying," Jack hissed back at her. "Stev – he's a berserker when he gets going, he'll've really crunched him up."

"So why waste all that time fixing Stev's cut and letting him gloat over what he'd done?"

"It wasn't a lot of time. Look – if you're gonna get all hysterical on me, don't come."

"I'm coming," said Gem grimly.

It took them less than five minutes to reach the service entrance of Woolworths. A small ambulance was parked all haphazardly among the dumpsters, lights flashing. Six or seven people were standing round, talking excitedly across the spaces between them, watching two women in white tracksuits gently lifting a thin limp shape on to a stretcher.

"Oh, shit," breathed Jack.

"He could be dead," wailed Gem.

"Shut up. Come on, back to the cellar."

"Was he moving?" Gem called out to a middle-aged

woman who was ogling the scene and sorrowfully shaking her head.

"Didn't look like it," the woman called back. "Out cold. Someone really done for him."

Jack dug his fingers into Gem's arm and tugged her away.

"OK, this is what we do," said Boxy, after Jack had relayed the news to him. "If the old bill come after Stev, you, Jack, and Big Mac, you too – say you were with him."

"But the gang'll say we weren't."

"And who they gonna believe, eh? You got a clean bill of health, you two. Mac stopping that mugger outside the school gates, and you with that gang that went after Gem. . ."

"OK, so it's three against four. But—"

"Just listen. I want you to say they was tooled up. I want you to say they had knives. So you had to do 'em over. You had to fight hard – to protect yourselves."

"And the kid in the ambulance?"

"You left him with the others, on the ground. You gave them all a shoeing, and moved on. You don't know anything about him being dumped by the service entrance of Woolworths."

"But the *blood*," Gem croaked.

"We all stick to the same story," went on Boxy, "and we'll be OK."

"The blood," she repeated. "Stev's blood, on him. On the ground, by Woolworths, maybe. And no one else's."

There was a long silence. Gem felt numb. Somewhere

deep inside there was fury at this, and horror, and disgust, but it was dormant, it was waiting, what mattered now was to make Stev take the rap for this, clear Jack of any involvement.

"She's got a point," muttered Karl.

Boxy glared at Gem. "We just have to hope it don't come to that, don't we? We have to hope the gang don't bother trying to press charges, we have to hope that little cockroach don't croak on us and give the old bill reason to investigate. Don't we?"

Then he looked round at the boys, and suddenly it was like a pre-match talk in the cellar. "Look, to most people, there's a thin line between a hero and a thug. You gotta act right, play the game, give the other bastard a chance – or you cross that line and you're a thug. But we don't think like that, boys, right? We know which side of the line we're on, cos we fucking draw it. We draw the line." He looked round at them again, reading their faces. "We play a match. Their number 8 puts the boot into Big Mac – puts it in bad, right in his face, gets away with it – *laughs*. Later, three of you happen to bump into him. In town. Dark, no one around. Two of you gonna stand by?"

The boys shook their heads. "Nah. We're gonna stick it right to him, scare the shit out of him. No permanent damage, but—"

"That kid has permanent damage!" Gem grated out.

Boxy whirled round on her. "You don't fucking know that!"

"You want to take a bet on it?"

"No. I want you to keep out of our *business*," Boxy

292

snarled, and turned back to the boys as though she hadn't said a word. "Right. You punish him for what he did. That's what Stev did. See what I mean, boys. You make the rules. Believe it. Believe you can. Now we gotta stick by Stev. Stick together. One in, all in."

Chapter 49

"So you're gonna lie, Jack, are you?"

"Gem – just get off my back."

"No, I won't. I wanna know what you're gonna do. When the police come after Stev, I wanna know if you're gonna give him a false alibi."

"Gem – you been watching too much crime telly. Just leave it, will you."

They were sitting side by side on a bench in a little park in the centre of town, the same park where they'd first really kissed each other, back in the autumn of last year, aeons away now. When everyone had left the cellar they'd walked off together, heading nowhere; then when they'd reached the bench they'd slumped down on it. Gem felt like some hideous madness had come down on them. Part of her just wanted to run home, get into bed and burrow under her duvet, but she couldn't move, she couldn't move away from Jack.

"I just wish there was a way of finding out," Jack muttered, "how the kid is. How badly damaged he is."

"Yeah, well, there isn't, is there?" snapped Gem. "Not

without it looking really suspicious. Anyway, what we saw looked pretty fucking serious, didn't it?" She kept seeing it. That thin, limp shape being lifted on to the stretcher.

"I s'pose it'll be in the local papers. If it's serious."

"Yeah. The *obituaries*."

Jack groaned, shifted away from her on the bench. Gem reached across, picked up his hand, and gripped it hard. "Jack," she breathed, "please think about this. You can't stand up in court and . . . and *perjure* yourself."

"It won't come to that. They'll patch him up and he won't press charges cos his type don't."

"But suppose it does come to that?"

"It *won't*."

There was a long silence. Gem let Jack's hand fall back on the bench. Then she said in a tired, tight voice, "That's not the point, anyway."

"What? What're you on about?"

"It's not about whether the kid's alive or dead or whether he'll press charges or whatever – the point is, if it came to it, you'd *do* it."

"*What?*"

"You'd stand up in court and lie for any one of that team, cos that's what you're all about. Wouldn't you? *Wouldn't* you?"

There was a long pause, then Jack said, "Yes."

Gem felt like her stomach was seizing, tightening inside her, choking her. "Boxy's got you. The team's got you. You'd do anything for them."

"You don't understand."

"I'm *sick* of hearing that – you don't understand, you

don't understand! I bloody *do* understand!" And suddenly the shock of the night, of seeing the boy on the stretcher and listening to Stev gloat and Boxy making plans to protect him engulfed her and she collapsed in on herself, sobbing. "*I hate it!*" she wailed. "I hate that fucking team! You're all mad – you're psychos, you don't care about anything but yourselves, you're like this little sick *club*, it disgusts me, the way you shut everyone else out, you don't grow, you don't change, and now *this* – I *hate* it! It's eating you up, Jack, it's making you *part* of it!"

Tears flew from her hands as she swiped at her eyes. But Jack couldn't comfort her, couldn't touch her. In some deep, unvisited part of himself he was wounded, betrayed. He'd spoken to her about what the team meant to him – he'd opened up that side to her. And now she loathed it, hated it, shredded it, trampled on it.

Gem was shaking. Everything in her longed for him to put his arms round her, comfort her, promise her it would change, he would change, things would be different from now on in. But he didn't.

"If I asked you to choose," she gasped out, "if I said, it's them or me – you wouldn't hesitate, would you? You'd choose them."

"You wouldn't do that. You wouldn't be such a . . . such a *mean-minded* little cow."

"But if I did ask you?"

"Then I'd choose them," he said, dully. "Because I wouldn't want to go out with you any more, if you tried to make me choose."

"Oh, stop *pissing* about," she erupted, "you know what I'm asking you!"

The small space between them on the bench could have been miles, miles of wasteland. Gem was clenched up into herself, trying not to cry out loud again. Jack was breathing fast and shallow, as though he were getting up the courage to jump across a ravine, down from a tower. "OK, Gem," he muttered, "OK, if you're asking me who I put first, you or the team – I gotta say the team. Because it's who I am, OK? It's what I am. And if you *hate* them that much – if you want me to turn my back on them – it's you saying you don't want what I am, you don't love who I am."

She shook her head, blasted, not trusting herself to speak.

"You're asking me to cut out what I am," he went on hoarsely, "turn my back on it, and I can't do that, I won't do that. I wouldn't do it to you, I wouldn't make you choose."

"Choose between what?" she croaked. She was reeling, sick, from what he'd said.

"Choose between me and . . . something that mattered to you. Like – I dunno. The time you spend with Chris. Shopping, and photos, and stuff."

"That's different. All that stuff doesn't . . . *fuck me up* . . . and anyway," she sobbed, "if you did, I'd choose *you*."

"Yeah? Well, you ought not to." He still couldn't touch her, put a hand on her. He'd gone cold, flint, inside. "No one has the right to make another person cut out something that's important to them, that's right for them. . ."

She wanted to argue back; she wanted to say that if you loved someone enough, you were ready to change, to grow together, to give things up . . . you *wanted* to . . . but she couldn't, everything inside her was aching and she just said hopelessly, "There's no point, is there."

"No," Jack muttered.

Chapter 50

And that was that. They were finished, severed.

Neither of them could talk.

Then Jack stood up and said, "I'll see you home."

"You don't have to," she whispered. "I'm OK."

"No, I'll see you home safe. To your door."

They walked side by side in silence. Everything in Gem was steeled against throwing herself on Jack, begging him to stay with her, because she knew what had just happened was right. It had come out at last and they couldn't pretend it wasn't there any more, the dark centre of what they were together.

It had been there all the time, waiting to come out; and now it had finished them. When he left her at her door they couldn't say goodbye, couldn't even look at each other.

Chapter 51

It was Tuesday night training, five days later, and Boxy and the boys were heading silently out to the field. With a kind of siege mentality, everyone understood that they couldn't discuss their business in the clubhouse.

"OK," said Boxy, when they all stopped. "No news yet. As far as we know, the street rat's still in hospital."

"Did you phone up?" asked Dosh.

"Oh, I'm really gonna do that, aren't I, Dosh. What do I say when some nurse asks me what my relationship to the patient is? Trainer to the patient's mugger?"

"I didn't mug him," growled Stev. "He had it coming."

"OK then, Boxy, how come you know?" demanded Dosh.

"I told him," said Will. "There's a kid a few doors along from me . . . he knows someone in the gang that went for Stev. The estate's full of it – how the gang got sorted."

Grins broke out and there was a rumbling of triumph; Iz clapped Stev on the back.

"But no one knows *who* sorted it, right?" demanded Boxy.

"No," said Will. "Not that I've heard."

"Let's hope it stays that way, and he gets out of hospital and keeps his gob shut. Cos we got more trouble, boys. There's been an official complaint from Ridgeside about the kid that got bitten on Saturday."

"Oh, *what?*" erupted Big Mac. "You're *joking*. Official?"

"Official. They want the lad who did it to own up and get banned for the rest of the season. Or the whole team gets banned."

"Oh, *pathetic*. What about the stud marks on Jamie? What about that headbutt? What about the fucking *fight* at the end?"

"Yeah, well, it wasn't a pretty game, we all know that. *Ridgeside*, of course, are making out it was our fault—"

"Wankers!" exploded Kyle.

"—but in my view it was down to the ref. He was out of his depth and things got out of control."

"You want me to own up?" said Iz. "I will do."

"I know you will, if I tell you to," said Boxy. "But no – I don't. They won't ban the whole team – they wouldn't dare. We face it out, together. Now come on. Let's get some training in. Come on, Jack – get 'em moving. Hey, Jack – you deaf? What's up?"

"Nothing," muttered Jack.

The Ridgeside officials were right, the last game had been a dangerously violent one. But they were wrong to pin all the blame on Boxy and his team, just as Boxy was wrong to blame the inadequate ref, because in reality, it was Jack's fault.

On Friday night, Jack had walked away from Gem not knowing how he was still breathing, moving. He went home and slept like the dead, then woke in the morning almost crazed with hurt. He knew he had to control this hurt – lock it deep down inside him – or he wouldn't function. He got up, got dressed and set off for the rugby ground.

He told no one what had happened. The boys in the changing room saw he was grimmer and darker than normal as he revved them up for the match and they thought it was the tension hanging over the team because of the kid Stev had put in hospital. Stev himself was wound up like a steel spring.

Jack ran on to the pitch like a berserker in the front line of battle. Before, he'd acted as a counterweight to Stev's violence – he'd kept the control, kept the team focused. But that day, he lost it. It was like he'd finally crossed over to Stev's side.

The team felt it; it infected them from the start. They tackled like madmen and ran in two tries in the first seven minutes. Ridgeside came back hard; Westgate responded harder. The ref began blowing up for every rules infringement, nearly always against Westgate. Their 12-point lead was soon wiped out by penalties kicked against them. Tempers flashed and flared, off the pitch and on.

By half-time, the ref was barely keeping control. Ten minutes into the second half, and the match was abandoned when the Ridgeside flanker scrambled from a scrum roaring. Iz, pinned down by a heavier weight and frustrated beyond control, had sunk his teeth into the flanker's back.

All hell broke loose, with the ref and the Ridgeside trainers and supporters demanding that the biter own up. Boxy insisted it was an old injury, bleeding afresh from being knocked. Iz took his cue from this and kept silent. Boxy, who'd been yelling abuse at the ref throughout, now refused to listen to or even look at him, even though he was practically jumping up and down with fury in front of him. A fight broke out between the two sets of backs that took fully five minutes to subdue, and the match was stopped.

When Len Hardcastle and Stan Head had confronted Boxy and told him about Ridgeside's official complaint and its insistence that the biter be exposed, they hadn't told him that the official complaint had some "advice" attached. Which was that in Ridgeside's opinion Alan Box was not a fit trainer. Ridgeside cited his lack of respect – amounting to sheer contempt – for the referee. They suggested his attitude was bad for the boys; that he was running an ill-disciplined and violent team. They suggested he needed to be removed.

Stan Head, who'd been chafing under Boxy's arrogant refusal to let players like Jack and Cory play for his Under 18s, called an Emergency Meeting to discuss the letter.

The alackadoos were closing in.

Chapter 52

On Wednesday evening, Boxy called up a celebration in the cellar. Word had got round Will's estate that the kid Stev beat up was out of hospital, and as he didn't want to press charges, the police were dropping the case. It seemed safe to assume that Stev had got away with it, and that, announced Boxy, merited a few beers.

Jack turned up just as the party was getting going. He hadn't told anyone about splitting up with Gem; he didn't want to talk about it, he didn't want to think about it. If he could've nailed it away in a box and buried it underground, he would have done. But something about the atmosphere of noisy relief in the cellar made him suddenly announce that he'd dumped Gem.

"*What?*" squawked Jamie.

"Bit out of the blue, innit?" demanded Iz.

"We had a bust-up," Jack said. "A real bad fight. She didn't want me to lie about being with Stev last Friday."

"Aah, you'll get back together again. You'll make up."

"We won't," said Jack. "It's over."

There was a gawping silence, then general cheering and laughing. "So Jacky-boy's a free man again!" crowed Boxy. "And Stev's gonna stay one."

"Yeah," grinned Stev. "Both of us outside the fuckin' jailhouse."

"Jamie – get the beers in – we got two things to celebrate now!"

A bit later, Boxy collided with Jack on the way into the toilets and asked him if he was all right. "Yeah," Jack replied.

"Good," said Boxy. "You done the right thing."

That was all the private conversation they had about Gem, and for Jack it was enough. He knew he could talk to him later if he wanted to but right now there was no need. Maybe there'd never be a need.

The party was lifting off. Texts went out and girls started to turn up, excited by all the drama. Some of them went up to Stev to congratulate him, some of them even kissed him, but only the few who felt as functional about sex as he did could stand him for long. It was Jack they were focused on. Jack without Gem was like the sweetie dish tipping out all over the table, begging you to dig in. It was all balm to Jack, obliteration. He went mad that night, drinking far more than usual, flirting and necking with the girls pressing round him.

Later, slumped exhausted and drunk in a corner with Dosh, he started railing at himself, saying how he couldn't believe he'd made the same mistake twice, how he should've learnt after Amy not to let a woman in again.

"Yeah, but you're OK now, mate, aren't you?" said Dosh, soothingly. "I mean – you got out."

There was a long, long pause, and then Jack muttered, "Yeah."

Even though it was absolutely not in her nature to do so, Gem was behaving exactly like Jack and burying the whole thing. She told Christian about the split over the phone, making a weak joke about how the relationship hadn't lasted as long as the rugby season. Trying to tamp down the excitement rising in him, he offered to come over, to meet her for a drink, a walk, anything . . . but she refused. She said she was knackered and just wanted to sleep. At school, when she bumped into him, she put a block on any mention of Jack. She said it was all too raw, she couldn't deal with it.

As soon as Holly heard about the split, she popped round with a present of a scented candle and some bath oil that she'd been given for Christmas and hadn't got round to using yet. "I've heard, babe!" she cried, as Gem opened the door to her. "You must be *so upset!*" Gem ducked back to avoid the arms reaching out for her. "Oh, Holly, that's really sweet of you," she muttered, taking the presents. "Thank you."

"It's nothing, darlin', OK? You need to pamper yourself!"

Gem managed to smile, and Holly said, "D'you want some company?"

"Well, I – I'm kinda better on my own at the moment, Holly. You know."

"You don't want to go bottling it up, Gem."

"I know."

"Let it out – and get over it. He wasn't good enough for you anyway. We all thought so."

"Did you?"

"Definitely. We used to talk about it. I mean – come on! A *rugby* player? What a meathead! You're too ... *sophisticated* for all that. For *him*."

Gem smiled weakly.

"You know what you need?" Holly demanded.

"What?" said Gem.

"A really good night out with us lot!"

"That'd be great," said Gem, and started gently closing the door on her. "Thanks Holly – I'll call you, OK?"

It was eight days before Christian finally got Gem on her own, when they doubled up in the photography darkroom. When he asked her how she was she said she was OK, she didn't want to discuss it, it was in the past and she wanted to move on. Then they made small talk. He felt he was talking to a robot who'd replaced her, just like the old film *Stepford Wives*, and something inside him finally accepted he'd never have her, ever, not the way Jack had.

And he gave up on her at last.

She left the darkroom first, and as he tidied away stuff into the drawer they shared, he came across the old negatives and contact prints of the match she'd photographed, and the photo of Stev gouging another player's eye. Looking at it, he felt full of hatred for Jack and his team, for Jack, with his arrogance and violence, being who Gem wanted. And the old saying about revenge being a dish best eaten cold came bleakly into his head.

Gem was shut down, shut off, coping alone. She wished she could do it another way, but she didn't know how to. She dare not open up to Christian because she knew it would bring about a closeness that wasn't right, that would mean too much to him. She wished she liked Holly better; she wished she had a real girlfriend she could talk to. She saw now that this was a weakness in her life, not – as she'd always thought – something that set her apart, something to be proud of. But there was nothing she could do about it.

She couldn't change the pattern with her parents, either. Much as she longed to cry, to have her mother coddle her and comfort her, the strong, independent daughter had to stay that way. She put up a faultless show of strength. "It's over with Jack," she announced, "and I'm fine. It could never have worked, we were too different."

And her parents, who totally agreed with that statement, were relieved, and pleased that she was being so mature about it all.

Alone in her room, Gem would wonder if this was how you felt when you were having a breakdown.

Chapter 53

The Emergency Meeting of the Westgate Rugby Football Club Committee took nearly three weeks to arrange, because the busy committee members had so many other commitments. But at last Stan Head rounded everyone up at six-forty-five p.m. Friday evening at the clubhouse with a promise that they'd all be out by seven-forty-five latest. Alan Box was not invited. When Len queried this, he was told that the committee felt unable to discuss Alan Box openly and frankly if he was sitting there in front of them.

By the end of the first thirty minutes, after a long list of Box's failures and a spider-graph of fears of what might happen if he stayed on as coach, it was mooted that he should be fired. Len suggested a temporary suspension and some kind of disciplinary action but he was argued down. "What would be the point?" demanded Stan Head, who was acting as Chair. "We've known the nature of the beast for some time now – we know he's not going to change."

"The boys'll take it hard, that's all," groaned Len. "They love him."

"*Love*," sneered Stan Head. "Hardly *love*! Look, Len – I'm not disputing that he's brought a lot of fire to the team – he's unified them. But there's been trouble and problems all along and this official complaint from Ridgeside – well. It's the last straw. Has any of the lads owned up to biting?"

"No," admitted Len, "not as yet."

"No, and they're not going to, either. And you know why, don't you? Because Alan Box never even bothered to ask them. Not properly. He wouldn't've made it a discipline issue. In his book, biting comes under the heading of *acceptable injury*."

"Now that's not true—"

"It's true enough. He's told 'em to face it out. If no one owns up, we'll be forced to ban the whole team – he thinks we won't let that happen." Stan Head sat back in his chair and looked steadily round at the other committee members. "And there's something else," he said, triumphantly. "This was put in my pigeonhole a couple of days ago."

With a flourish he pulled a large black-and-white print out of his briefcase and laid it dramatically on the table for all to see. It showed Stev deliberately gouging his thumb into an opponent's eye. Christian had done an excellent job of enlarging it.

Horror and disgust murmured round the table. "You sure it's genuine?" faltered Len. "You can do amazing things with photos nowadays. . ."

"Oh, I think it's *genuine*!" erupted Stan Head. "And I think if a copy of this gets into the hands of any other club, and we haven't taken action both against both Alan Box and this player here, Stev Kroeger, we're for the isolation pit!"

"Stev Kroeger should never have been on the team in the first place!" erupted one of the members. "I warned everyone when he joined up, he had a bad reputation, he—"

"I agree, Tom, but we're dealing with it now, OK?" said Stan Head. "Well – I think that's conclusive evidence, don't you? Martin here has to get off to a dinner party – we all have to get off. Are we going to take a vote?"

There was a surge of head-shaking, rumbles of "No need."

"Good," said Stan Head grimly. "I thought as much. Sorry, Len, but when the writing's on the wall, you've got to read it out loud and clear, in my opinion. As from *now*, Alan Box is off the job. I'll contact him tonight. I'll take over for the game against Petersgate tomorrow. I'll deal with Stev Kroeger tomorrow, too."

"Stan," groaned Len, "you're asking for trouble. . ."

"Sorry, Len," replied Stan, smugly. "Decision's been made."

Which was how it happened that the boys turned up at the grounds at ten a.m. the next morning to find Boxy wasn't there. They hung around waiting for a quarter of an hour, sure he'd be there at any minute, until at last Dosh said, "I'll try his phone."

"The one time before when he was late," said Jack, "he phoned me."

"Yeah, well, maybe something big's happened," Dosh said, mobile clamped to his ear. Seconds later he pulled a face. "Turned off," he said.

311

"Something big musta happened," said Mac. "Something—" He broke off. Stan Head, who normally disdained to do much more than nod at the Under 17s, was heading straight for them. "Morning, boys!" he boomed. "Good to see you all here! Why aren't you getting changed?"

"We're waiting for Boxy," bridled Dosh. "I can't get hold of him, I've tried his mobile but—"

"Hasn't he been in touch with you?" demanded Stan Head.

"No – why should he?"

Stan Head cleared his throat. He'd prepared for all eventualities: the boys not turning up as a protest at Boxy's dismissal; the boys turning up angry at Boxy's dismissal; the boys not knowing about Boxy's dismissal. It was clearly situation three, and he'd decided that in that case, he was going to tell them after the game, when he'd also dismiss Stev Kroeger. No sense in inflaming things before kick-off.

"Something's come up, boys," he said, firmly and genially. "Alan Box won't be along today."

The boys looked stunned. "Why not?" asked Jack. "What's happened?"

"Is he OK?" demanded Karl.

"He's fine, boys, fine. Look – the other team has arrived already; we're bringing kick-off forward to eleven o'clock. Play your hearts out, and we'll have a little chat after the game."

The boys exchanged glances. "Let's have the little chat now," growled Stev.

"No time. Look – you have a responsibility to your

visitors. To get changed and get warmed up. And give them a damn good hiding, OK?" He grinned chummily at the boys, who stared stonily back. "Come on. You're just going to have to manage without *Boxy*." Stan Head hadn't meant to, but he laid sarcastic emphasis on the word *Boxy*. "OK?"

There was an ominous pause. Then Stev said, "No. Not OK."

"Tell us what's happened," said Jack.

Stan Head squared his shoulders at Jack. "For heaven's sake, this is getting ridiculous. There isn't time. You're the captain – get them organized."

Jack squared up back at him. "Tell us what's going on," he said, "or we don't play." The team shifted, voicing its agreement.

"I'm disappointed in you, Jack," snapped Stan Head.

"Like he cares," muttered Big Mac, while Jack repeated, "Tell us what's going on."

"*Fine*, you leave me no alternative," erupted Stan Head. "Alan Box has been *fired*. He's no longer your trainer."

There was an explosion of anger and disbelief, swearing, demands for answers. Stan Head raised his hands, backed away from the team, and shouted over the noise: "I spoke to him last night, told him not to turn up today. The events at last week's match – the biting, the brawl at the end, the way he reacted to the ref – it was the last straw. Indefensible."

Uproar. Dosh shot forward, thrust his face right up to Stan Head's. "You can't just fire him!"

"I'll think you'll find we can. He's employed by the Club."

"Yeah, but we're not," snarled Jack.

"Now come on. You're hurting no one but yourselves with this reaction. Now get changed and—"

"*We're not playing.*"

The team roared its agreement. "Oh, don't be *ridiculous!*" bellowed Stan Head.

The visiting team jogged out of the training room, all kitted up. "Why aren't they changed?" their captain asked.

"'*Why aren't they changed?*'" mocked Stev.

"Boys—"

"Don't you *fucking* 'boys' us!" exploded Jack. "You fire our trainer – and expect us to mince out on to the pitch like nothing's happened! We ain't playing till we've spoken to Boxy."

"Well – he's not here to speak to. Is he?"

"He'll be here. He won't let us down."

"Really? Well it's nearly kick-off and he's not here. Or apparently reachable by phone. Is he? Your precious *Boxy.*"

This was too much for Dosh. He lifted both arms and shoved Stan Head backwards, hard.

Afterwards, no one could quite put his finger on how it all kicked off. When Stan got shoved, the visiting team's coach came racing over, demanding fussily, "Is there a problem here?" and got shoved too. So the visiting team raced over to protect him and soon there was an all-out punch-up going on.

You could only just hear the police siren over the din of it.

Chapter 54

"I swear to you, Gemmy, honour of God, I'm not lying. They *all* got arrested. They're down at the station now."

"What, for having a punch-up?"

"Yeah, but it was *total carnage!*" Holly insisted. She was sitting in a café in town, mobile clamped to her ear, enjoying the stir she was causing at the nearby tables with her words. "Sarah called me – she's been seeing Karl – she turned up to watch the match and there was this *massive battle* going on. Some of the other team got really hurt. One of them had a broken nose, and another had his ribs cracked. . ."

Gem was desperate to know if Jack had got hurt, if he'd tried to stop them, but she didn't want to say his name to Holly.

"And when the police car came in, Stev – you know that insane one?"

"Yeah," said Gem, "I know Stev."

"—well he raced over and *jumped* on its *bonnet.*"

"*Whaaat?*"

"Seriously, Sarah said he was like this freak or

something, a *monster*, he just took off the ground and landed on both feet on the car. He was, like – *leering* through the windscreen, at the policeman – *challenging* him. Then he jumped off, and ran into the clubhouse, and some of the team ran after him, and Sarah said they were just kind of rampaging through, wrecking everything!"

"What d'you *mean*?"

"*Wrecking* everything!" Holly gloated. "They trashed the bar – and the changing rooms – and all the time this huge *fight* was still going on! More police turned up – reinforcements – *and* an ambulance. They managed to stop the fight but then the rest of the team ran into the clubhouse and just went *mad*. Someone smashed the case with all the cups and medals in it. Glass everywhere. It was a *riot*. When they got it under control Stan Head insisted the *whole team* got arrested." Holly paused, savouring the drama. "Jack too. He's down there, at the station. I know you're not going out with him any more, Gemmy, but I thought you'd want to know."

"*Idiot*," hissed Gem, throat tight. "I can't believe it – what an *idiot*." She was so full of feeling she could barely talk. Anger at Jack, and disgust, and something else, something like a leap of hope she didn't understand.

"It'll mean the end of the Under 17s, of course," Holly drooled. "Sarah said Stan Head was going on about it, how not one of them would set foot in the clubhouse ever again. Banned for life. Well, you can't blame him, can you? His lovely glass case smashed up and everything. Sarah was crying her heart out when she told me about it all. She went to the police station too, to be with Karl. I mean – she was upset with him, of course she was, letting himself down like that, but she wanted to be with him, you know?"

"Yes," croaked Gem. "Thanks, Holly. I'll see you, OK?"

And she hung up.

"I still can't believe it," groaned Len, into his second pint of beer. "I can't come to terms with what went on. They're not some bloody gang. They're not some bunch of deprived kids out to get their kicks from making trouble. They had *discipline*. They had *sport*."

Len looked so defeated, hunched up over the clubroom bar, that Martin, who'd also been at Stan Head's Emergency Committee Meeting, was on the verge of putting a comforting hand on his shoulder. But he thought better of it, and said, "It just goes to show. Scratch the surface and they're all the same, all bloody little animals underneath."

Len shook his head. "I can't believe that. I won't."

"It's the evidence of your eyes, Len."

Both men took a long pull of beer, then Len suddenly erupted, "That Alan Box has got a lot to answer to! Walking out on the boys like that! *Abandoning* them."

"Len – he was *fired*."

"Yes, but he could've talked it over with the lads, couldn't he? It was like he set them up for that riot! It was like he wanted it to all go up in flames!"

"And that excuses what they did, does it?"

"I'm not saying that, of course I'm not. Nothing excuses it. But if he'd stayed on, talked it through with them – they were so *angry*. They were all pumped up for the match –

and then it just gets landed on them that Boxy's been fired – they had all that pent-up energy—"

"And you're saying it had to have somewhere else to go."

"Well it did!" Len took a swig of his pint. "No one's heard from him, you know. No forwarding address, nothing. It's like he's disappeared off the face of the earth."

There was a pause, then Martin said, "There's rumours."

"What rumours?"

"Stan Head's been doing a bit of digging. Seems Alan Box left the army under a bit of a cloud."

"Now *look*. I checked his record when I took him on here. There was nothing against him, nothing at all."

"Oh, there's nothing *against* him. Nothing official. But he wasn't doing well in the army, seems he couldn't hack it, couldn't fit in. Most people thought he was a bit of an oddball – disliked him for causing trouble, that kind of thing. He came up for an assessment, and it was . . . well, his leaving was mutually agreed. Put it that way."

Len subsided lower still on to the bar. "I was always uneasy at the amount of time he spent with the lads."

"Well, seems like he didn't have a lot of other friends."

"He was out to prove something, maybe. With our boys."

"Maybe. No sense in mulling it over now, though, is there? It's over. Come on, mate. I'll get another round in."

When the fresh pints were put in front of them, Len seized his and blurted out, "It's just – it's downright bloody tragic, that's what it is. They were such a good team. You

318

know how tight they were. How loyal – to Boxy and each other."

"You said it," said Martin gloomily. "Gang mentality. The gang means everything – it's family. They stick by each other whatever comes, do things together they'd never dream of doing on their own."

"The court case is next Friday," Len muttered. "You going to go?"

"Certainly. You?"

"I'm giving character witnesses. Someone's got to stand up against Stan Head. He's out for blood."

"They'll be all right, won't they? They're under eighteen, and it's a first offence for most of 'em. . ."

"Martin, a couple of the lads on the other team got really hurt. There's talk of custodial sentences. And I don't want any of my boys banged up in a young offenders' institution."

There was a silence, which Len broke by musing, "They were like a little army, weren't they. Strong, focused, used to putting their bodies on the line for each other . . . which made them all the more dangerous. When the time came." He took a long pull of his warm beer. "I s'pose all things considered," he said, "it could've been worse."

This time, Martin did put a hand on his shoulder. "It could've been a *lot* worse," he said.

Chapter 55

The following Friday, the public gallery at the town magistrates' court was full to overflowing. People had to be told not to sit on the steps, as it blocked the emergency exits, should there be a fire. The boys were coming up in front of the magistrate one by one, but parents, girlfriends and friends all wanted to see the trial of the whole team.

The boys had been warned not to discuss the case between them, but the warning wasn't necessary. They didn't want to talk about it; the prevailing feeling among them all was a kind of shame. They avoided each other's eyes. Stev was the only one who wanted to talk, to relive what had happened, but everyone shunned him. He seemed suddenly diminished, pathetic almost. Jack looked at him and was ashamed he'd ever felt a kinship with him. He felt nothing like that now.

Outside on the long benches waiting to go in, Dosh muttered to Iz, "I hope I don't get asked to explain what happened. Cos I haven't got a fucking idea."

"Me neither," Iz muttered back. "It just kicked off, right?

Like a red mist came down. I thought I might bring up the berserkers."

"The *who*?"

"They were the Viking nutters who were in the front line of battle. They'd just go ape – berserk. I saw it on that Viking programme."

"Right. And that's gonna get you off, is it, you tosser?"

"Probably not. Oh, shit, this is fucking awful. It's like our whole lives have just . . . *gone*. No more cellar, no more rugby. . ."

"Any news of Boxy yet?"

"No. But he'll be here. He'll stand up for us. He won't let the team down."

Dosh didn't answer him. Deep down, he felt like he'd woken up – as if some kind of dream was over. And the dream may have been amazing, but once you'd woken up, you could never go back.

Thrilled by the drama, Holly squeezed into the court alongside Sarah, and kept Gem informed of events by mobile in the brief breaks. The hearing lasted three days. On the last day, after Holly had rung to tell her that Jack was about to appear, Gem sat on her bed wringing her hands. Thoughts and feelings were coursing through her, no pattern to them, no sense. She knew that no solitary walk, however long, could sort these thoughts out, could resolve anything. She left the house and got the bus to the magistrates' court.

The magistrate took into account Len Hardcastle's fervent

and positive character references for each one of the boys. He took on board the problems with Alan Box, especially the fact that he couldn't be reached and had neglected to attend court to speak for any of them. Then, after due consideration, he referred them all to the Community Service Order Officer who would, he said, allot to each boy a sizeable number of hours' community service, depending on how much damage had been caused and how violent he'd been. He confidently expected Stev to receive the most hours. He made much of Jack's failure of responsibility as captain; he expected his allotment of hours to be second only to Stev's.

It was all over when Gem got there. Jack was standing in the entrance hall under a marble bust of a pompous-looking dignitary, with his parents on one side and a handful of the team on the other. They'd come over to commiserate with him, to say they knew it wasn't his fault. It was all very awkward, very strained – what they wanted was to get away from each other and lick their wounds – but they had to make that contact, say the words that meant they'd meet up again one day in the future, and maybe understand it all then.

Nothing could prepare Jack for the shock of seeing Gem standing there in the doorway, the blast to his heart that followed. He muttered a few words to excuse himself from the group, and walked over to her. "Hi," she whispered.

"Hi," he croaked back. "Were you in there?"

She shook her head. "Holly phoned. I just. . ."

"What?"

"I just wanted to see you. How you were."

"If you've come to gloat, Gem, you can fuck off, OK?" It was out before he could help himself.

"And if you think that's what I'd do," she snapped, "you can fuck off back!"

There was a long silence, both of them looking at each other, fighting not to rage, cry, grab hold of each other, all three. Then Jack grated out, "Gem, d'you wanna go somewhere? D'you wanna talk?"

Chapter 56

They sat side by side in a scoured and faded little café a few minutes' walk from the magistrates' court. It would have been too much to sit opposite and face each other. They hadn't touched yet but an electric aura surrounded them as they sat there, heads close, both staring down at the same spot on the table in front of them. Gem listened as Jack told her about Boxy being fired and what had happened at the Club. He related it flatly, as though it had happened to someone else, and somehow there was no need for Gem to comment on it, no need for her to talk about her disgust with it all. All that was there between them, taken as read.

When he'd finished his story, she asked, "So – what did you get?"

"Dunno yet. It's up to the community service officer. He works out what he thinks we should do . . . the magistrate reckons I'll get thirty hours at least."

"Shit!"

"S'all right. I'm gonna try and do big lumps of it together, six Saturdays on the trot, maybe – get it over with."

"God. Giving up all your Saturdays."

"Well I won't be needing 'em for rugby, will I?"

"They gonna make you fix up the clubhouse?"

"Nah. Stan Head won't let us near it. There was talk of this project going on Newbury Estate, fixing up an old kids' playground . . . it's been derelict for years." Jack paused, huffed out a bleak laugh. "They were saying maybe I'd be put in charge of the team, to use my *leadership* skills."

"So you might be with some of the boys. . .?"

"Nope. That was made crystal clear. We're bad news together, we'll all be doing separate stuff. The team's finished."

"I can't see you giving up rugby, Jack."

"Dunno. Maybe not. They'll still make me play for school – unless I get kicked out over this. But I do know the team's over – if we do play it'll be for different clubs. Mac said he's giving up, and Karl . . . quite a few of them were talking about it."

There was a long pause. Then without saying anything, Jack picked up his and Gem's mugs, walked up to the counter with them and got them refilled. When he sat back down she took in a breath and blurted out, "You'll really miss it, won't you. The team, Boxy, the cellar, Saturday nights – everything."

"Course I'll miss it. But it's over now – it's in the past."

Gem took a sip of the hot, sweet tea. "I can't believe Boxy didn't turn up at the court."

"I guess he thought he'd cop a lot of flak if he did turn up."

"Too right he would! Holly said they were going on and on about the bad influence he had on you."

"Yeah. A lot of that was shit, but some of it . . . I dunno, some of it wasn't." He twisted his mug around on the table. "Stev reckons Boxy didn't tell us he'd been fired cos he wanted it to kick off. He was going on about how we did Boxy proud at the end, shit like that—"

"He *would*. How does he explain Boxy just *disappearing*? Not turning up at court?"

"He doesn't. We haven't really been talking much, to be honest."

She sat back in her chair. "I'm not surprised. You all must feel just incredibly . . . *betrayed*."

Jack twisted his mug through another half-circle. "I been thinking about it a lot, Gem. It wasn't just about what happened at the end; it was the whole thing. It was all sorts of stuff I could blame Boxy for if I think about it."

There was a long silence that Gem decided not to break with any more questions. They were leaning so close together now that their heads were almost touching. Then Jack mumbled, "God, I've missed you, Gem."

"Me too," she whispered back.

"I couldn't handle it, the way we split up. I couldn't talk to anyone about it."

"But Jack, you never talked about stuff like that!"

"Shut up – I did to you! Well – I was starting to." She pushed her face briefly against his shoulder. "I remember you saying once," he muttered, "that I was scared. Of you, of what I was feeling. I thought if I just kept it all pushed down, it somehow—"

326

"Wouldn't be so real."

"Yes."

"Well, it was. Wasn't it."

"Yes."

Gem took in a breath and said, "I was scared, too."

"What of?"

"The way you made me feel. I used to be all – self-sufficient. In control. Then with you – I wasn't."

"And you didn't like that."

"Sometimes I did. Sometimes I thought I'd just been . . . I dunno, not really feeling anything before. And sometimes I hated it because I thought you didn't feel the same for me, and sometimes I thought I was cracking up."

Sliding her eyes sideways, Gem could see Jack smile. "I've decided you were right," he said.

"About what?"

"About dumping me. Over Stev, and that kid he beat up. . ."

"Jack – you dumped me! You said the team came first!"

Gem laughed, and at last Jack turned to look at her, and said, "Hey, if I didn't dump you, and you didn't dump me, does that mean we're still together?" She shut her eyes so he couldn't read them. "Does it?" he persisted, and closed his hand round her wrist.

She could feel everything inside her being taken over, just like before. She wanted to stand up, take him back to her room, make love with him . . . she resisted it, fought down the feeling. "I dunno," she croaked. "It's just – we're so *different*, Jack."

"I know. I know we are. But that's what makes it good,

doesn't it? I mean – that's why you don't wanna be with Christian, isn't it?"

"Maybe. But all those rows we had. . ."

"Over the *team*, Gem. And Boxy."

"So you're saying, it'll all be different now. You're different now."

"Well, I'm bound to be, aren't I? Everything's changed." Jack's face was charged with urgency. "Gem – let's give it another go. *Us* another go. You can come and meet me after I've done my community service."

"Lucky me!" she sneered, laughing – and he honed in and kissed her.

Gem felt exhausted, exhilarated, as though she'd been swimming a long distance and had reached land at last. She took hold of his arm and said, "OK. But it's not just about the team not being there – *you* gotta change. It can't be like before."

"It won't be."

"You've got to stop being so scared of me . . . *eating your soul.*" Jack laughed, and she went on, "You've got to *talk*. If you're different from someone, you gotta keep the channels open, you got to make the effort to understand them, or you just fight all the time. . ."

"Gem, I *swear*," he said, so fervently that she craned up and kissed him back.

"There's one thing, though," he muttered, as they broke apart. "I been thinking about it. I'm not sorry it happened. The team and everything. Even though there were things wrong with it and even though it ended up like this. OK? I'm glad it happened."

328

Gem drew back. Set her face, considering.

"Look – I don't need it any more," Jack went on urgently, "and I've thought about it a lot and I reckon Boxy was a bit of a wanker, to be honest. But what happened was – it was good, what we had, what we made. I'm glad I was part of it. It's part of me now and . . . and I'm glad about that too." He looked at her, and everything in him was distilled down to a need for her to know what he meant, to know *him*. "Are you OK with that?" he demanded. "Are you?"

Gem looked back at him. "I dunno," she said. "I dunno, Jack." She took in a deep, shaky breath, and realized she couldn't even begin to imagine what it would be like now, her and Jack, and no team. The space in front of them was dizzying. She took his hand and muttered, "Let's just see how it goes, shall we?"